What It Must Be

BOOK 3 IN THE OFF ICE SERIES

GRAYCE RIAN

Dedication

To every oldest sibling: this one is for you.
Thank you for leading by example, paving the way, and shaping your siblings' lives.

Content Note

This book contains mature themes and potentially triggering content, including off-page descriptions of the loss of a parent and grief. There is also explicit language and sexual scenes, some of which include bondage. Despite being a romance novel with a happy ever after, readers should be aware of these themes.

CONTENTS

Playlist		VII
Prologue		1
1.	Scarlett	24
2.	Bennett	34
3.	Scarlett	39
4.	Scarlett	48
5.	Bennett	53
6.	Scarlett	67
7.	Bennett	77
8.	Bennett	88
9.	Scarlett	105
10.	Scarlett	116
11.	Scarlett	124
12.	Bennett	140
13.	Scarlett	147
14.	Scarlett	156
15.	Bennett	168
16.	Scarlett	183

17.	Scarlett	188
18.	Bennett	199
19.	Scarlett	211
20.	Scarlett	223
21.	Scarlett	231
22.	Bennett	239
23.	Scarlett	248
24.	Bennett	257
25.	Scarlett	265
26.	Bennett	273
27.	Scarlett	280
28.	Scarlett	288
29.	Bennett	296
Epilogue		304
Extended Epilogue		309
Also by Grayce Rian		316
Acknowledgements		317
About the Author		319

Playlist

you look like you love me – Ella Langley, Riley Green
Can't Take My Eyes off You – Frankie Valli
Spin You Around (1/24) – Morgan Wallen
Sober – Hudson Westbrook
Cold Beer Cold – Callum Kerr
Wind Up Missin' You – Tucker Wetmore
Hurricane – Luke Combs
Let's Get Married – Jagged Edge, RUN, Lamarquis Jefferson
Guilty As Sin? – Taylor Swift
Next Thing You Know – Jordan Davis
never til now – Ashley Cooke, Brett Young
World on Fire – Nate Smith
Mine – Bazzi
My Boy – Elvie Shane
More Hearts Than Mine – Ingrid Andress
Maroon – Taylor Swift
Call Me When You Get Home Friends – Tenille Arts
Wanted – Hunter Hayes
Your Body Is a Wonderland – Taylor Acorn, David Ryan
Think I'm In Love With You – Chris Stapleton
8 Letters – Why Don't We
Say Don't Go (Taylor's Version) (From The Vault) – Taylor Swift
Before You – David J
Beautiful Crazy – Luke Combs
You Are In Love (Taylor's Version) – Taylor Swift

Love You Anyway – Luke Combs

Paper Rings – Taylor Swift

Yours - Wedding Edition – Russell Dickerson

My Person – Spencer Crandall

Paris – Taylor Swift

Crazier – Taylor Swift

Forever and Ever and Always – Ryan Mack

Love You Right – Chanin

Feels Like Home – Chantal Kreviazuk

From the Ground Up – Dan + Shay

Prologue

BENNETT - MAY

Six Years Ago

How did I find myself standing at a hole-in-the-wall bar in crocodile cowboy boots, cut-off jean shorts so short I fear my dick will fall out, and a cropped top flannel?

For starters, my fuckface brother chose my outfit for the first night of our childhood friend's bachelor party.

Griffin Turner is getting married next month, and this is the first of a three-night combined bachelor and bachelorette weekend. We're celebrating the festivities over Memorial Day at the cabin of my other teammate, and Griffin's future brother-in-law, Carson Wilder. The timing of this trip not only means the lake will be packed, but also that we lost in the first round of playoffs during my first season as the captain of the Minnesota Wolverines.

If I had done my fucking job, we would still be on the ice. Therefore, Griffin wouldn't have been able to have this last-minute bachelor weekend, nor would he have asked me to get ordained before his shotgun wedding next month. For fuck's sake, who gets married after only being engaged for two months? Don't couples typically want to take their time planning a wedding?

But when it comes to McKenna Wilder, Griffin has never thought rationally. The moment he moved in next door to his little sister's best friend, he was smitten. We all grew up in the same town, which meant I played on the same team as Griffin and McKenna's twin brother, Carson. Hell, McKenna even played on our team for a few seasons before she switched to girl's hockey.

The cabin we're staying in is a few hours north of home. Being born and raised in Minnesota, also known as the state of hockey, it was always a dream of mine to grow up and play professionally. Did I ever imagine I'd be playing for my home state's NHL team with my little brother and two of our childhood friends? Hell no. Am I incredibly grateful to have been drafted by the Wolverines straight out of high school? Fuck yes. Am I humbled that in my sixth season with them, they appointed me team captain? You're damn right. Am I also pissed beyond measure that we lost in the first round of playoffs? Fucking livid.

I slam back another shot of whiskey, gritting my teeth as the Jameson burns its way down my throat. My preference is sipping on an aged pour of Buffalo Trace on the rocks, but desperate times call for desperate measures. Usually, I'm not one to get a buzz, let alone attempt to get shit-faced, but I look like a fucking rodeo clown right now.

My younger brother, Jackson, decided it would be a great bonding opportunity to create a fantasy football league with only him, myself, and Carson last season. Being absolutely clueless when it comes to the NFL, I, of course, came in last place. This is how I wound up at the mercy of Jackson and Carson regarding my wardrobe this weekend. Penance is a bitch.

Jackson also happens to love planning and throwing themed parties, so he helped with the weekend's festivities. Tonight is Reverse Cowgirl, where everyone dresses as cowboys and cowgirls. Tomorrow is Golf Pros and Tennis Hoes, where the guys dress in golf attire and the girls dress in tennis attire. Finally, we round out the weekend with the Blackout, where everyone but the bride and groom dresses in black. I'm pretty sure they can't embarrass me as much as they have tonight—or at least, I hope fucking not.

Tonight's disaster of an outfit is courtesy of Jax. He dressed me in cutoff jean shorts that are so short I had to resort to tucking my dick in my waistband so it wouldn't pop out the hem of the shorts and land me in jail for indecent exposure. My fucking shirt is a cutoff flannel that also happens to be a goddamn cropped top. And to top off the outfit, he chose a fucking straw cowboy hat that looks like it belongs on a scarecrow.

I'm not a poor loser, so of course I'm following through with my punishment for losing the league, but if the day ever comes for me to get payback, Jax is fucked.

The moment we stepped into the hole-in-the-wall bar on Lake Mille Lacs, heads turned our way. Thankfully, my god-awful outfit has saved me from being recognized by Wolverines fans.

Jax, Carse, and Griff are at a table in the corner waiting for the girls to show up, but I'm bellied up at the bar drowning my sorrows, which will likely be the only way I get through tonight.

I'm momentarily pulled from my sulking when someone bounces into me from behind. A low growl of frustration escapes before I can bite it back, but when I turn to find the offender is a woman, I sigh and attempt to soften my face.

"Oh my goodness, I'm so sorry!" the woman exclaims as she steeples her hands to cover her mouth with a gasp. "Are you okay? Did I hurt you?" she asks.

Hurt me? That's laughable. I'm a six-foot-five defenseman in the NHL. She couldn't hurt me if she gave it her very best.

Oddly enough, I find her genuine concern endearing. If that feeling wasn't foreign enough, I also find it somewhat unsettling how adorable I think she is. Rich copper hair frames her face and falls in waves down to her trim waist. And there's a spattering of freckles covering her cheeks and the bridge of her nose, leaving me strangely curious to know where else freckles lie on her body.

"While I appreciate your concern, I think it'd take a bit more than your, what, five-five frame to hurt me," I rasp, quirking a brow at her as I look her up and down.

A low chuckle escapes me when her whiskey-colored eyes widen as she takes me in. She slowly lowers her hands at the same time as her eyes roam down my body. Her mouth hangs slightly open as we not-so-subtly check each other out. She looks gorgeous in a black tank top tucked into a pair of high-waisted jeans. I watch as she bites her plump lower lip when her gaze narrows in on my exposed, toned stomach. My stomach flexes on its own accord, which seems to snap her out of her daze.

"I'm actually five-seven. Add in these heels, and I'm closer to five-ten," she points out as she lifts her foot so I can see her strappy heels.

I swear to god I'm not a creep, but the way her red polished toenails match the red lipstick she's wearing has my pulse racing.

Catching her checking me out again, I don't miss her quick inhale just as the emcee for the night announces karaoke will be starting soon. Furrowing my brow, I bite my cheek in annoyance that nobody shared it was karaoke night.

"I take it by the look on your face you're not planning to partake in tonight's festivities?" she questions. Her voice has a melodic quality that I find myself drawn to.

In an attempt to get her to talk some more, I answer her. "Honestly, I didn't have a clue until just now that it's karaoke night."

"Not much of a singer?" she asks, and curiosity sparks behind her amber eyes—a shade I've never seen before, like a pool of liquid caramel.

"No, not if I can help it. Though, my mom's always told me I have a great voice."

"Doesn't she kind of *have* to say that?"

I scoff. "My mother is a saint; she'd never lie to my face."

The woman before me throws her hands up in surrender. "Woah, woah, woah. I didn't call anyone a liar—I just meant to point out the fact that no mother is going to tell her child they have a horrible voice."

"Well, for starters, I'm actually a pretty good singer, so her telling me otherwise would make her a liar," I state.

"And second?" she asks.

"Second, what?" I shoot back.

"You said for starters, which usually implies there's a second. But maybe you've just had too much Jameson tonight," she points out as she nods toward the empty shot glasses before me. "What sorrows are you trying to drown out . . . what did you say your name was again?"

I cackle at her theatrics. "I didn't. I'm Bennett," I tell her, holding my hand out for her to shake. She looks down at it and narrows her eyes before gazing up at me through dark lashes. "And I'm not drowning my sorrows, just trying to help myself forget that I'm wearing this ridiculous outfit for my buddy's bachelor party."

"I don't know, Benny. I think you look kinda cute," she teases as she takes my hand.

Hearing her call me my nickname has me humming in response. "And you are?" I ask, trying to ignore the way her touch sends currents of warmth up my arm.

"Not sharing," she tells me as a mischievous smile lights up her face.

"Playing hard to get, Little Red?" I rasp the question as her new nickname slips out.

Her eyes widen for only a second before they narrow slightly again. "Oh, Benny Boy, for some reason, I don't think I'm the closed-off one between us."

"Hmm," I murmur. "Well, if you won't tell me your name, tell me what brings you out tonight."

"It's my best friend's twenty-first birthday. We're staying on the lake for the weekend to celebrate," she informs me.

"Tell me something else about you," I request.

She picks up one of the beers the bartender just set down in front of us and tilts the neck of the bottle at me. "You're pushing your luck, but I'll play along. Hmm. Okay, I've got it. I fall into a slight depression every time I watch my favorite movie," she admits.

I snort as I take a sip of my beer. "If it makes you depressed, why would it be your favorite movie?"

"Because my favorite movie is *10 Things I Hate About You*, and Heath Ledger was a generational talent that died far too soon," she explains.

"Shit," I mutter before agreeing. "He was a generational talent."

Out of the corner of my eye, I see Carson make his way over to the two of us. Red must notice too, because she says, "Come find me later, Benny."

With that, she waves as she walks toward the front of the stage, where a group of girls wrap her in their embraces.

"Wilder, get your ass over here," I command, my eyes remaining trained on her retreating form, as Carson immediately does as he's told.

"What's up, *Benny*?" he asks, singsonging my nickname like an asshat.

"You and I are going to sing a duet, *Carsey*," I inform him.

"Yeah, as much as I'd love to give you the assist up on stage . . . I'm a shit singer," he tells me.

"Do I look like I care if you're the next American Idol? I wasn't asking," I deadpan.

Carson has always been intimidated by me, and I fully plan to take advantage of that now. "Right. Not asking. Cool, cool, cool. So, what exactly are we singing?"

Smacking him on the back, I call out over my shoulder, "You'll see when we get up there."

I watch as Carse beelines back to Griff and Jax while I go up to the emcee to add our names to the lineup for karaoke night. We're first on the fucking list, but at least that means we don't have to follow someone like Jackson.

The shots have me feeling warm and a bit hazy, but I'm still in control—just how I like it. As the captain of our team, I've quickly garnered the control freak label, but I'm more than okay with it.

Standing off to the side of the dance floor as I await our turn, I take in the groups of dancers. The bride-to-be, McKenna, is dancing with her two college volleyball teammates and Dakota.

Dakota is McKenna and Griffin's daughter's nanny, who just so happens to be living with Carson. I seriously can't keep up with all the crazy shit they've got going on, but they're some of the few people I let into my close circle.

The emcee says it's our turn, so I nod to Carson before going on stage.

When the starting notes of "Can't Take My Eyes Off You" sound through the speakers, my cocky smirk accompanies a rueful wink toward Little Red. She shakes her head at my antics but raises her beer to me in salute.

My hands tremble with nerves. God, it's been a long time since I've been up on a stage singing. Taking a deep breath, I bring the mic to my mouth and sing the opening lines, all without taking my eyes off the auburn hair bombshell.

She stares back at me, utterly bewildered at the fact that I can, in fact, sing. When she mouths, "I'll be damned," to me, I have to fight back the chuckle rumbling to life in my chest.

As I sing the song's last bars, Red tucks her beer bottle into her arm, brings both hands up to her mouth, and lets out a shrill whistle. After securing the mic back in the stand, I make my way over to her.

"So, was my mom lying to me my whole life?" I inquire.

"She may have been telling the truth. But it's hard to know if I'm just nice and buzzed or if you actually sounded good. Perhaps a private show is needed," she jokes, or at least I think she was joking. When her eyes widen, I realize she most definitely didn't mean to say that last part.

I attempt to bite back my chuckle before asking, "How am I supposed to give you a private show if I don't even know your name?"

"What about this—if fate puts us in the same place at the same time again, I'll not only tell you my name, but I'll give you my number too," she suggests, stepping closer to me.

Holding back my groan of frustration, I sigh instead. Anyone who knows me knows I don't leave anything up to fate—doing so means I forfeit control of a situation, and I don't lose control.

"You're killing me, Little Red."

She tries to hide her cheeky grin as she takes a pull from her beer, but I don't miss how her nose wrinkles and the upturn of her cheeks. I'm so fascinated watching her red lips wrap around the lip of the bottle that I don't realize her friends have called out for her.

"Looks like we're headed to the next bar on the birthday girl's list," she tells me. "Thanks for serenading me tonight, Benny."

I'm not sure what possesses me to do so, but I grip the top of my straw cowboy hat with one hand and nod my head in goodbye to her.

What the fuck has gotten into me?

Red just shakes her head at me before turning to walk away, her hips swaying with each step.

I'm not a man who believes in fate, but if she were placed in my path again, I don't think there'd be a chance in hell I'd let her slip through my fingers so easily. The odds of that happening, though, are slim to none.

One Month Later

Loosening the collar of my dress shirt, I curse Griffin for about the tenth time today.

I'm a great public speaker, but I'm shit with emotions, so I can't for the life of me figure out why he and McKenna asked me to be the officiant of their wedding. Not only did he wrangle me into that, but I'm also performing their first dance song with Jackson.

I managed to officiate my first—and last—wedding ceremony without too many hiccups. Not that I expected any different, but the groom didn't wait for my queue to kiss his bride—not once, but twice.

Slamming back my second shot of Jameson, I set the glass on the bar and turn to find Jax.

"You ready for your big debut, brother?" he mocks, knowing I hate that I'm about to perform on stage in front of people. I'm not nearly buzzed enough for this.

Turning back to the bartender, I nod for a refill.

"One more," I murmur to Jax.

"Go easy, B. I don't need you increasing your odds of yacking on stage. You were stone-cold sober the night of the high school talent show," he reminds me as if I need that mental image at this fucking moment.

Narrowing my eyes at my idiot brother, I throw back the shot without breaking eye contact. The whiskey burns down my throat, and I welcome its familiarity.

I grab my Martin acoustic guitar and head to the makeshift stage set up in the backyard of McKenna and Griffin's cabin. The ceremony was in the backyard of McKenna and Carson's parents' cabin, but the reception tent, if you can even call it that, is in the adjoining yard next door.

Jackson joins me on stage and sits on a barstool next to mine, adjusting our mic stands before giving me a reassuring nod.

With one deep breath, I strum the opening chords of Restless Road's "Growing Old With You." Jackson's heavy baritone resonates through the tent and I harmonize with him as Griff swirls Kenna around the dance floor. Allowing myself to get lost in the music—the familiar feel of the strings beneath my fingers—I don't feel nervous when my deep bass voice booms through the speakers as we finish singing the song's bridge.

The second I strum the final chords of the song, I push aside the mic and set my guitar on the stand before making a beeline to the bar.

"Whiskey, neat, please," I tell the bartender, who nods before looking over my shoulder. Leaning against the bar, I see he's looking at Dakota.

"Oh, um, I'll have a tequila sour, please," she requests before wringing her hands together and looking up at me. "Who knew the karaoke night wasn't a one-off?" she asks me.

I turn and face her, quirking a skeptical brow.

"Good job up there. I didn't know you could play the guitar," Dakota rambles.

"Thanks," I murmur just as an elbow nudges my arm.

"Hey, Benny. Isn't that the girl you were drooling over at Griff's bachelor party?" Carson asks, coming up out of nowhere.

My head whips to where Carson is pointing across to the other side of the bar, and I notice a woman standing with her back to me. Her long, auburn hair flows to the middle of her back, just above the hem of her backless navy dress. I watch with rapt attention as the redhead turns around. My jaw drops as recognition sinks in.

"How is she here right now? I thought only family, close friends, and teammates were invited. Does McKenna know her? She has to, right? I mean, why else would she be here?" I rattle off. Nervously rambling like this is completely out of character for me, and Carson must notice too.

He gives me a skeptical look before shrugging his shoulder. "I don't know. Maybe she lives on this lake, and that's why she was at the bar that night, and now she's . . . I don't know, wedding crashing or something. I have a good idea—why don't you go ask her?"

I shoot an unamused glare at Carson. "Funny."

"Well, if you're not going to shoot your shot, I'm going to at least shoot mine," Carson says, turning toward Dakota with an outstretched hand. "May I have the honor of this dance, my lady?" he asks, and Dakota's cheeks heat before she nods.

Grabbing my whiskey from the bartender, I take a drink before making my way toward my mystery woman.

I try to compose myself as I approach the redhead who has taken up residence in my head over the past month. But my mouth dries as I take in the way her backless dress showcases her creamy skin full of freckles.

Bending down, I whisper in her ear, "So are we wedding crashing now?"

Her spine stiffens before she turns, her eyes widening as she takes me in. "Benny? What are you doing here?" she asks incredulously, a dazzling smile spreading across her red lips.

"I've gotta admit, I never had faith that fate would intervene, yet here we are. So tell me, Little Red, are you wedding crashing now, or are you here for the bride or groom?"

"A bit of all the above, I suppose. My parents are friends of both the bride and groom's parents, but I'm not sure I was necessarily invited. I finished my summer class early and was able to make it up here for the reception. Though it looks like I missed some of the action, I was hoping to make it in time for the first dance, but no such luck."

"Summer class? Which college do you go to?" I ask as I bring my glass of whiskey to my lips.

"Oh, no. It's actually for high school."

I nearly spit out my drink. Using the sleeve of my dress shirt, I wipe my lips before sputtering, "Excuse me? I think I misheard you."

"Yeah, no. The girl whose birthday party I was at—she was my nanny growing up."

My eyes widen as a foreboding feeling settles in my stomach. *High school?* I mean, when I assumed she was only twenty-one, that made me hesitate. But high school? No, she was drinking that night. Looking down, I see a glass of champagne in her hands. She takes that moment to bring the delicate glass to her lips and winks at me over the rim.

"You're fucking with me?" It comes out more of a question than a statement.

Her answering laughter has me narrowing my eyes at her.

"You're such a brat," I tell her, shaking my head at her antics.

I don't miss the way her eyes flare when I call her that or how she bites her bottom lip.

"Make it up to me?"

"And how would I do that?" she asks, quirking her brow.

"Dance with me." Taking the glass from her hands, I set our drinks on a nearby table and hold my hand out for her.

She only hesitates a moment before placing her hand in mine and letting me lead her to the dance floor. I spot Jax on our way and nod toward the stage. A shit-eating grin eclipses his face, but he seems to understand what I've asked of him.

He grabs my guitar and sits on a barstool on stage. Seconds later, the opening chords of Morgan Wallen's new version of "Spin You Around" fill the tent. I pull my mystery woman to my chest, grasping her one hand in mine and sliding my other around her waist.

The seemingly innocent contact shouldn't have me buzzing with nervous excitement, but it does nonetheless. Clearing my throat, I ask, "Which college do you attend?"

"Abbott University."

"Ah, I've got a buddy that went to Abbott U. What are you studying?"

"My undergrad was merchandising. I'm just finishing one prereq I needed for my accelerated MBA program that starts this fall."

I hum in admiration. "Beauty and brains, I knew you were a catch."

She tucks her chin, but not before I see the apples of her cheeks heat. "What about you? Did you go to college?"

I stiffen at her question because it hasn't occurred to me until right this moment that she has no idea who I am. She knows my first name is Bennett, and she's likely got to be clued in that there are professional hockey players here—what with her parents knowing Griffin and Carson's parents. But I don't think she's put the puzzle pieces together about who I am.

Pushing aside the voice in my head telling me this is all wrong, I shake my head before telling a little white lie. "No, college wasn't in the plans for me. I decided to get a job right out of high school." It's not *technically* a lie. I did get drafted first overall right out of high school and signed the next season instead of playing college hockey. Though, I am attending online courses now.

She's so beautiful looking up at me right now, I can't stop myself from brushing a strand of hair off her face. Her cheeks heat and she glances toward the lake, breaking our eye contact.

Clearing my throat, I squeeze my hand resting on her lower back. "Fate intervened. I think that means you owe me your number and your identity."

Her eyes narrow as her nose scrunches up in the most ridiculously charming way. With a deep breath, she tells me her name on an exhale. "Scarlett."

A wide grin spreads across my face. "Scarlett," I repeat, liking how it rolls off my tongue.

"What? You're not going to make some silly joke about how our names rhyme?"

"Not much of a jokester," I inform her. "Besides, you call me Benny anyway."

Just then, her eye catches on something over my shoulder and as I turn to see what's caught her attention, she pulls on my loosened tie and draws my eyes back to her. "Do you wanna get out of here, *Benny*?" she asks with a spark of mischief in her amber eyes.

I try to process her question, but my brain feels like it's short-circuiting. Not wanting her to misinterpret my silence as turning her down, I swallow past my suddenly dry throat. "Where to?"

She steps away from my grasp and meets my gaze. "I was thinking wherever you were planning to stay the night."

Still temporarily stunned by her question, I simply nod in response and she leads me away from the dance floor.

Scarlett

A short Uber ride later, Bennett rests his hand on my lower back as he guides me through the lobby of his hotel. When we're in the elevator, he presses a button, but I'm not paying much attention to which one.

Instead, my eyes rake down his body as I take him in. His brown hair is cut short on the sides, leaving the top longer but smoothed back and giving him a polished look. He has the perfect amount of trimmed scruff that somehow enhances his sharp jawline. The suit he's wearing is tailored to fit his muscular frame like a glove. I'm a sucker for a tall guy, and he's well over six feet. As he unbuttons his suit jacket, I can't help but fixate on the size of his hands. Everything about this man is broad and powerful, and I can only hope this elevator ride leads me to a night full of him using that strength to pick me up and bend me over every surface of his hotel room.

Once we're shut inside, our eyes lock from across the elevator, and before I know what's happening, my feet move to Bennett of their own volition. An impish grin takes over his face when he sees how turned on I am.

I lunge toward him, and he easily lifts me with one arm, my legs wrapping around his waist at the same time that he tangles his other hand through my curls and softly tugs on my tresses. His lips crash against mine and it's at this moment that I realize how utterly fucked I am. I know this man is about to ruin me for all others. The moment Bennett's tongue swirls against mine, a trail of burning heat shoots to my core. Trying to ease the ache, I shamelessly grind my hips against his until my clit begins to pulsate and I think I'll come right here, right now, just like this. From dry humping a stranger in an elevator.

I don't even know his last name. The thought is gone as fast as it appeared when a low growl of approval rumbles through Bennett's chest as he presses me against the wall of the elevator, allowing him to work his hips even harder against mine.

Oh Jesus, thank you for this night. For putting me in this man's path once again. Thank you for divine-fucking-intervention.

Bennett balances me against the wall as he hikes up the silk skirt of my dress before slamming his hips against mine once more. The feel of his erection through his suit pants rubs perfectly against my exposed clit.

His fingers dig into the bare skin on my hips before he pulls away and groans, "Fuck, Scar. You're not wearing any panties?"

"I didn't want any lines to show through my dress," I explain, panting as I try to catch my breath just as the elevator chimes and the doors open.

Bennett carefully puts me down and makes quick work to adjust my dress, but there's no need, the floor his room is on is deserted.

He grabs my hand and leads me through the entryway of his room after swiping his keycard.

I drop his hand and act as if I'm taking in his suite, but I can't make sense of a single detail, completely distracted by how wound up my body is. The moment he turns the deadbolt, he faces me and then our bodies collide once more.

We're a tangling mess of limbs as we strip each other out of our clothes. I break the kiss and wander into the bedroom, but I don't get more than a few feet before Bennett clasps my wrist and pulls me toward him.

"Come here, baby. I want to watch you fall apart for me," he rasps with my back pressed against his chest. I have to bite back a whimper when I arch my back and his cock nudges my ass.

Turning my head, I arch a brow at him and taunt, "Ah, shucks. Forget my name already? You had so many redeeming qualities, well, really just one, if I'm being honest." I bite my lip as I look down at his thick cock that's begging to be sucked. Slowly trailing my fingernail up his thigh, I grip his shaft and am thrilled to find my hand can't clasp around it. *This is going to be a fun ride.*

"Scarlett," he growls out my name as he carefully brushes my hair over my shoulder before placing slow, open-mouthed kisses along my collarbone. "How could I forget the name of the woman who has invaded my every thought for the past month?"

I let out an unattractive snort, unwilling to believe that statement, and start to chuckle.

But my laughter dies in my throat as Bennett wraps my hair around his fist and yanks it back.

"Careful, Little Red. I'd hate to have to spank that snark out of you," he warns.

My answering whimper tells him all he needs to know about how I'd feel about being spanked.

"Hmm," he hums. "Perhaps you want to be punished. Does that turn you on, Scar? The thought of me turning this creamy skin red?" He pauses to palm my ass and I can't stop the moan that slips past my lips. He steps closer, caging me in against the bedroom wall and his broad chest. "Yeah, me too."

Bennett is hard all over. Every inch of his body is defined and looks like he's spent years in the gym. *Maybe he has a manual labor job. Construction?*

All thoughts evacuate my brain as Bennett drags the head of his cock between my legs from my opening to my clit.

The feel of his hot skin against mine has my skin erupting in goosebumps. The anticipation is killing me, I can't take it another minute.

"Condom?" I ask.

"Whoa, why the rush?"

"I don't know, most guys aren't into the whole foreplay thing, I figured you were one of them."

Bennett stills behind me, his chest stiffening as he speaks. "You figured wrong, Little Red. Wrong for thinking you should bring up other guys right now, and wrong for thinking I haven't been daydreaming about what I would do to the girl who got away if I ever caught her in my orbit again. I've fucked my fist countless times to thoughts of tasting your sweet pussy. So I'm going to need you to get on that bed on your hands and knees with your ass up for me, baby girl."

He pushes me toward the bed and lightly spanks my ass as I go. I'm completely unashamed of the moan that slips past my lips at the contact.

Bennett chuckles in response. "I knew it."

This is sure to be one of the best nights of my life.

Bennett

"If I could live anywhere in the world, it'd probably be either Stars Hollow or Paris," Scar says as she clasps her fingers through mine. The sun is just starting to peek through the small gap in the curtains, painting her creamy skin with a golden glow.

"Where is Stars Hollow?" I question somewhat absentmindedly. I'm distracted, my focus set on counting the number of freckles on her left shoulder.

Rolling up onto her knees, she straddles me and looks down at me in shock. "You can't be serious. You don't know where Stars Hollow is?" she presses.

"No," I admit, letting out a yawn as I stretch and then fold my arms under the back of my head. "Is that out east?"

She laughs at that, and I get lost in the songlike sound. "That's because it is a fictitious town from *Gilmore Girls*."

"You're a little brat," I tell her, playfully swatting her ass before I grip her hips and bring them back down on me.

The feel of her slick heat against my cock has me ready for another round, but unfortunately, we ran out of condoms sometime in the middle of the night. But that didn't stop this siren woman from sucking the soul from my body as her pussy suffocated my face in the most glorious way.

"Don't look at me like that," I warn her. "We've got to leave this room so I can feed you something. We need sustenance. And condoms. A lot more condoms."

"I don't know, Benny. Last night was fun and all, but you're starting to sound like a stage five clinger with this talk of breakfast and next day condoms runs."

She's fucking with me again. *Right?*

An adorable snort escapes her, and before she can cover her mouth, I see the slip of her poker face.

I shake my head at her. "I'm going to let your smartass comment slide for now, but your pussy is going to pay for it later. Now get dressed so I can take you to breakfast."

"I'm less of a breakfast gal, and more of an inject-a-pot-of-coffee-straight-into-my-veins kind of lady."

"Breakfast is the most important meal of the day. Besides—"

"Yeah, yeah. *Sustenance*," she mocks, cutting me off before lifting herself off my lap. Grabbing my dress shirt off the floor, she wraps it around herself like a robe and stumbles into the bathroom.

Why do I find it oddly endearing and not completely terrifying that she didn't shut the door behind her? *What is happening to me?*

I've just slid into a pair of gym shorts when her phone buzzes on the nightstand.

Walking over to it, I holler over my shoulder, "Hey, Scar, someone named Gibby is calling you. Do you want me to bring you your phone?"

Scarlett's voice is muffled by the sound of her brushing her teeth, but I'm able to make out, "Oh, that's just Gibson, my driver. Can you answer it and let him know which hotel we're at and that he can plan to pick me up later?"

Driver? Weird, but whatever.

"Hello?" I answer.

"Oh, hello, sir. Is Miss Carlisle with you?"

Carlisle? Is that her last name? Shit, I didn't even realize. I guess we bulldozed right over proper introductions and straight to my hotel room.

"Uh, yeah. Scarlett's right here. She's just brushing her teeth . . ."

Putting her phone on mute real quick, I peek my head into the bathroom. "Hey, are you using my toothbrush?"

Turning to face me is a completely unashamed Scarlett with my toothbrush between her smirking lips.

"Brat!"

"Yet you can't seem to get enough," she throws back in a muffled voice.

She's right. I can't get enough of her. It should be alarming how easy things are between us. But the conversations between our rounds in the sheets last night were as natural as they come.

"Sir? Where is Miss Carlisle? Her father is requesting her attendance at the bride and groom's brunch this morning."

Unmuting her phone, I turn and head back into the bedroom. "I'll take her."

I wasn't planning on attending the brunch this morning, even though I was invited, but I suppose if it means more time spent with Scarlett, I'll go.

"That is quite unnecessary, sir. If you'll just put Miss Carlisle on the line, I would be more than happy to take her off your hands."

Take her off my hands? Who even says shit like that nowadays?

"Listen, Gibs, I officiated the ceremony yesterday for the newlyweds. I was invited to brunch as well, so let's save the environment and I'll plan on bringing Scar when she's ready."

I'm just about to hang up when I hear the guy sputter on the other end.

"M–Mr. Wilson? What are you doing with Mr. Carlisle's daughter?" Gibson stutters out the question and my hackles rise on high alert.

Clearing my throat, I ask, "How do you know my name?"

"I think I'd be remiss if I didn't know the star player and newly appointed captain of my boss's team."

My blood turns to ice as the realization sinks in.

Mr. Carlisle. As in Mr. Charles Carlisle. As in the owner of the Minnesota Wolverines. Also known as the guy who signs my fucking paychecks.

Fuck. *Fuck.*

"The Whitley Hotel," I grind out.

"I'll be there right away, Mr. Wilson. Please let Miss Carlisle know I will be there in ten minutes," Gibson says before the call disconnects.

Miss Carlisle. Miss. Fucking. Carlisle?

I stand frozen on the spot, the phone still at my ear, when I feel a pair of arms snake around my waist and she presses her lips between my shoulder blades.

"What did he want?" she asks. When I don't answer, she says, "Now that you mentioned food, I realize I'm starving. Where would you like to eat?"

She unclasps her hands and walks around to face me. Her brows crease in confusion when she takes in whatever look is on my face. "What's the matter?" she asks.

Tossing the phone onto the bed, I turn my back on her and run my fingers through my hair. "You know, for a second there you actually had me believing in fate—that the two of us meeting again was kismet. But nothing about our meeting was by happenstance, was it, *Miss Carlisle?*"

"What are you talking about, Bennett? Why are you saying my name like that?"

"I can't believe this," I scoff, shaking my head in disbelief as I turn to face her.

No one can ever want me for who I am. How could they when I hardly know myself? Because who am I outside of the serious hockey captain?

I clearly don't know the answer to that, but Scarlett fucking Carlisle sure as shit isn't going to be the one to find out.

"Gibson will be here to pick you up in ten minutes, Miss Carlisle. I had a good evening with you, but I think it's best if we go our separate ways."

"Ben—"

"Was this all a game to you? Was I some pawn you thought you could use to your advantage? Were you mad at your daddy and needed to lash out? Whatever your reasoning, the show's over."

Her head shoots back as if she's been hit. "Will you tell me what the hell you're talking about? Why are you talking about my father right now?" she asks, running her fingers through her hair in exasperation.

I'll give it to her, she actually manages to look genuinely confused. The girl must've been an actress in another life—hell, maybe she's one now.

Shaking my head, I let out a grunt of frustration. "I'll tell him I had a temporary lapse in judgment, I mean, it was an honest mistake. I had no idea who you were. But that wasn't the case for you, was it?"

Without giving her a chance to respond, I toss on a shirt and slide my shoes on before grabbing my phone and wallet off the dresser. "Please see yourself out, Miss Carlisle," I tell her before slamming the hotel room's door behind me.

I've never been known to lose my head over a woman before, so why the fuck did I think now was a good time to start?

1

Scarlett

AUGUST

Present

"Fuck!" I hiss under my breath after stepping on my second Hot Wheels car of the morning.

"You said another naughty! That's a quarter in the swear jar," Gunner squeals, holding his hand out as if to say *pay up*. His hazel eyes stare up at me, and I can't find it in me to be mad at the little guy who has stolen my heart.

"As if, Bug. You should have to pay me for every injury I obtain from your cars and LEGO pieces," I toss back, placing my hand on my hip.

"Those little bricks are the actual worst. But I'm afraid it's a hazard of the job, sis," Gemma calls out.

Hazard of the job? More like just another day in the life of Scarlett Carlisle.

"Well, it's not a hazard we have time for this morning. We've got Gunner's kindergarten open house followed by your new student orientation at St. Christopher Academy."

"Is it too late to plead my case for me to attend public school? I don't want to be another private school snob," Gemma whines.

"Gems, we've talked about this too many times to count. I went to St. Christopher and so did Dad. This isn't up for negotiation," I say with finality.

Gemma scoffs before moving off her stool at the kitchen island, stomping up the steps, and slamming her bedroom door. *Ugh, teenagers.*

"What are we gonna do with her?" I ask mostly to myself, though Gunner is quick to reply.

"Dunno. Please don't take her computer again. She gets meaner when it's gone."

Biting back a groan, I tell him, "You're right. But I can't take her phone away or I won't have any way of getting ahold of her after school, and she won't be able to check her sugar levels. Life is about to get busy for the three of us."

That's the understatement of the century.

"Let's get you upstairs and ready to meet your new teacher."

"But I like you as my teacher," he whines.

"Me too, Bug. But I promise you, this will be so much fun! You'll have new friends to play with, tons and tons of art supplies, and your teacher even said they have magnet tiles."

"Alright," Gunner agrees begrudgingly.

After I get him dressed and leave him to play in his room, I go across the hall to mine and settle into my favorite part of the day—my morning shower, where I get ten minutes of gloriously uninterrupted time to myself.

As I lather the shampoo in my hair, I can't help but reflect on what led me here.

My life was steered completely off the rails five years ago when my father's private jet crashed, killing him and my stepmother, Angela, therefore leaving me the sole guardian to my younger siblings, Gemma and Gunner.

Loss swallowed me and my sister whole those first few months, though I had already experienced the loss of losing one parent. Gemma and Gunner are my half siblings; my dad married Angela when I was eight and they tried for a few years to get pregnant before having success with IVF and having Gemma. Angela was told she wouldn't be able to have any more children, so they were content with it just being the four of us. That is, until the little miracle named Gunner came along. When my father and Angela told us they were expecting, we were shocked. Hell, I was twenty-one at the time, but I was happy for them nonetheless. It looks like I wasn't the only one who had a good night at the Turner wedding that summer . . .

A few months after Gunner was born, my dad surprised Angela with a trip to Banff for a weekend getaway. I was thrilled to spend some time with Gemma and soak in all the snuggles I could with my new baby brother before my internship with Nike began that fall.

Our lives changed in the blink of an eye that weekend. I went from being a newly graduated MBA student about to start her career, to a stay-at-home guardian to an infant and ten-year-old.

Over the past five years, we've been granted the luxury of staying at my family's cabin estate in northern Minnesota. I homeschooled Gemma while learning to raise an infant on my own. My grandfather became the interim owner of my father's professional hockey team after his untimely death, with the hopes that when life settled down for the three of us, I'd take over for him.

The problem was that life didn't seem to slow down or settle for us. Instead, we've been met with wave after wave of complications and unforeseen circumstances. I discovered Gunner had a tongue tie, so he wasn't properly taking a bottle after having nursed for most of his first few months. Gemma was diagnosed with type 1 diabetes last year at the age of fourteen. We went from homeschooling as a temporary transition to it being a necessity until we could figure out how to regulate her blood sugars.

It felt like the second we got our heads above water, the tide came and pulled us right back under.

I was drowning.

And now? A tsunami was brewing in the wake of the news my grandfather gave me last month. He was diagnosed with early-stage dementia, which meant our time for living in our little bubble was over.

Instead of pursuing my dreams in fashion merchandising, I would be thrown headfirst into the world of sports ownership and management. I'd be spending this next year under the wing of my grandfather learning the ropes before taking over at the start of the next hockey season.

I didn't have the first clue about owning a professional hockey team—it was never the path I'd planned to take. My dad had always supported my dreams to pursue a career in the fashion industry. He'd been the one to buy me sketchbooks and my first sewing machine. He'd sat on my bedroom floor with me and helped as I made mood boards from hundreds of magazine clippings. He was truly my hero and my best friend, and the sinking feeling that comes whenever I remember I'll never get to call him for advice or receive another one of his priceless hugs again is all-consuming.

Shaking myself out of my grief spiral, I turn off the shower and towel dry before walking over to my vanity to moisturize my skin and comb my hair.

Next, I walk across my bathroom to my happy place, my walk-in closet that is the size of most people's primary bedroom. I'm not ashamed to say this is my favorite space in our new home—fashion has always made me feel more connected to my mother who was a renowned model until she died from complications following my birth.

Loss has surrounded me my entire life.

I've never missed my mother, stepmother, and father as much as I did when I took guardianship of Gunner and Gemma. I didn't have them to call for advice when Gunner was colicky, or anyone to babysit them when I needed a moment to myself, or any family to celebrate the big milestones with. No one to FaceTime when Gunner took his first steps or Gemma stood up on water skis for the first time. Our holidays were spent with our only family, our grandparents, and while they tried their best to help when they could, they just couldn't keep up with the needs of two young children at their age.

I mindlessly flip through the hangers in my closet, which is wasted time because I already know what I'll wear today. Knowing I need to make a good impression on Gunner and Gemma's teachers, I decide on a white, lightweight blouse that is sleeveless and tucked into my favorite navy, wide-leg trousers. I finish off the look with my gold Chanel belt and earrings.

After I finish blowing out my hair, I add a reminder on my phone to schedule hair appointments for the three of us. My makeup doesn't take long and is as natural as possible, allowing for my freckles to show through. I used to resent that feature, being fair-skinned with red hair meant I was an easy target for the mean girls growing up, but as I've grown older, I've learned to love them.

I've just slipped on my favorite pair of nude Louboutin pumps when Gunner comes running into my room. "Scar, tell her to give them back!" he shouts.

"Whoa!" I hold out my arms to catch him. "Give what back, Bug?"

"My lucky crystals! She stole them from my collection and I need them for my big day," he explains.

Before I have to seek her out, Gemma appears at my bedroom door.

"Gems, come on, give him his crystals back. How would you like it if he took one of your composition notebooks?" I ask.

With a roll of her eyes and scoff, she holds out her hand to Gunner to give him his crystals back.

"Here, I'm sorry," she says to him with genuine remorse.

"Why did you take them when you knew I needed them today?" Gunner whines.

Gemma throws up her hands. "Look, maybe I needed them too. It's not like anyone is going to be nice to the nerdy girl who's been homeschooled practically her whole life."

My chest squeezes with worry and my stomach sinks with unease hearing her reasoning.

"Well, I have two. One for me and one for you," Gunner tells her as he holds a crystal out for her.

Gemma hesitates. "Are you sure, Gun? I don't want to make your big day any harder."

"I'm sure. Besides, my crystals are the strongest in the whole world!" he squeals as he takes off down the hallway with his fist raised in the air like a superhero.

God, I love that boy.

Gemma echoes my thought, adding, "I wish I could be more like him—so carefree and fun-spirited. Sometimes I'm just so *angry*."

I've been taking Gemma to therapy regularly for a few years now, not only to cope with the loss of our parents but also to help her accept her diagnosis.

I wrap her in my arms and give her a tight squeeze while I inhale the scent of her mint and eucalyptus shampoo.

"So much has happened in such a short time, it's okay not to be okay, sis. But just know, we're going to rock this year, I can feel it," I reassure her while also hoping I can convince myself too.

We did it, I was able to successfully get the kids off to their first day of school this morning after yesterday's orientations went well. We're off to a good start, and I'm feeling good about this year.

My morning is already productive, I just got off the phone with my grandfather's secretary, Marissa, to confirm my meeting with him this morning. It'll only be my second week in the office, but so far so good.

As soon as the call disconnects from my car's speakers, I park outside my new favorite coffee spot in the city, Spencer's Coffee Co.

I'm waiting in line but am surprised to hear my name called by a barista holding up a coffee order. Looking around, I figure it must be for another Scarlett. That is, until the shop's owner grabs it off the pickup counter and walks it over to me in line.

Spencer Quist, or Spence, as he's asked me to call him, saunters over to me with a shy smile on his face.

"Good morning, Scarlett," he says as he holds out the cup for me. "A triple shot hot white mocha with oat milk, extra foam, and no whip. Right?"

Somewhat flabbergasted that he remembered my very specific order after only coming here the past few days, I try to hide my shock as I grab the drink from his hand. "Y–yes. That's exactly right. Wow, thank you."

"You're welcome," he replies as he grasps the neck strap of his apron on either side and rocks back on his heels. "Listen, I'm just going to come right out and ask. Do you have time to stick around for breakfast with me?"

Again, I'm completely caught off guard, this time by his forward question.

"Um, no actually. Unfortunately, I've got a meeting this morning that begins shortly on the other side of the city." I hold my cup up in front of us before reaching into my purse for my wallet. "I just have enough time to pay for my coffee. Perhaps another time?"

"Yeah, a rain check?" he asks.

"Exactly," I say as I look around for a spot to set down my coffee so I can dig around in my wallet for some cash.

Spencer must sense what I'm trying to do because he shakes his head at me. "On the house, Scarlett." He winks before wishing me luck at my meeting.

I thank him and hurry back to my car, cursing myself for completely losing my ability to flirt with an attractive man. Even though Spencer isn't the type I typically go for, he's still good-looking and seems sweet.

My game is rusty, it's been far too long since I've flirted with a man. My lifestyle change hasn't exactly left a lot of time for dating the past few years.

After setting my coffee in the cupholder, I start up my Mercedes-Benz GLS-Class, grip the steering wheel, and close my eyes to take a deep, calming breath.

I've got this. I can do this. It's just my first day full of official meetings with board members and management.

At a job you're unfit for, for a sports team you know nothing about, my subconscious shouts at me as I make my way across the city to my grandfather's office, which is right next to the arena.

I shake those negative thoughts, push my shoulders back, and move through the lobby of the building a few minutes later.

"This is going to be great," I whisper to myself once I'm closed inside the elevator. But I can't seem to believe my own sad excuse at pumping myself up.

This is already going horribly, unless I just heard my grandfather incorrectly.

"You can't be serious. I don't have any prospects, how am I supposed to do that within a year?" I ask incredulously.

"You're the brightest light I know, Firefly. You'll be just fine," he tries to assure me; however, that seems like an impossible task.

There's a tall, dark blur in my peripheral that catches my attention.

And suddenly, I realize things have just become infinitely worse.

What the hell have I done to receive this karma?

My stomach sinks to my toes as I look out the glass door of the conference room only to find my one-night stand who so rudely dismissed me over six years ago.

The square edge of his jaw is clenched and his eyes narrow suspiciously when they meet mine from his spot in the hallway, where he's paused with his hand grasping the door handle.

But why? I can't for the life of me understand why Bennett is looking at *me* like that. If anything, I'm the one who should be upset with *him* for giving me the night of my life before promptly kicking me out of his suite the next morning.

Suddenly, Bennett's face shifts as he opens the door, and it's as if he slips on a mask of indifference.

"Ah, there he is. Come on in," my grandfather turns and waves him in.

"Joseph," Bennett says as he holds out his hand for my grandfather to shake.

How does he know my grandfather? And why in the hell is he here?

I do my best to keep a neutral expression, but I'm sincerely so fucking lost right now.

"Bennett, this is my granddaughter, Scarlett Carlisle. Scarlett, this is Bennett Wilson, the captain of the Wolverines."

Record scratch. Come again? Did he just say *captain*?

Bennett's jaw ticks as he holds out his hand for me to shake, and when I do, I can't help the shiver that slips down my spine from his warm touch. Unwarranted memories from that night six years ago cloud my vision.

"One more. Come on, Scar, give me one more," he says as he adjusts my positioning so I'm hovering just above his face. "I'm famished, Red. I'll perish if you don't sit down and take what you deserve from me."

Without warning, Bennett pulls down on my thighs and I can't stop my hips from rocking in response.

Holy fucking shit, I've never been so wholly devoured in my life. The way Bennett's mouth, tongue, fingers, and scruff of his beard work my pussy is enough to cause black dots to spot my vision.

"Oh, fuck! I'm so sensitive, I can't," I pant.

Bennett lifts me just enough to growl, "You can. Now sit the fuck down and fuck my face, baby girl."

Well, with a demand like that . . . I hold on to the hotel headboard with one hand and grasp a hold of his brown hair in the other.

I'm thrust out of my trip down memory lane when Bennett says in an icy tone, "Pleasure to meet you, Miss Carlisle."

Fuck my actual life. This should be interesting . . .

2

Bennett

Standing before me is a surprise I didn't see coming. Though I'm not sure why I'm so stunned, she is the owner's granddaughter, after all.

Scarlett Carlisle.

In place of the cute college student I met all those years ago, is a put-together woman in a white blouse, charcoal pencil skirt, and stilettos. Her once long and curly tresses have now been slicked back into a tight ponytail, though I'm glad to see she hasn't cut the locks I have longed to wrap around my fist once more.

Snap the fuck out of it, man.

I let go of her hand, but I didn't miss the way her features went from confused, to shocked, to furious within a matter of seconds.

She should've been a drama major with the way she's able to make me feel like a fool even all these years later.

"Captain?" she questions as she smooths her skirt.

"Yes, this will be his eighth season wearing the C on his chest," Joseph tells her.

"And you said his name was Bennett. Bennett Wilson," she repeats, more to herself than to her grandfather. Her brows are pinched and she's blinking rapidly, almost as if she's putting the pieces of the puzzle together for the first time.

Wow, someone give her an Oscar, she's knocking this performance out of the park. I'd give her a round of applause if it wouldn't pique Joseph's curiosity.

She's snapped from her role-playing of an innocent woman, when her grandfather suggests, "Why don't you take Bennett to your office and go over the schedule changes for the preseason we discussed."

Her jaw falls open as she stares back at her grandfather in shock.

"That won't be necessary, we can discuss any changes here, Joseph," I tell him, but he just shakes his head.

"No, I insist. It will be good for Scar to get a feel for interacting with the players," he replies.

Why does she need to interact with the players? And did he suggest she take me to her office? Since when did she get an office? Is she working for the team now?

For the past six years, Scarlett Carlisle has been a ghost. Well, more so for the past five years since her father tragically passed away. I sought her out at his memorial that the Wolverines put together to give my condolences, but she hadn't shown up.

Without saying a word, Scarlett nods at her grandfather, grabs her laptop, and heads out the conference room door down the hallway that I assume leads to her new office.

I quickly say goodbye to Joseph before sauntering after her.

Once we're inside her office, I quietly shut the door behind me, looking up to find her pacing in front of the floor-to-ceiling windows as she rubs her temples with both hands.

"This can't seriously be happening," she murmurs to herself, still pacing and rubbing her temples.

When I clear my throat, her spine stiffens as she snaps to attention. She turns to face me, and I curse my stupid attraction to this woman when my chest squeezes in, what . . . *yearning*? Fuck.

"Please have a seat," she offers and gestures at a chair across from her desk. I take the offered seat, manspreading to get comfortable before leaning forward with my elbows on my thighs.

"Before we begin, I'd like to propose a reset. We can just leave the past in the past—forget that night ever happened, as far as I'm concerned."

"And how exactly would you like me to do that? Find a hypnotist to erase the memories of you moaning my name and begging for me to fill your mouth with my cum?"

Her eyes widen in shock. "Th-at is not at all what I was requesting, Mr. Wilson."

"Mr. Wilson. Miss Carlisle. Can we skip the bullshit formalities? I think we know each other too . . . *intimately* for that, yeah?"

"Why?" she asks, shaking her head in exasperation.

"Why what?"

"Why didn't you tell me who you were that night? Or the next morning?"

"You're a damn good actress, Scarlett, you know that?" I tell her as I stare at her pointedly. "Even sitting here across from you and knowing the truth, you've almost played me the fool."

She huffs then lets out a low chuckle. "And what truth is it you think I know? Because I can assure you that up until ten minutes ago when my grandfather told me who you were, I had no clue that you were on the roster of my family's professional hockey team."

"How is that even possible?"

Sitting back in her chair, she crosses her arms and shoots me with a look I can't quite read. "Be honest, did you know who I was the night we met? Or the night of the wedding?"

"You can't be serious." I scoff. "No, of course, I didn't know."

She raises a skeptical brow. "And why is that?"

"Your father wasn't exactly the sharing type. He didn't parade you around team events or at games, so I had no clue that he had an older daughter."

"Exactly."

Exactly what? Instead of stating that, I crook a brow at her bullshit.

"My point exactly. You didn't know he even had an oldest daughter because I was so far removed from anything to do with the team. I won't pretend to be a huge fan of the game. I won't sit here and lie to your face by telling you I'm an avid spectator of Wolverines games. This was never the plan for me," she admits.

"And what plan is that?" I ask warily because I think I know where this is headed.

"Well, I'm not entirely sure I'm at liberty to discuss that with you, Mr. Wilson."

When I narrow my eyes at her, she sighs in defeat. "Bennett."

"Why do I get the impression that you're keeping something from me? I don't like secrets, Scar." I grit my teeth when I realize her nickname slipped past my lips. I take a deep breath and continue. "When it comes to my team, I know everything. So whether you tell me now or not, I'll be clued in. Might as well save yourself the trouble. I hear keeping things bottled up doesn't do anyone any good."

"Yeah, as tempted as I am to spill all my deepest secrets to a complete stranger, I'll pass." Scarlett shuffles some papers around on her desk before finding the one she was looking for. It is a calendar with a schedule of events and ice times on it. "Now, let's get back to the matter at hand. We've discussed changing the preseason practice schedule to be able to incorporate a couple of team events. One is an old tradition that we'd like to bring back—the team friends and family preseason skate. The first few seasons as an organization, the Wolverines players and staff would bring their friends and families to the arena for a fun evening of skating and socializing as a way to get to know everyone. We'd like to bring this back."

"And why is it that you need to get to know the players? Your grandfather had mentioned you needed to get a feel for interacting with the players. Are you joining the organization?" I press.

She sighs in defeat before bracing her hands on her desk. "Yes, I will be working alongside my grandfather this season."

I sit back in my seat and bring my ankle up to rest on my opposite thigh, hoping I look calm and collected, when really I'm freaking the fuck out. The realization sinks in that I'll be seeing Scarlett on a regular basis.

My chest does that pathetic clenching thing again and I curse it for being so weak.

Even if she didn't realize who I was all those years ago, the feelings I had for her after only two encounters are worrisome. She's a distraction I can't afford. Joseph said it himself, this will be my eighth season as a captain of this team, and I'll be damned if it's not the season I finally hoist the cup in the air.

3

Scarlett

Training camp has been going well and the first few weeks of working alongside my grandfather have gone better than I'd anticipated. Gemma started her sophomore year at St. Christopher Academy, and so far she hasn't had any diabetic episodes, so I'm calling that a win. However, what isn't a win is the way she's shut down on me this week. I'm not sure what to make of her shift in her mood quite yet. Gunner's teacher said that he is thriving academically, but he's been a bit shy and reserved when it comes to making new friends. I can't help but feel guilty for keeping him home with me for as long as I did. After all we'd been through, I couldn't stomach the thought of sending him to daycare.

I buckle my seatbelt and glance back at Gunner in the rearview mirror. His light brown hair is trimmed short on the sides, leaving the wavy hair on top a bit longer. Gemma's hair is red like my own, however, hers is a bit of a darker auburn than mine. The three of us just got haircuts for our upcoming picture days. Gunner and Gemma both have school pictures next week, and I've got my first NHL media day headshots scheduled for tomorrow morning.

This afternoon is the team's friends and family skate, so I suppose there's a chance the three of us will be pictured by the team's social media crew as well.

Gemma crosses her arms over her chest in the passenger seat beside me and pleads her case one final time for me to let her stay home.

"You can't miss this event, Gems. Come on, it'll be fun to get out on the ice again," I say enthusiastically. "Besides, Gunner hasn't had the opportunity to skate yet. I need your help to teach him how."

Gemma used to figure skate before her diagnosis and she was beyond talented, like on track for the next Olympics talented. Since she gave up competition last year, she hasn't stepped foot on the ice. It wasn't a medical requirement that she give up the sport altogether, however, with how unsteady her sugars were, we spent months in and out of the hospital, and being the competitor she is, she decided to give up the sport when she felt she had fallen behind.

"I don't even have skates that fit me anymore," she counters.

"When I ordered Gunner's skates, I got you a new pair in your size too," I inform her.

That earns me an annoyed growl from my little sister.

"Fine! I'll help Gunner, but don't expect me to talk to anyone else, or pose for any stupid photos," she grumbles.

"Deal. No talking to strangers and no photos," I agree, winking at Gunner in the rearview when he sticks his tongue out at Gemma and makes a silly face to the back of her head.

I swallow the laughter that wants to slip out at his antics.

"I'm just going to stop by the house so we can get changed into warmer clothes, then we need to head over to the arena so we're not late."

This was the case the first few days of school as we adjusted to our new routine. Being late is a horrible habit I've been trying to break for as long as I can remember. My father told me growing up that it's the one bad trait I inherited from my mother. According to him, she was chronically fashionably late to events. He used to tell me I had to be ready thirty minutes before we really needed to leave to try to get us out the door on time, and even in doing so, I'd still manage to make us late.

When I pull up to our gated neighborhood, I wave at Frank, the security guard on duty, as he opens the gates for us. Living in a family home in the suburbs with a manicured lawn wasn't exactly what I had envisioned for myself in my twenties, but I'm glad our family is fortunate enough to provide stability for Gunner and Gemma's sake.

As we walk through the front door, I'm forced to face another bad habit of mine—I become chaotically disorganized when I'm overwhelmed, which is exactly how I'm feeling after all of the changes the past two months. When we moved from the cabin to this house, enrolled in new schools, and started a new career path all in a matter of a few weeks, my mind shut down on me. Sometimes I get so overwhelmed that it feels like my brain is an internet browser with hundreds of tabs open, so overwhelmed I start to short circuit, not knowing where to begin.

Looking around the main floor at all of the clutter, I make a mental note to look into hiring a housekeeper. Growing up, my father had a live-in housekeeper who also acted as a nanny to me until I went to school. Her name was Ruth and I loved her dearly. She is married to my former driver, Gibson. Shortly before my father passed away, Ruth and Gibson retired to help care for their first grandchild, but we still talk often. I'd love to find someone as loving and caring as Ruth to help around the house and perhaps with Gemma and Gunner if I need to work late.

Once we're changed, we head to the arena and I park in the underground parking reserved for players and management.

I grab the bag of our skates and a helmet for Gunner from the trunk of my SUV and lock it before grabbing Gunner's hand. "You excited, Bug?" I ask him.

"Yeah, let's do this!" he squeals. I don't miss the small smile Gemma tries to hide when she hears the excitement in his voice. I'm looking forward to sharing this experience with them. Perhaps I'm even excited to see a certain someone I've only been able to catch glimpses of in passing this week. It's been boring not giving him a little hell.

Bennett

I see her copper hair flowing around her before I register anything else.

Like the small boy beside her taking timid steps onto the ice. Or the other girl with darker auburn hair, who looks to be in her teens, skating up to the two of them with a skate trainer for the boy.

Scarlett is here.

Jackson chooses this exact moment to skate up to me and spray ice that makes it all the way up to my lower stomach.

"You're an asshole, you know that?" I growl at him under my breath as I dust the powder off my jacket and pants.

"Funny, I don't think I've heard that one before," he throws back at me.

Letting out a sigh of annoyance, I try to subtly look over his shoulder to see if I can spot Scarlett again. I must do a shit job because Jax turns to see where I'm looking and when he spots her, he sucks in a deep breath.

"Is that Little Red Riding Hood?" he questions.

Motherfucker. This is exactly what I didn't need today. "Who?" I ask, trying to feign ignorance.

"There." Jax points and I train my gaze to where he's motioning to the redhead across the rink standing beside the benches.

"Don't know. But it wouldn't be surprising, I guess, considering she is family to the owner of the team," I reply with as much nonchalance as I can muster.

"Yeah, that's definitely her. Since when does Scarlett Carlisle come to team events?" Jax asks curiously. And just as the words leave his mouth, Carson and his wife Dakota skate up to us with their twin son and daughter in tow.

Lainey and Leo Wilder are four now, but they're able to stride on the ice without too much assistance and they're both in full hockey gear. Leo is the spitting image of his dad, with honey-blonde hair and piercing blue eyes. Lainey looks more like her mom with dark, wavy hair braided into a ponytail flowing out of her helmet, though she also has her father's eyes. I'm actually surprised to see Dakota on the ice, she isn't the best skater and Carson just shared with us a few days ago that Dakota is pregnant again. That's likely the reason Carson is glued to her side instead of the twins's. I hope for their sake that it's only one baby this time around—the thought of four kids is daunting to me, but they're a great team so they'd probably take it in stride.

"Wait, did y'all just say Benny's girl is here?" Carson asks in a tone that is the equivalent to what I imagine a Golden Retriever would sound like if they could talk.

"Y'all?" I quirk a brow at him in question. And for fuck's sake I had sex with the woman over six years ago. She's not my girl. She's nothing but a new inconvenience.

"Yeah, y'all. I'm married to a beautiful Texan and we happen to split some of our time there. Sue me for using slang that, by the way, makes a hell of a lot more sense than saying 'you all,'" he replies in a defensive tone.

"Touché, Carsey. Don't let this grumpy ass bring you down; he's just freaked out to see his one that got away show up out of the blue," Jax explains.

Ha! He's so fucking wrong. Though, I can't seem to stop my gaze from veering in her direction. And when Carson mutters, "Huh, I didn't know she had a kid," I can't deny the way my stomach sinks and my chest squeezes in disappointment. That is, until I take a better look at the young boy she's seemingly teaching how to skate. What the fuck?

Panic consumes me when I take in his features—brown hair far too similar to my own, and as I skate closer, I see his hazel eyes look up at me with recognition.

Wait, why am I close enough to this kid that I can make out the color of his eyes?

The thought evaporates the moment he opens his mouth and shyly greets me. "Heya there."

I kneel in front of the trainer he's leaning on and take him in a little more. The only resemblance to Scarlett I can see in him is his slanted smile and button nose. Other than those features, he looks eerily similar to . . . me.

Clearing the anxiety from my throat, I hold my gloved fist out to the kid so he can give me knucks. "Heya there, bud. I'm Bennett. What's your name?"

"Gunner," he replies.

"Nice to meet you, Gunner. And how old are you?" I can't stop myself from asking.

"I'm five. How old are *you*?" he tosses back.

Somehow a chuckle slips past my lips, though I'm not sure how, considering my stomach is in knots and my throat is now even more clogged with anxiety. "I'll be thirty-one in a few months. When's your birthday?" I manage to choke out the question.

"March twentieth. I'll be six then."

I mentally tally his age and the world stands still as the numbers and dates align in my head.

Holy shit. He was likely conceived in June. Just over six years ago in June.

My head snaps up to see a skeptical Scarlett's narrowed gaze on me. *Oh really?*

"Can I have a word with you, Miss Carlisle?" I question as I stand from the ice.

"I thought we were past the formalities, *Mr. Wilson*," she replies in a snarky voice, crossing her arms over her chest. As if she has any right to be annoyed right now.

"I'd like to discuss some additional scheduling items that have recently been brought to my attention," I tell her in a low, even tone, letting her know I mean business.

Scarlett skates over to the other girl and I miss what she says to her due to her hushed tone. The girl nods before skating over to Gunner. I wonder if she's his nanny, though she looks a bit young for that role.

Once Gunner is out of ear's shot, Scarlett faces me. "I'm all ears, Mr. Wilson. What is it you wanted to discuss?"

"Can we go somewhere more private?"

"Lead the way," she says, gesturing toward the bench. I lead us off the ice to the team's locker room, and once I've confirmed we're alone, I turn to face her.

"Is he the reason you disappeared?" I ask after a moment of hesitation.

"Who? My father?" She appears taken aback.

"No, Gunner—*your son*," I bite out.

She blinks at me once, twice, before breaking out into a fit of laughter. She's full-on belly laughing at me right now—bent over, choking on her chuckles as she slaps her leg. "Oh-ho my god, that's some good shit!" Once she's able to stand again, she bites her lip to stifle her laughter when she sees my less-than-enthused expression. "Before you ask, no, Gunner is not your son. He's my little brother!"

My body stiffens even further as her words sink in. Her little brother. Meaning he's not mine. Well, thank fuck. After seeing how much Griffin missed from the first year and a half he didn't know Cadence existed, I couldn't stomach missing out on five years of my child's life.

"Now that we've cleared that up, do you have anything else you'd like to discuss, or can I get back to my siblings so we can enjoy the family skate?" Her haughty tone now matches the one I'd used with her. Scarlett shoulders past me, but pauses when she gets to the double doors of the locker room. "And to answer your question, yes, Gunner and Gemma are why I 'disappeared' as you put it. Becoming the sole guardian to two orphaned children at the ripe old age of twenty-two left me reeling. I think it's pretty understandable that we took some time to ourselves to adjust to our new normal."

My apology is on the tip of my tongue, but I don't manage to get it out before she shoves through the doors. Now I'm the one left reeling from her confession.

I've gotten it all wrong for far too long when it comes to Scarlett. For years, I've been under the impression that she knew exactly who I was that night. That she hooked up with me to get a rise out of her father. When, in reality, she didn't have a clue as to who I was. And then, if that wasn't bad enough, I just accused her of having a secret baby and disappearing from the face of the earth to keep him from me. Essentially eliminating what little progress we'd made the past few weeks.

What has gotten into me? When it comes to Scarlett, I can't stop myself from acting like a complete fucking ass.

I decide right then and there to do anything and everything I can to make it up to her.

4

Scarlett

"**B**ennett Wilson is so cool!" Gunner squeals as he climbs into his booster seat, and I can't help the sigh that slips out. "Did you know he didn't start skating until he was five?"

"I didn't know that. How did you find that out?"

"And now he's the captain, Scar," Gunner continues in amazement without answering my question.

"I know he's the captain, Gun. But how did you know he didn't start skating until he was five?"

"He told me. Duh!" I'm having a hard time buckling Gunner into his seat with how excited he is.

"Really? And when did he do that?" I've barely asked the question when there's a knock on the rear window of my vehicle. I step back, surprised to find Bennett standing a few steps away.

"Hey, Cap!" Gunner yelps, popping his head out the door.

"Hey there, Champ," Bennett greets him as if they're longtime buddies. He holds up a teal, bedazzled cell phone and says, "I think this might belong to Gemma. I wasn't trying to be nosy, but there was a Dexcom notification going off about a low sugar reading."

Panic flares to life inside my chest until I look over and see Gemma opening up a packet of gummy bears she keeps in her crossbody bag.

"Don't worry, I'm on it, Scar," Gemma assures me, but it's not enough to override my anxiety.

I place my hand on my chest, close my eyes, and take a deep, calming breath.

She's okay. She's in tune with her body. She isn't having an episode. She doesn't need to go to the hospital. You didn't fail her . . . at least, not this time.

I'm pulled from my spiral when I feel the warmth of Bennett's hand clasp my own. "Hey, it's okay. She's got it handled, don't you Gems?"

Gems? How does he know her? And since when are they on a nickname basis?

"Sure do, Benny," she replies, her mouth still full of gummy bears.

"Look, like I said, I wasn't trying to be nosy, I was just concerned. My little cousin has type 1 diabetes too, so I know how important glucose monitoring is," Bennett says in a soothing voice that is so polar opposite to the tone he'd used with me in the locker room only hours ago.

Instead of acknowledging what he just said, I turn to Gemma. "Why are your sugars low right now? Did you have anything to eat while we were at the event?"

She looks sheepish when she shakes her head. She doesn't meet my eye as she confesses, "No, I kind of got caught up in being on the ice again. It felt . . . good. I hadn't realized how much I'd missed it."

I bite my lower lip, taking time to weigh my response. "I'm so happy you were able to skate again today, Gems. Next time, just be sure to take breaks to nourish and hydrate as you need them."

"Not sure yet if there will be a next time. But, yeah, I'm sorry I got caught up in the excitement," she replies, finally looking at me. I see genuine remorse shining in her eyes, and I hate that for her.

"No need to apologize. Let's get home and you can perform that song for me you've been working on," I suggest.

When her eyes flare and her cheeks heat with embarrassment, I immediately realize my mistake. I've just let a secret passion of hers slip in front of a complete stranger. "I'm just going to grab your phone and then we'll take off. Give me a minute," I tell them as I shut the door and move to the rear of the vehicle where Bennett is standing, looking unsure of himself as he holds Gemma's phone in one hand and grips the back of his neck with the other.

"I'm sorry if I overstepped. It wasn't my intention to upset any of you just now. And I'm also sorry for how I acted earlier in the locker room. I was an ass," he admits, looking awfully bashful and so unlike the confident Bennett Wilson I've come to know him as over the past month.

We haven't had to interact much, but my grandfather seems to call him into his office or have him sit in on meetings that other players and alternate captains aren't privy to. I haven't worked up the courage to question my grandfather on it yet, but I've definitely noticed that Bennett is held with higher regard than other players in my grandfather's eyes.

It's interesting, to say the least.

Feeling unsure of myself is something I've become all too familiar with since becoming their guardian, so as I stand before Bennett's imploring gaze, I find myself shifting on my feet to get recentered. "You didn't overstep. At least not just now. The locker room is a whole different story—"

"I'm so sorry, Scar," he cuts in.

Holding my hand up to silence him, I continue, "Let's just pretend that the locker room incident didn't happen. I appreciate you bringing Gemma's phone out here."

Bennett holds out my sister's phone for me to grab. As I do, his fingers brush mine, and a surge of heat shoots up my arm and pools in my chest, leaving me a bit breathless.

Unsure of what else to say, I turn around and take a step toward the front of my vehicle.

"You're doing a great job with them," he says, so softly I wonder if I'm imagining things. With my brows pinched, I face him again. "While you were talking to the social media team, I gave Gunner a couple of pointers. He's a good kid, told me he loves hockey, so we hit it off. Gemma was more reserved at first, but once she started talking, she went on and on about how amazing you are. And my god, she's so talented."

"About that, could you keep what you overheard me asking her about to yourself?" When he stares back in confusion, I clarify, "She's a bit self-conscious about her songwriting."

"Oh, I was referring to her talent on the ice, but yeah, I can keep that tidbit to myself. It sounds like she has quite a few creative passions," he murmurs.

"I keep telling her the songs are amazing, but she says I have to tell her that as her older sister."

"If I recall, you said something about my mother lying to me about being a good singer the night we met," he tosses back with a cocky smirk.

My cheeks heat in response to the playful lilt of his voice and the reminder of that night.

God, what I wouldn't give to be able to go back to being a carefree twenty-one-year-old hitting on a sexy man dressed in a ridiculous outfit for even just one night.

"Well, I still can't recall if she was telling the truth or not. I was pretty buzzed. But when it comes to Gemma, I'm being completely unbiased when I tell you she's so incredibly talented. Her songs are filled with such emotion, and when she sings them while playing the piano, my heart can hardly take it. She says she wants to learn how to play guitar, but I haven't gotten around to signing her up for lessons. Maybe that'll be a good Christmas p-present," I stutter to a stop when I realize I'm rambling, and Bennett likely wants to get on his way.

He tilts his head to the side. "She wants to learn guitar?"

"Yeah, but I'm sure you don't want to hear about all this. I'm going to get them home. I'll see you when I see you, Bennett," I tell him, but he surprises me with his next words.

"I'll teach her." His offer leaves me speechless, so I just stare back at him like an idiot.

"How to play guitar, that is," he clarifies when I still haven't said a word. "I could come to your place to teach her, or if she's ever around the office, I could bring my guitar there."

What would that be like? To have Bennett in my home, taking up space with his broad body, and polluting the air with his crisp masculine scent, all while teaching my little sister to play the guitar. It sounds like a terrible temptation that I should absolutely turn down.

But I don't, because why would I have any sense of self-preservation? Instead, I find myself nodding in response while biting back the emotion threatening to spill out from his kind offer.

As I round the vehicle, Bennett calls out, "Drive safe, Scar. I'll text you to set up a time that works best for your schedule."

I can't help but smile softly to myself. "You don't have my number."

A moment later, my phone buzzes in the pocket of my jeans.

Unknown:

I've got my ways, Little Red. Talk soon.

5

Bennett

Me:

How does Thursday evening sound for Gem's first guitar lesson?

Little Red:

She doesn't exactly have a guitar yet, and I doubt I could get one before then.

Me:

She could use mine for the first lesson. We'll just be going over basic chords and positioning. Is she right or left-handed?

Little Red:

Right.

Me:

Same, she can use mine. Then if she likes it, I can go with you to pick one out for her.

Little Red:

That's awfully kind of you to offer. And I'm too clueless and desperate to turn you down.

Little Red:

> Wow, that came off wrong . . . What I meant to say is, I'd appreciate the help. Thanks!

Me:

> Send me your address and I'll see you Thursday night. Does 6pm work?

Little Red:

> Works great! See you then, Benny.

I'm smiling to myself like a complete idiot at her use of my nickname when I hear a throat clear.

"Wilson, are you even listening to me?" Coach Evans asks through gritted teeth.

Pocketing my phone, I meet his eye and apologize. "Sorry, Coach. It was just my father checking in. You know how he is." The lie makes my stomach sink, and just thinking of my dad makes my mood sour.

"Don't I know it. How is Senator Wilson doing these days?" he asks.

Miserable as ever. Though, I don't voice that thought.

"Thankfully, he's been busy lately," I reply, which is also the truth. And thank fuck for that.

"No wonder Jackson is having such a great preseason. Your father isn't making him second guess his every decision on the ice," Coach says, shaking his head. "If it wasn't impossible, I'd try to have him banned from attending Wolverines games and events."

I scoff at that. "I can just see the headlines now, 'Minnesota Senator Banned from Attending the State of Hockey's Team's Games.' Don't think that'd go over so well," I deadpan.

"No shit. And I'd like to keep my job if I can help it," Coach tosses back. "Anyway, we're getting off track. I was asking you how things with Connelly are going."

Ah, right. Nathan Connelly. The eighteen-year-old rookie, drafted first overall in the latest draft, and starting center for our team's second line. He's also the franchise's youngest rookie ever, with me coming in at a close second. I turned nineteen in December of my first season in the NHL. Connelly just turned eighteen in June.

Navigating the start of my NHL career straight out of high school was a difficult transition for me at first. The pace of the game was definitely a hurdle I had to get up to speed on, but trying to figure out the lifestyle of a professional hockey player at such a young age kind of fucked with my head. And that was twelve years ago when social media wasn't quite as big of a beast as it is currently. Damn, that makes me feel old. But my point is, now, for Connelly, he's got to deal with the pressure of being one of the league's youngest rookies of all time, in addition to adapting to having his life put under a microscope for fans to scrutinize his every move.

Though, thankfully for him, he homeschooled and played juniors instead, so he was able to graduate early and play a year of college hockey before signing his first contract.

Coach asked if I'd take the kid under my wing and mentor him this season. I told him I'd be honored, and so far, I've enjoyed the hell out of the experience. The rookie is a good kid, and not that I'd tell him this, but he's probably on track to become a generational talent. The way he possesses the puck is unnatural, and his speed and edge work are unbelievable. He's six-foot right now and needs to work on putting on more muscle, but I know he's not done growing yet.

"Things with Connelly are going great," I assure Coach.

"Glad to hear it. He seems like he's got a good head on his shoulders, and his focus and drive remind me of yours. Even though I wasn't your coach for the early seasons of your career, I remember coaching against you, and you always had a look of determination that intimidated opponents."

I'm caught off guard by his compliment. Coach isn't a prick by any means, but he's also not a guy who adds any fluff to a conversation.

"Thanks, Coach. I think Connelly will become an offensive weapon, creating scoring opportunities for our second line that we've been missing. We needed the depth on the second power play unit as well."

"You're exactly right, Bennett. I appreciate you taking him under your wing. You've got a knack for developing players and bringing out their potential."

Again, I'm surprised by his praise. "Thank you," I say simply, because I'm somewhat uncomfortable when given compliments or praise. I've been raised to thrive under criticism.

"If you can't take criticism, then you don't deserve praise," was something my father always told us growing up, and the saying has stuck with me over the years. But if my father ever actually handed out praise, it would be an eighty-degree day in the dead of a Minnesota winter.

"Have you ever considered coaching after you retire?" Coach asks.

"Um, I've actually considered potentially going into team management for a franchise. General manager, that sort of position."

"Put that well-earned degree to use, I like it. You'd do well in the C-suites," Coach replies.

He's not wrong, I did work hard to earn my masters in business while playing professional hockey. It might've taken me damn near ten years to do it online, but I did.

"That's the hope," I admit. "But not before we win a few championships. We've struggled the past few seasons, but I've got a feeling this year will be our season."

It has to be.

While I'm not necessarily old in terms of NHL players still in the league, I do feel more desperate to hoist the cup over my head than I've ever been. Eleven seasons without a deep playoff run will do that to a guy. I'm determined to make my twelfth season the one where it all comes together.

"Well, I won't keep you. I know you've got places to be and I've got to prep for morning skate tomorrow. Have a good one, Wilson," he says before waving me off dismissively.

I shake my head and chuckle at his goodbye that is so far from the Midwest farewells I've grown up with—the ones where it takes a half-hour to leave if I'm lucky.

Grabbing my trusty old duffel bag from my locker, I feel like a walking hypocrite as I sling the bag I've had since I was in high school over my shoulder and head out of the practice facility to unlock my matte black Range Rover that still has the new car smell. What can I say? I'm a guy who not only enjoys luxury cars and top-shelf whiskey, but also a guy who refuses to replace a good thing. This bag has traveled with me to countless arenas throughout the years—it's one of the only things I find myself attached to. The social media team likes to give me crap for it any time they take arrival photos.

I've just clicked the unlock button on my key fob, but before I get to my vehicle, I have to dodge out of the way of a white Mercedes as it screeches to a halt.

A wide-eyed Gemma is behind the wheel and a panicked Scarlett is in the passenger seat one moment, and then they're both flying out of the SUV the next.

"Oh my gosh, are you okay?" Scarlett asks. Before I can assure her I'm fine, Gemma begins to freak the fuck out.

"I'm so sorry! Don't sue me. Oh my god, Scar! Is he going to sue me? Can I go to jail for almost hitting a pedestrian? I didn't hit you right?

I don't even have my license yet. Will this keep me from getting my license? He's famous and on your team. Is Grandpa going to fire you? My life is so *over!*"

Scarlett turns her back to me and places her hands on Gemma's shoulders. "Gems, calm down. You're not going to jail, I'm not getting fired, and Bennett isn't suing you. He's alright, you didn't hurt a hair on his pretty head. You're fine, right Cap?" Scar asks, looking at me over her shoulder.

She's right, I didn't get hit by her car, but fuck if the way she looks right now and the way her whiskey eyes assess me doesn't strike me right in the chest. And hearing her call me "Cap" most certainly turns me the hell on.

Scarlett looks stunning in an off-the-shoulder cream sweater that shows off one of my favorite features of hers—her freckled shoulders and collarbones. Her top is fitted and tucked into a pair of wide-leg jeans that cling to her ass in a way that has me finding it hard to look away.

And now that I know the truth of our meeting all those years ago, the resentment and frustration that I'd been hanging on to has been replaced by sheer want for this woman all over again.

Snapping out of it, I clear my throat. "You think I'm pretty? I'm flattered, Little Red."

"The ego on this one," she mutters to Gemma, turning to face me with her hand on her hip. "It's a shame you didn't hit him to knock him down a peg or two."

"Gems wouldn't do that. We've got guitar lessons to look forward to."

"He's right. I'm actually pretty excited to have lessons," Gemma admits before her eyes widen. "Are you actually alright? You're, like, kind of old. Scar said you're *thirty.*"

I scoff in offense. "I'm going to ignore the old comment, and to prove I'm alright, how about this: if you're free tonight, why don't I run home to grab my guitar and I'll swing by your place this afternoon to get us started a few days early," I suggest.

Gemma looks back at me in awe, but when I glance at Scarlett, she looks frazzled, and I'm not sure what to make of that.

"Really? I'd love that!" Gemma squeals, turning to her sister. "Can he? We don't have anything going on this afternoon right?"

"Um, yeah, I think we're free," Scarlett mumbles.

"Oh, shoot! Is your date with that coffee guy today?" Gemma asks. My mood immediately sours at her question.

Scarlett's eyes narrow before she gives Gems a gentle shoulder nudge. "No, I'm just getting coffee with a guy, and that isn't until Thursday morning. Bennett said he would give you lessons Thursday evening, so no problems there."

"Ah, a hot date? Who's the sorry sucker?" I can't stop myself from asking as I fight the strange urge to puff my chest like an asshat.

"Don't you mean who's the lucky man that has the privilege of having coffee with me?" she retorts.

"Isn't that what I said?"

"Not quite, but that's none of your business," she bites back.

"Got it. Well, if you're okay with me coming over today, I'll run home real quick to grab my guitar and then I'll head to your place." As I wait for her response, I shift my weight back on my heels.

Scarlett lets out a sigh, blowing the bangs off her face that I hadn't noticed at first, before she reluctantly replies, "Yeah, fine by me. Can you just give us, like, an hour or so? I've got to swing by my grandparents' place to pick up Gunner."

"You betcha," I tell her as I adjust the strap on my duffle and begin walking backwards toward my car. "See you in a bit."

I watch as Scarlett hurriedly moves to the driver's side and gestures for Gemma to get in the passenger seat before they buckle up and take off.

My phone rings just as I'm leaving the parking garage, and I answer using my steering wheel once I see Jackson's name on my car's display.

"Yep," I say in answer.

"Wow, what a way to greet your brother. Hello to you too, sweetie," Jax retorts.

"Oh, I'm sorry, is this better? Hey, dear brother, to what do I owe the pleasure?"

"Much better. See, was that so hard?"

"Cut the shit, Jax. What's up?"

"Nothing, just wanted to call to say hi to my big brother. And maybe ask for your advice on something."

My brows shoot up in surprise, usually Jax and I butt heads when it comes to some of the decisions he makes. I can't remember the last time he came to me for advice. "Always," I tell him.

"What are your thoughts on me asking McKenna's college friend, the one she played volleyball with, to go out?"

I'm taken by surprise yet again, knowing Jax hasn't really dated anyone seriously since high school. "Which one, Brooke or Alexa?"

"Alexa, obviously. Brooke is engaged."

"Oh, I didn't know that. I don't keep up with that shit. But I don't see any problem with you asking her out. She seems cool whenever we've hung out. More your type, too, with how outgoing she is."

"And I think we'd be on the same page with things."

"What do you mean by that?"

"Keeping things casual. Nothing serious," he clarifies.

"It wouldn't be the worst thing in the world to settle down, you know."

"Says my single older brother who thrives in the bachelor lifestyle. Have you ever had a relationship?"

"I've dated a few women, but haven't found someone I want to be serious with," I answer, but what I don't tell him is that I would've absolutely asked a woman I was with over six years ago to be in a relationship with me had I not fucked it all up. Instead, I steer the conversation back on his love life, or lack thereof. "Are you still avoiding relationships because of her?" I don't say her name because I know it'll only set him off. Even after all these years, he still can't speak about her.

"Don't go there," Jax grits, just like I thought he would.

"Alright, sorry J. Let me make it up to you. Meet me at the Wolf Den tonight for a bite to eat and I'll buy you a beer."

"You buy dinner too and you've got yourself a deal," he throws back.

"Fine, dinner too, you frugal fuck."

"Not all of us got a big fancy contract like you, big bro. What time?"

"Um, not sure yet. I'll text you."

"Wait, why? Do you have other plans? You never have plans."

"I'm, ah, giving guitar lessons this afternoon and I'm not sure how long it'll take."

The line is silent on the other end for so long I think the call disconnected.

"To who?" Jax finally asks.

I'm hesitant to reply. "Gemma Carlisle."

"As in the little sister of the girl who got away?"

"As in the owner's granddaughter. I'm just giving her a few lessons as a favor to Scarlett."

"Oh ho ho, this is going to be good. Can't wait to hear how your *favor* for Little Red Riding Hood goes. Text me the time later."

Before I can respond, he hangs up and I grip the wheel, already annoyed with all the shit he's going to give me tonight.

Just over an hour later, with my guitar case in hand, I pause in front of a set of large oak doors. After I ring the doorbell, I hear who I think is Scar holler, "Shit, is he really here already?"

A moment later, the doors open and Gunner peeks out before yelling over his shoulder, "Yep, he's here!"

"Hey, Champ. How's it going?"

"Heya, Cap! It's okay, Scar is kinda going crazy that you're coming over."

I chuckle as his eyes widen and he folds his lips in on themselves like he wasn't supposed to let me in on that last bit.

"Don't worry, I'll keep that last part to myself." I kneel and set my case on the ground, waving him closer. "Why is she going crazy?" I whisper.

"She says the house is messy."

"Ah, well that's understandable. You guys have been busy," I tell him, giving him a pat on the back. "Think she'll be less flustered if I do Gemma's lessons on the front porch?"

"What does fluss-ed mean?"

"Flustered," I correct. "It means—" I stumble over how to define the word in terms a five-year-old will understand. "I'm asking if she'll be less crazy if we do it out here."

"Who are you calling *crazy*?" Scarlett asks in a tone that raises the hair on the back of my neck. Shit.

"No one. Certainly not you," I say just as Gunner throws me under the bus. "He was calling you a flust-ed crazy lady."

"A what?" she questions, looking slightly deranged as she narrows her gaze on me.

"Thanks for the assist," I deadpan.

Gunner clearly doesn't pick up my meaning when he gives me two thumbs up and squeals, "Good luck!" over his shoulder before running up the steps.

Christ, here we go.

Standing up, I dust off my pants and grab my guitar case. "Hey, Scar. I was just asking Gunner if you'd rather Gemma and I do the lesson on the front porch. It's a nice night and it looks like there's plenty of room for us to sit out here if you'd prefer I don't come in."

"And why would I prefer you not come in?"

"Uh—" I nervously shift my weight from being put on the spot. "Gunner mentioned you guys haven't settled in yet. Which is understandable considering how busy you all are and Joseph mentioned you only moved in a couple of weeks ago. Besides, I sprang this change of plans on you last minute."

Before I can continue rambling, Scar holds up her hand to stop me. "I think Gemma would probably prefer to do the lessons inside for now. She's somewhat shy about her songwriting and piano playing. I'm guessing it will be the same with playing guitar for now. I don't mind if you come in. I'm sorry if Gunner made it seem like I didn't want you to come inside. I'm not the cleanest person by nature, so I was just tidying up."

"Yeah, me neither," I tell her but she shoots me a look that shuts me up.

"Says the guy with the cleanest locker and weirdest pregame rituals. I bet you're a neat freak. You probably organize your closet by colors."

Guilty.

She gasps, covering her mouth. "Oh my god, you totally do, don't you?" Her laughter rings through the entryway when she gestures me inside, and my heart rate picks up speed at the sound.

"What about my pregame routine is weird? And how exactly do you know about my rituals?" I question.

Scarlett moves closer, lowering her voice for just us to hear. "I've decided to make it my business to know exactly what makes the captain of my team tick."

My heart beats double time as her words register.

"Your team?" I press, after I've cleared my throat.

"My family's team," she corrects, before turning to the steps and cupping her mouth. "Gems! There's an old guy in our entryway with a guitar offering you lessons. Get your butt down here before I have to make more awkward conversation."

She turns back to face me and bites her bottom lip to muffle her giggling.

"You think you're so funny. What's with the two of you calling me old? I'm not old."

"To her, we both are. Don't you remember a time when you thought your parents were old? Well, that's pretty much how she thinks of everyone. When I turned twenty-one, I was *so old*. When I turned twenty-five, she checked me for gray hair. You're thirty, so in her eyes, you've practically got one foot in the grave."

What did I get myself into?

"Cute. Is this what I have to look forward to?" I grumble.

"Precisely." Her voice is laced with humor at my expense.

Gemma comes skittering to a stop at the base of the stairs. "Hey, Bennett. Thanks for offering to do this."

"No problem. I'm happy to do it. You ready to get started?" I ask her.

"Yep, we can go in the living room," she suggests, leading the way into the open-concept living space down the hall.

We pass under the entryway staircase and I take everything in. Even though they only moved in a few weeks ago, Scarlett's managed to make this place into a home with little touches like the framed artwork on the walls and a large black and white portrait of the three of them making silly faces together. Next to that are portraits of each of them zoomed in on a feature of their face. Starting at the bottom is Gunner's smile missing one of his bottom teeth. Above that is a close-up of Scarlett's scrunched nose, speckled with my favorite feature of hers—freckles that stand out in stark contrast to her creamy skin due to the black-and-white composition. At the top are Gemma's eyes, the striations of her retinas emphasized and framed by long lashes.

I get caught staring at the photographs, and Scarlett softly shoulder checks me. "This way, Benny Boy."

Hearing her call me that earns her a smirk accompanied by the quirk of my brow.

"Are we back on nickname basis, Little Red?"

She rises to her tiptoes, leaning in to whisper in my ear, "For now. Until you do something to royally piss me off again, like when you assumed I'd only fucked you as revenge because I had daddy issues."

Fuck me. Hearing her talk about our night together gives me mixed feelings. On one hand, I'm riddled with guilt for assuming she knew who I was. On the other, my mind is filled with lustful memories from our night together. Memories that I've recalled in vivid detail while I'm alone.

Not the kind of thoughts I should be having right now.

She pulls away, and the smirk she gives has my cock twitching beneath my zipper. She knows exactly what she's doing—the effect she has on me.

I've already come to terms with the fact that I'm completely fucked when it comes to this woman. Distractions be damned. Scarlett Carlisle can consume my every waking thought for all I care.

6

Scarlett

We're running late this morning—shocking, I know. By the time I dropped off Gemma and Gunner, I was nearly twenty minutes late to my coffee date with Spencer.

My coffee date which was a complete disaster, might I add. And that doesn't bode well for me considering the news my grandfather shared with me less than a month ago. News that I still haven't come to terms with. A stipulation I can't even fathom.

"Knock, knock." Looking up, I lock eyes with Bennett's captivating hazels. He's the picture of relaxed with his shoulder resting against the doorframe, one ankle crossed over the other, and his hands in the pockets of his dress slacks.

"Bennett. What can I do for you?"

"Nothing, I was just meeting with your grandfather."

"I wasn't aware we had a meeting this morning, my apologies for missing it."

"Joseph called me in to discuss a possible fundraiser for the local dog rescue—a players and puppies calendar. He also wanted to go over the first regular season away stretch; it's one of our longer ones this season. Thankfully that isn't until next month. But I hear you'll be flying with us to Chicago next week."

My world comes to a screeching halt—my heart stops beating and panic seizes my lungs. Bennett is still talking about the details of the trip, but I can't focus on anything he's saying as my mind replays one word. Flying.

In the past five years, I have not traveled anywhere that I can't drive to. Getting on a plane has been completely out of the question after what happened to my dad and Angela.

When the ringing in my ears finally subsides to a dull buzzing, I hear Bennett ask, "Scarlett? Are you okay?"

No. Nothing about this is okay. I'm twenty-seven and have spent thousands of dollars on therapy over the past five years, only for each one of the coping mechanisms I've learned to fly out the window simply because of one word.

How could my grandfather do this to me? He knows I haven't flown, that I've refused to since their accident.

"Scarlett," Bennett says, gently tilting my chin up to look at him. I hadn't even noticed he moved across my office to where I sit at my desk. "Did I say something to upset you?"

Clearing the raw emotion from my throat, I shake my head. "No. It's not you. It's just, I haven't—" I close my eyes, afraid he'll see the panic in them. "Not since—" Biting my lip until I feel a sting of pain, I blink back the tears trying to make their escape.

"You haven't flown since your father's accident?"

My head shoots up so quickly, it's dizzying. "How did you—"

Instead of replying, he places his hand over the one I have gripping the arm of my desk chair and squeezes it. The gesture is so delicate, so sincere, it takes me by surprise.

"I can't imagine the devastation you, Gemma, and Gunner have gone through due to their loss."

The tears welling in my eyes make their escape and I stand abruptly, turning my back to Bennett because this moment is entirely too much for me—especially at eleven in the morning. Grabbing a tissue from my desk, I dab my eyes, careful not to smudge my winged liner.

I take a calming breath and turn back to face him, offering him a soft smile. "It seems I'm full of apologies this morning. I'm sorry about that. Now, to what do I owe the pleasure?"

Bennett doesn't say anything, moments tick by as he stares at me expectantly. I square my shoulders in anticipation for, what, I don't know.

"May I have a seat?" he asks.

"Of course," I gesture to the set of armchairs in the corner of my office and follow him to take a seat beside him.

Bennett breaks the silence first. "Did Gemma say if she liked her first few lessons?" he asks softly before dipping his head, playing off as if he's adjusting the cuff of his dress shirt.

Bashful Bennett is making another rare appearance, and it's unsettling how much seeing this side of him affects me. He's come over each night for the past three days to give Gemma lessons, with another planned for tonight. Watching him interact with her and Gunner has quickly become the highlight of my day. I didn't realize he was so good with kids, and I have to admit seeing that side of him does things to me.

"She said she had a lot of fun and she's up for the challenge of learning a new instrument. I heard you even helped her put a few chords to one of the songs she's been working on. Thank you for doing that—she told me she can't wait to get her own guitar so she can start practicing."

"No need to thank me. It was fun teaching someone to play the guitar again. I hadn't done that since my brother and sister were little."

"How old is your sister? I know Jax is about the same age as me, but do you just have one brother and one sister?"

"Yeah, just the two. Jax is twenty-eight and Walker turns twenty-one early next year, god help us all," he says, shaking his head and I can't help but chuckle at the exasperation in his tone.

"Such a stereotypical older brother response," I tease.

"Yeah, well, if you met her, you'd understand. And I know I don't have any gray hair, but if I do get any in the next few years, she'll without a doubt be the cause."

"Oh, quit it. She can't be that bad. She made it through the teenage years."

"Walker is wild at heart, and I love that she's free-spirited, but I've lost countless hours of sleep worrying over her now that she's out on her own."

"Is she in college?"

Shaking his head, he answers, "No, much to my protest. She lives in LA—she's a professional dancer and does some modeling."

"That's amazing! What style of dancing?"

"She's a trained ballerina, but she's always loved ballroom and contemporary as well. She was just promoted from apprentice to dancer at the Los Angeles Ballet. I'm really proud of her."

His beaming smile reveals a new layer of himself.

"You're also the oldest, so I'm sure you know how it is. I want the best for both of them, but I'll also never stop worrying about them, even when things are going seemingly well." He lets out a big sigh. "I do sound like an overprotective older brother don't I?" Bennett chances a quick glance at me, and I fail to hide my bemused smirk.

"I think it's cute, how much you care for them," I admit before I can stop myself.

A sly smile spreads across Bennett's face and I can't deny the reaction my body has to the devastating sight. My stomach pools with heat, and a dull ache surges to life in my core, causing me to clench the muscles of my thighs and abdomen.

Bennett leans forward in his chair, his large frame suddenly taking up far too much space. "That's the second time in only a few days you've called me cute or pretty. If I didn't know any better, I'd think you actually like me, Little Red."

My breath hitches hearing him call me that again. "That would be highly inappropriate, not to mention extremely unprofessional," I murmur as I sit back to create some distance. His tone sounded flirtatious, but that can't be right.

His answering chuckle is downright sinister. "I said 'like,' as opposed to hating me."

Bennett stands and buttons his suit jacket before turning to face me.

"Oh, I almost forgot to ask, how was the hot date this morning?" he asks as he places his hands in his pockets, the picture of nonchalance.

Well, he's not fooling me. As much as I'd love to tell him it went amazing, and I've got a second date lined up, I'm not going to lie to the man.

"It went about as horribly as it could've gone," I admit.

He frowns for a second before schooling his features. "Wait, really? Why was it so bad?"

"Well, for starters, I showed up about twenty minutes late because morning drop-off was a bit hectic. Gemma forgot to charge her phone last night so I turned around to grab her Dexcom receiver in case the little phone battery she had didn't last throughout the day. Then, when I explained that to Spence—"

"Spence? What kind of name is that?" he interrupts.

"A name. His name. Now, can I continue or are you going to interrupt me again and then lecture me like my date did this morning?"

His brows furrow. "Wait, he lectured you?"

"Yes, he told me that 'the early bird gets the worm,' and that had I been more prepared, Gemma wouldn't have needed to be tardy to school and I wouldn't have been late to our date. Needless to say, I was ready to dump my iced latte on him and leave."

"Tell me you did," Bennett says, fighting back a smile.

My cheeks heat with embarrassment. "I did, but only after he told me our relationship wouldn't be going anywhere because he wasn't interested in having children that weren't his own. I stood up, told him I wasn't aware a coffee date meant we were in a relationship, told him I'd be finding a new coffee shop, and poured my latte over his head."

"Oh my god. You're savage," Bennett mutters through his chuckles.

"I could've told him I hoped he was sterile so no woman or kids had to be stuck with his sorry ass, but I kept my composure," I point out in a sticky sweet voice.

"Yeah, sure. Composed," he deadpans. "Either way, I'm glad you dumped your latte on that dickwad's head. It was well-deserved. And, hey, at least it wasn't a hot drink or you would've been fresh out the slammer."

"Oh my gosh, are you a Swiftie? Gemma will lose her shit when I tell her."

"I mean, I'm not *not* a fan of hers, but between you and me," he leans in and lowers his voice. "And I mean this has to stay between the two of us, I'm more of a Taevin Gray fan."

"Stop, really? She's my favorite artist. Gemma's too!"

"I'm serious, I keep that close to the chest."

"Your secret's safe with me, scout's honor," I say, crossing my heart.

Bennett lets out a sigh and rolls his eyes. "You were clearly never a scout, they don't cross their hearts like that."

"Alright, you got me, but I can keep my mouth shut. So long as you tell me your favorite song of hers."

"'Martyred,'" he replies and my jaw drops.

"Shut up, that's mine! Did we just become musical besties?" I squeal.

"We most certainly did not." He sounds offended at the suggestion, but he unbuttons his jacket and sits back down, which tells me I haven't run him off quite yet.

"Sure, sure. Yet you're making yourself right at home in my office. Do you plan to stick around for the afternoon? Should I order us lunch, *bestie?*"

"I almost forgot how much of a brat you are," he resigns.

Why do I like it so much when he calls me a brat? I'm seriously depraved.

"I was kidding about the bestie part, but I'm famished, so I'm going to have my assistant order some lunch. Do you want anything?" I ask, though I'm not sure why. It's not like I want him to stick around. It's just nice . . . having someone to talk to. Before starting this job, I hadn't had a lot of adult interaction over the past five years. It's not that we were isolated at the cabin, but I didn't necessarily make new friends, and I was at a completely different phase of life than all of my college friends.

Bennett looks at his watch and shrugs. "Sure, I don't have anything going on aside from an afternoon skate with Connelly in two hours."

A half hour later we're passing takeout boxes back and forth from my favorite Chinese restaurant across my desk. Bennett's taken off his suit jacket and has the sleeves of his shirt rolled up his forearms. Carved forearms that are most certainly distracting me in the very best way.

"So," Bennett starts, but pauses to steal the piece of sesame chicken from my chopstix with his own before plopping it in his mouth.

Until this moment, I didn't realize I could be turned on by the sight of a man eating. The way his strong jaw clenches while he chews, and the way his Adam's apple bobs as he swallows has me wiggling in my desk chair.

I could be quite literally drooling right now.

"So?" I toss back halfheartedly, still distracted by the show he is completely unaware he's putting on for me.

He brings his fist up to cover his mouth as he clears his throat. "So any other hot dates you've got coming up?"

"Why is that any of your business?"

"It's not. I just wanted to see if we had to schedule Gemma's guitar lessons around any more dates."

I wrinkle my nose at his logic. "Correct me if I'm wrong, but the lessons thus far were the past three evenings with no interruptions and one more tonight."

"Yeah, so?"

"So . . . quit beating around the bush and just ask me if I'm single."

Bennett seemingly chokes on a mouthful of rice at my request. After taking a swig of his water, he clears his throat and looks across my desk. "Are you?"

I flutter my eyelashes innocently. "Am I what, Benny Boy?"

"Single. Are you single?"

"Yes, I'm embarrassingly unattached. And my current relationship status has made things that much more difficult for a predicament I've found myself in," I admit, sighing in frustration.

"And what predicament is that?"

"A large problem."

"Humor me. What problem? How can I help?"

"Yeah, well, this is a problem you couldn't possibly fix. I've already had every lawyer at my family's disposal look into it. And it's some fucking archaic bullshit, if you ask me, pardon my French."

"What's the problem, Scar?" I stare back at him, my eyes searching his to find nothing but genuine concern in his expression.

Rolling my lips together, I hesitate before asking, "Can I trust you to keep your mouth shut?"

"Who am I going to run and tell your problems to?"

"Your teammates," I point out.

"I won't. Your secrets are safe with me. Now, tell me what's wrong."

"My grandfather was diagnosed with early stages of dementia. I am working as his apprentice this season with the hopes that I'll take over ownership by next year."

Bennett's face falls and he clears his throat. "I'm so sorry to hear about Joseph. If you're worried about getting up to speed with the team, I'll help in any way I can. But what does that have to do with lawyers? Can't he legally hand over ownership to you while he's still in the right frame of mind? Before it progresses?"

"That's not the issue. It's the terms of ownership that my grandfather only just shared with me earlier this month. You can't help my biggest problem, though. No one can. And you wanna know why?" I pause for a beat, taking a deep breath that fails to calm my racing heart. "Because I've got to get *married* within the next year in order to take over ownership." The word tastes bitter on my tongue and I swallow before continuing. "The sooner the better according to my grandfather. And I've got zero prospects. Besides, even if I did find time to date, the whole 'single guardian of her two younger siblings' thing is probably *really* attractive to a lot of guys. So, no, unless you're willing to sign your life away and marry me, you cannot help me."

Complete silence fills my office as I end my rant. Bennett stares back at me, not saying a single word, head turned to the side like he's trying to see inside my head.

"I'll do it."

The laugh I let out in response is slightly hysterical, bordering on unhinged. "You'll do it. Do what, exactly?"

"I'll marry you."

Now it's my turn to stare back in silence, mouth agape.

I'm not sure how long I gawk at him across my desk, or how long my jaw remains dropped to the floor, but when Bennett finally breaks the silence, I have no idea what to think anymore.

"Sorry, that's not what I meant."

Oh, thank god. Because it's one thing to marry someone out of mutual convenience. I don't need to love the man I marry. I just need him to respect me and keep his distance from Gemma and Gunner. But Bennett? He'd be a risk. A six-foot-five, chiseled risk I couldn't afford. Because while I might not fall in love with him, I already know the way my body responds to his touch. And there would be nothing mutually convenient about the arrangement. He's a millionaire professional hockey player with women lining up to have him in every city he plays in.

"What I meant—what I mean to say is, that isn't any way to propose to a woman. I-I can do better." He takes a deep breath, and I'm too stunned to ask the million questions running through my mind.

Before I can blink Bennett is standing and gathering our garbage. When he gets to the door, he pauses and says, "Don't worry, Scar. I'll take care of everything. See you tonight for Gemma's guitar lesson."

What does that even mean? *Dear Lord, help me.*

7

Bennett

SEPTEMBER

What in the fuck am I doing right now?

Instead of finishing my two hours of ice time with Connelly, I'm sitting in a jewelry store beside the rookie looking at engagement rings while my leg bounces incessantly.

"You alright, Cap? You're looking like you might be sick," Connelly supplies.

"I'm fine. I just didn't realize there were so many options to pick from. Why can't it just be as simple as 'I want a diamond ring, she's got skinny fingers,' they tell me what they think will look best, I purchase the damn thing and walk outta here?"

He nervously chuckles beside me. "Yeah, that's definitely not how this works. Didn't you do any research first? Also, why didn't I realize you had a girlfriend? Was she at the family skate?"

"She was," I say curtly without elaborating.

Connelly's brows wrinkle in confusion. "Oh, I don't remember you bringing anyone."

"Didn't realize you watched my every move, rookie," I retort, quirking a brow. God, I'm an ass, but I don't have it in me to care right now. I'm too busy freaking the fuck out because I'm sitting in a jewelry store prepared to buy a ring to propose to a woman I've known for a month.

"For a guy about to propose, you're especially grumpy today."

"Why did I bring you again?" I ask gruffly.

"Good question. I think you just forgot to drop me off at my place before you came," he replies before shaking his head. "That's got to be it, otherwise shouldn't, like, Jax be doing this with you or something?"

"Shit. Should I have brought her with me? Are women supposed to have a say in the ring?" I ask, pulling the collar of my dress shirt from the sudden bout of claustrophobia.

"Nah, I think if you wanna go about this the traditional way, you're supposed to pick out the ring so it's a surprise—she's not supposed to see it coming. Haven't the two of you discussed getting married? What kinda ring did she say she wanted? Oh, does she have Pinterest? My mom and sister are constantly on Pinterest. What's her name? Let's look her up," he suggests as he pulls out his phone, but I rip it from his hand.

"Not happening. I doubt she's a Pinter girl."

"It's Pinterest," he corrects before grabbing back his phone. "Come on, just look her up," he says as he opens the app and hands the phone over to me.

The salesperson helping us excuses himself, so I grab the phone and type her name in the search bar.

"How many siblings do you have anyway?" I ask him as I wait for the results to load.

My eyebrows do a shit job of containing my shock at seeing her profile appear in the search results.

"Two, a younger brother and sister. Did you find her?" he asks, trying to look over my shoulder but I turn the phone away from him and nod in response. "Cool, cool. Scroll through her boards and see if she has any wedding ones or ring ones. Sometimes my mom calls them weird names, but as long as she doesn't mark them as private, you should be able to see if she has any rings pinned."

Sure as shit, Scarlett has dozens upon dozens of boards that I scroll through. She's got a board for just about everything except wedding stuff. She's got one for pretty much every room in her house. A whole board dedicated to crafting ideas for Gunner. One titled 'healthy but fun snack ideas,' and another called 'date night ideas for someday.' I make a note to come back to that one later when I can download the app on my phone.

"I'm also the oldest with a younger brother and sister," I tell him as I continue to scroll.

"Really? I always thought you and Jax had a younger brother."

"We're not too keen on the team knowing we've got a younger sister. She doesn't need to be around all you assholes."

He scoffs, seemingly insulted. "How am I an asshole? You barely know me."

I'd hate to break it to him, but my baby sister would chew him up and spit him out.

"You're a hockey player. Enough said. We're all assholes. No one is good enough for my baby sister, but especially not a hockey player." I look over and narrow my eyes at him to be sure he gets my message.

Connelly lifts his hands in surrender. "Easy there, Cap. I'm not interested in anyone's sister. My sole focus is hockey. Swear to god."

I fight back a smile at his scared shitless expression and focus back on his phone. Just as I'm about to give up on finding anything ring related I stumble upon a board titled 'Forever & Always' that's filled with all sorts of wedding ideas.

My stomach tightens as I scroll through the different pins she's saved. "This feels wrong," I tell Connelly. And it does, it feels like I'm getting a peek into all of her hopes and dreams she's envisioned for a special day in her life that I'm not supposed to be a part of.

"How else are you supposed to know the type of ring she wants? If she didn't want you to see, she'd have made the board private," he assures me.

"Fine," I grit out. The kid must be on to something because as I continue to scroll, the same type of ring is pictured in pin after pin. When the salesperson sits back down, I turn the phone to him and say, "I think she wants something like this."

"Ah, she's got lovely taste. Let me grab a selection and you can determine the carat and setting. Do you think she'd like white gold, yellow gold, rose gold, or platinum?"

My brows knit in confusion. "I don't know. I guess I didn't realize there were so many choices. What happened to just silver or gold?"

"I'll tell you what, I'll just grab a few of each and you choose what you like best," the salesperson suggests.

When he's out of earshot, Connelly leans closer and murmurs, "You've got that sick look about you again, Cap." He claps my shoulder and chuckles. "Lighten up, you're making me nervous for you. What's the worst that could happen? It's not like she's gonna say no. You're Bennett freaking Wilson."

Why do those feel like famous last words?

Scarlett

I open the front door to find Bennett pacing the length of my front porch. When he looks up and notices me, he pauses his steps. His dark hair has a mussed-up look, different from his normal slicked-to-perfection style, but if anything it's only amplified his sex appeal. He's wearing slim dark khaki pants that cling to his muscular thighs, crisp white tennis shoes, and a navy button-down with the sleeves rolled up, showcasing his delicious forearms.

Damn, he looks good.

"Sorry, I didn't hear the doorbell. Have you been out here long?"

"What? No. I didn't—I didn't ring the doorbell."

Ugh. He's acting weird and it has everything to do with me opening my big mouth today. Why did I think he'd maybe get a small bout of amnesia and forget all about our conversation? So much for wishful thinking.

"Do you think we could talk for a moment before Gemma and Gunner notice I'm here?"

Confused by his request but knowing Gemma and Gunner are occupied doing a craft, I nod and shut the door behind me before stepping off the front porch and following Bennett to the back of the house.

"Where are you going?" I ask as I try to keep up with his quick pace. My bare feet feel cool against the grass as he disappears around the other side of the large willow tree in my backyard.

I stop short when I round the tree and find Bennett standing in the middle of a bed of white rose petals surrounded by a dozen or more vases lit up with flameless candles.

I'm unsure if it's nerves, butterflies, or trepidation swimming in my stomach right now.

"Bennett, what—" I start but he cuts me off.

"I realized pretty quickly that I didn't go about things the right way in your office," he pauses and holds his hand out for me in invitation to join him just beneath the willow tree. I walk over to him, and when he takes my hands in his, I feel a slight tremor to his. This breathtaking man is shaking with nerves and I can't for the life of me understand what the actual hell is going on right now.

Bennett takes a deep breath. "I know we're only just getting to know each other, and I know this is probably the last thing you anticipated happening this year, but my gut is telling me we could make this work." He pauses when I hold up my hand.

My brain finally catches up to what I'm seeing and hearing. "Let me stop you right there. I know what *I* have to do. But I can't do this to you. I won't trap you. A marriage between the two of us would not be mutually beneficial to both parties. I'd be the only one gaining anything from the arrangement. Besides, it's not just me you'd be signing your life away for. I have to think of Gemma and Gunner. What would they think? They already know you. I mean, you're giving Gemma guitar lessons for crying out loud—"

Before I can continue, Bennett shocks me silent once again when he drops to one knee and reaches into the pocket of his pants and pulls a small burgundy velvet box. He doesn't open it, he just holds it in one hand, taking my left hand in his other.

"If you agree to this, I'm all in. Yes, we will have a contract marriage, but the only two people who would be aware of that would be the two of us. As far as you, Gemma, and Gunner are concerned, the three of you would be mine. And I would be yours in return. They will never know anything except that I chose them when I chose you. I'll be there for them in every capacity that they need me and however makes you most comfortable. I haven't gotten where I am today without giving my all when I set my mind on something. If you'll have me, I'll do everything I can to be the partner you deserve. We'll be teammates in this arrangement. So what do you say, Little Red—will you take a gamble on me?"

I'm stunned speechless, staring down at this man before me on one knee as he opens the velvet box with his thumb, his hands are steady now as he holds the most beautiful diamond ring up to me and says, "Marry me, Scar."

I swallow deeply past the lump forming in my throat. "That didn't sound like a question."

He half chuckles, half scoffs. "I'm not asking."

"It sounded more like a command," I tell him, narrowing my eyes.

"Nope. It's a demand."

I scoff at his audacity. "You don't even know me, Bennett."

"I know enough. And what I know, I like a whole lot," he replies with a cocksure grin that starts incredibly arrogant but turns more boyish the longer I hesitate with my response.

Fighting the sting behind my eyes, I blink past the emotions swelling to the surface. "What if I'm some sort of psychopath?" Alarm bells ring in my head that this will end badly. If not for me, then surely for Gunner and Gemma.

He chuckles at that, shaking his head at my nonsense. "You're not. But you are a pain in my ass for making me sit here this long."

"For how long? How long are you willing to be married?" I clarify.

"However long you need," he answers.

He sounds so nonchalant over the fact that he'd be practically signing his life away, or putting it on hold at the very least, for me. *Me.* The person he calls a brat and is practically strangers with.

Mulling it over, I bite my bottom lip. "Three years. That should be enough to gain and maintain ownership," I explain, nodding my head more to reassure myself than him.

"Deal," he answers without hesitation, which is shocking.

"Okay."

"Okay?" he questions.

"Okay, sure. I'll roll the dice with you, Benny Boy."

An electric grin eclipses his face and the sight causes butterflies to soar through my chest. He stands to his full height and I look up into his eyes as he slides the ring onto my finger. My emotions are all over the place as I recognize the sincerity shining in his.

What have I done? I just agreed to use this man—to take complete advantage of his selflessness—for him to receive nothing in return.

"I'm shocked, I didn't think it'd fit, but it looks like it might be just the right size," he says once he's slid it on.

I chance a glance down at my hand and when my eyes land on the stunning ring, my stomach sinks. It's my dream ring—an elongated cushion-cut diamond ring that has to be close to four freaking carats with a hidden halo.

"Bennett, I can't accept this ring."

"You don't like it?" His forehead creases in confusion and I'd probably think it's adorable if my head wasn't spinning at the moment.

"It's too much. You had to have spent a fortune on this." What I don't say is that wearing my dream ring for an essentially fake marriage makes me sick to my stomach.

"You're about to be the one signing my paychecks, I assure you I can afford it. But if you don't like it—if you'd prefer something different—we can go to pick out a different one."

"Bennett, no. It's perfect. I just—" I take a moment to compose myself, my thoughts a jumbled mess. "What does this all mean to you? Shouldn't we draw up a mutually beneficial contract before we agree to something so serious?"

"What do you want, Scar? What do you *need*? This will mean to me whatever you need it to."

God, what do I need? When was the last time someone asked me that? When was the last time I did something as selfish as this? Probably the night the two of us were together all those years ago, that was the last time I acted selfishly—did something just for myself. And marrying Bennett would be for entirely selfish reasons. Not only would I be the sole benefactor from this arrangement, but I'd be marrying a man who is a total catch. Asshole tendencies aside, Bennett Wilson checks all my boxes when it comes to the qualities I'm looking for in a man. Not only is he extremely successful, but I've come to learn in the past few weeks we've spent together that he's smart, kind, caring, annoyingly charismatic, charming, and if this action says anything about him, he's also selfless. Like when he stays after practices to help the guys who need extra work and has also become a mentor to Connelly. Or how about the fact that he's offered to give free guitar lessons to Gemma simply because I mentioned she wanted to learn?

"This isn't just about me, Bennett. Why would you sign your life away for me? Don't you want a real marriage? A family of your own?"

I have to imagine he would want all of those things eventually, I know I want those things someday.

"Do you happen to know who my father is?" he asks instead of answering.

"Of course I do."

"So then you know that my father, Senator Wilson, makes almost all of his decisions for his political gain, whatever is in his best interest, this includes who his children date or marry."

I try to swallow past the sudden dryness in my throat. "What are you trying to say?"

"I'm saying that this marriage would be a mutually beneficial arrangement. While you're mostly a pain in my ass, I think I could become fond of your sass over time, and it'd be a hell of a lot better than being attached to someone my father or his advisors hand select for me."

"You could grow fond of me . . . just what I've always hoped my fiancé would tell me as he's proposing," I deadpan.

He sighs and rubs the back of his neck, his sheepishness giving him a boyish look. "Look, if you want the truth, I didn't see marriage and babies in the cards for me. It's not that I am opposed to the idea, it's just that I've only felt explosive chemistry with one person before, and it turns out I fucked that up pretty badly. And I didn't have the best example set by my parents for a loving marriage. But I think we could be a good team, the two of us. I think we have a shot at making this work."

My chest tightens as his words sink in and jealousy I have no right to feel takes over. "Honestly, hearing about your one that got away isn't exactly what I want right now."

"You did get away from me once, Scar. I'm not about to make the same mistake twice."

I have to hold my abdomen to contain the riot of butterflies threatening to take flight from his words. I'm not sure what to make of them. "What are you insinuating?"

"I'm saying you knocked me on my ass six years ago and I'm going to do my best not to fuck up my second shot with you."

Needing to shift the conversation from the sudden seriousness, I give him my best sass. "Don't you mean your third shot with me? If I remember correctly, you didn't even get my name the first night we met."

"And look how the tides have turned. Not only did I get your name, but now you'll have mine," Bennett boasts, sending a playful wink my way. Goddamn. My fiancé is fine as hell when he's flirting with me.

Fiancé. Bennett is my fiancé. This is so surreal.

"Hey, Cap?"

"Yeah, Little Red?" he tosses back, stepping into my space and clouding my thoughts with his cologne that smells like my own personal brand of pheromones.

"This changes nothing between the two of us," I tell him, my voice unsteady due to his sudden proximity.

"Wrong. This changes everything," he assures me, rubbing his thumb over the ring he just placed on my finger. My traitorous heart squeezes and picks up speed at his words instead of taking them as the warning they are.

8

Bennett

The team has just loaded onto the plane and we're set to depart to Chicago any minute now, but we're waiting on one passenger. My fiancée.

Well, no one besides the two of us knows she's my fiancée, but Scarlett is late and I'm beginning to question if it's due to the perpetual tardiness she warned me about, or if something is wrong.

She told me she hadn't been on a flight since her father's accident, and now that I think better of it, I wonder if this oversight on her grandfather's part was due to his progressing dementia. Surely he wouldn't put her in this situation—flying for the first time since the accident with a plane full of her employees and coworkers—while knowing she's been too terrified to travel for the past five years. And with our new arrangement, her stress is sure to be off the charts.

Since I proposed last week, I've continued Gemma's guitar lessons and snuck in a few lunches with Scarlett either at her office or the lunch spot down the street from the arena she said she loves. I won't lie, I thought things between us would be stiff and awkward, but I've never been happier to be wrong. Our conversations flow naturally, and I'm enjoying getting to know her more, which doesn't happen for me much outside of my small friend group.

A few moments later there's commotion at the front of the plane before a flash of copper catches my eye. I stand on instinct, my feet moving toward her before I know what I'm doing.

"Sit with me?" I ask as I approach her, surprising myself with my question.

"Oh, I don't want to mess with your pregame routine," she replies, nervously tucking her hair behind her ear with her left hand. I notice her ring finger is bare like it has been all week, but I don't mention it . . . for now.

"You won't. We don't play until tomorrow. Follow me, I sit in the back."

She worries her bottom lip and I fix my gaze on her mouth. "I should probably sit up front with the rest of management."

"We've got much to discuss, boss. Come on." I nod toward the back of the plane and move into an empty row so she can walk ahead of me down the aisle. When she huffs out a sigh of defeat, I internally fist pump in victory.

"Thought you're not supposed to wear white after Labor Day," I tease as I follow her down the aisle, taking in the white pencil skirt that clings like a second skin to her ass. She's paired it with a black polka dot blouse beneath a matching white, fitted blazer. She looks incredible, and I have to fight back the urge to claim her in front of all my asshole teammates whose heads turn as we walk by them.

"You couldn't last two minutes," she points out, pulling my glare away from my teammates.

"If memory serves, I'm not sure what gave you that impression." I don't bother hiding my cocky smirk when her head whips around.

She scoffs, rolling her eyes in annoyance at my innuendo. "I meant you couldn't even go two minutes without giving me shit for something. As for the other thing . . . my memory unfortunately doesn't serve me that long ago."

Now it's my turn to scoff before suggesting, "Maybe we'll have to bring it top of mind then."

Scarlett merely hums in response, and her nonchalance is somehow sexy as hell.

"We're right here," I tell her as I place my hand on her lower back to guide her into our row. "Do you prefer the window or aisle?" I ask her.

"Um—I-I'm not sure. I think window. If that's alright with you," she says hesitantly, her mood shifting to unease.

"I'm alright with whatever will make you most comfortable," I tell her, offering her a gentle squeeze on her thigh once we've sat down, which I hope is reassuring.

As we fasten our seatbelts, I notice her hands trembling. When the captain tells the flight attendants to prepare the cabin for takeoff, Scarlett's breathing becomes shuttered and her grip on the armrests tightens.

I lace my fingers through hers without thinking about it. Easing her worries is my only priority right now. "Eyes on me, Scar."

She turns her head and I'm met with her stricken gaze. Forget frightened. Scarlett is terrified.

"What's something no one else knows about you?" I ask, attempting to distract her.

"W–what?"

"Let's play a game of twenty questions. Except instead of asking twenty questions to guess one correct answer, we ask each other twenty questions to get to know one another better. If we're going to be married, I should probably know more about my fiancée."

"Okay," she agrees, shaking her head up and down almost as if she's giving herself a silent pep talk. "Well one thing most people don't know about me is that I make seasonal bucket lists for me, Gemma, and Gunner to complete."

A genuine smile spreads across my face picturing the three of them doing seasonal activities together that Scar planned. "That sounds fun. What is something you're looking forward to crossing off your fall bucket list with the two of them?"

She takes a deep breath. "We haven't gone to a pumpkin patch in years and I was hoping to go all out decorating for Halloween this year now that we're at the new house. A few of the neighbors told me the entire neighborhood gets really into it and everyone votes to choose a winner for best decorations."

"Do Gemma and Gunner like Halloween?"

"They love it, though Gunner gets scared of some of the costumes and decorations we've seen over the years. But this year he's taken an odd liking to the scarier costumes. Like, he just told me he wants to be Pennywise. I told him absolutely not because I'm terrified of clowns."

"So if a clown showed up at your office, that would be a bad thing?"

She gives me a scathing look that oddly puts me at ease, knowing it's replacing her look of terror. Definitely storing that information away for later though.

"When do you see getting married falling on your bucket list?" I ask, looking down at our intertwined hands, a little bashful but curious to hear her answer.

"To be honest, I hadn't really thought about it until earlier this week."

I hum in response before shooting her another question. "If you could get married anywhere, where would it be?"

"Paris. In the spring when the trees are in bloom." Her answer comes without hesitation, and she has this far away look in her eyes.

"Hate to break it to you, Little Red, but you're about to become the owner of an NHL team. Hopefully, we'll be making a deep playoff run in the spring. We could have a summer wedding in Paris. Maybe we'll have the cup on a table instead of a cake."

"I didn't say that's where *we* would get married," she clarifies. "That's just been my dream since I was a little girl. My mother lived in Paris for a few years during the height of her modeling career."

"And does she still live there? Your mother?"

"No, she passed away from complications following my birth. I only have secondhand stories and photographs of her. But every time I visited Paris growing up, I got this sense of everything feeling *right*. Do you have a place like that?"

The honesty of her answer surprises me. I wasn't anticipating such a detailed answer, given the nature of her fear of flying.

"I'm not sure I do," I admit, peering at her from the corner of my eye to find her eyes on me once again. Clearing my throat, I change my answer. "I suppose the ice. When I'm on the ice, I feel a sense of belonging—of peace—I don't otherwise feel. It doesn't matter if it's a game, practice, or I'm just skating by myself, regardless of who is with me, I feel better on the ice."

She playfully nudges my shoulder with hers. "Then I guess it's a good thing you've got the career you do."

"Doesn't it make you angry that you're not able to choose your career path now?" I ask.

She pulls at her bottom lip as she considers her response. "I'm thankful the team will remain in the family, however, I'm not ecstatic that I'm the one who has to hold down the fort until someone else is old enough to take over."

I consider that and look out the window over her shoulder. "So what you're saying is, you're going to hold ownership until either Gemma or Gunner is old enough to decide if they'd like to take over? That would put you in your late thirties or well into your forties. Is that really what you envision for yourself?"

"I told you, none of this is what I envisioned. But it's not just about me. Stability is what Gemma and Gunner need. A change of leadership is what is required of me now that my grandfather's condition has been diagnosed and is progressing. Do I wish I had a capable, long-lost cousin that could take over? Absolutely. But that isn't the case. It's just me," she finishes with a shrug.

Scarlett's selflessness and her ability to change shitty circumstances into a glass-half-full perspective are quickly becoming traits I didn't realize I was looking for in a woman. The manner in which she's handled each hurdle she, Gunner, and Gemma have had to overcome is awe-inspiring.

As the plane turns off the tarmac onto the runway, Scarlett's grip tightens on mine and she presses her head back against the headrest, closing her eyes as she attempts to gulp in air through her unsteady breathing.

Without knowing what else to do, I lean in and press a kiss to her temple, and when I do, I breathe in her sweet floral scent. The familiar perfume she's wearing has lust flooding my stomach with a sense of longing for moments from a night six years ago when I held this incredible woman in my arms under far different circumstances.

I keep my lips pressed to her temple as the aircraft picks up speed and we ascend into the sky. I don't think about the fact that it is broad daylight and anyone could see us in this intimate moment; my sole focus is ensuring Scarlett is okay right now—that she can get through this flight without breaking in front of a plane full of her employees.

Fighting past a sudden tightness in my throat, I ask, "Do you want to watch a movie together? I've got your favorite movie on my laptop—well, I'm not sure if it's still your favorite, but I downloaded *10*

Things I Hate About You. If we start it now, we should finish right about the time we land."

Scar looks taken aback by my question, and my skin prickles with unease. Shit, maybe I overstepped when I asked her to sit with me. Is she pissed I kissed her temple in front of the guys?

"I'd actually really like that. I can't believe you remembered after all this time that that's my favorite movie."

"I might've been attempting to drown my sorrows over that ridiculous fucking outfit, but I haven't forgotten a single moment we spent together. I'm just sorry I fucked up my only shot at a chance for something real with you when I assumed the worst."

"You know what they say about those who assume," she muses and I'm happy to hear the snark in her tone. *Hit me with your best shot, Red.*

Instead, her next words are a sideswipe I didn't see coming. "I could be convinced to give you another shot for the sake of our agreement, but it's either the third time's a charm or third strike and you're out. So what's it gonna be, Cap?"

My brows rise in surprise as her question registers and I don't hesitate before answering. "I've been told I'm as charming as they come, Little Red."

"I'm not sure who fed you that bullshit, but I suppose you've had your moments here and there. Tiny as they may be."

"Nothing about me is tiny and you know it." The smirk-wink combination I send her way lands exactly how I intended as her pale cheeks heat, and I marvel at the way the color spreads down the column of her throat to the barely-exposed skin of her chest. I decide to really test my luck when I lean in and whisper, "Stop thinking about how big your fiancé's dick is and focus on the screen. I'm not sure I've ever seen the full movie."

Scar lets out a mock gasp that I know is her way of trying to distract me from the fact that I just called her out. That's fine, I'll let this one slide in hopes that she doesn't try to settle the score.

"We should probably discuss that at some point," she surprises me by saying.

"Discuss what? My dick size?"

She chokes on a laugh. "Oh my gosh, no. I meant we should discuss boundaries, maybe even put some rules in place."

Not sure I'm going to like where this is heading. "Rules . . ."

"Yeah, you know, like rules for our marriage of convenience. We've already established it'll be a three-year timeline."

"Right."

"And maybe we should add some other guidelines."

"What do you have in mind, Little Red?" I question, unease pricking my spine.

Wringing her hands together nervously, she suggests, "We should probably agree to not cross the line physically. I mean, I'm sure we'll have to kiss at some point, and obviously on our wedding day, but we should probably draw the line there."

Quirking a skeptical brow, I ask, "Why? You worried you'll fall head over heels in love with me and beg me to make our arrangement permanent if I fuck you too good?"

She smacks my chest and huffs. "You're such a cocky little shit."

"Wow, boss. You sure look professional, but that mouth of yours . . ." I *tsk* but can't stop my gaze from falling to said mouth, and I mentally smack myself for the added temptation when she flicks her tongue out, wetting her lips.

"There will definitely be no falling in love. Consider that a hard and fast rule of this arrangement," she says, though her voice lacks finality.

I'm not sure what happens to me in her presence, but I can't stop myself from taunting, "We'll see about that, Scar. I'm pretty damn lovable."

"I can see why, you're a real ray of sunshine most days," she deadpans.

"Okay, so no crossing the line and no falling in love. Anything else?"

"We already agreed that Gemma and Gunner will never know this was an arrangement, but I'm still trying to process the fallout they'll experience once our agreement comes to an end. Maybe we can talk about that more on the flight home?"

"Deal," I tell her, holding my hand out for her to shake.

She locks eyes with me and after a moment takes my hand in hers. "You've got yourself a deal, Mr. Wilson."

As we settle in for the movie and the opening credits play, I move my hand to rest on my thigh but Scarlett surprises me once again when she takes it in hers. "Is this okay? I'm still pretty nervous."

I give her hand an assuring squeeze. "Always. You can hold my hand whenever, Red."

She gives me a shy smile before refocusing her attention on my laptop.

"This counselor is out of control," I tell her after a few minutes in.

"I know. And bratwurst? Who would want to read that?"

"You should ask Dakota if she'll add that in her next book," I suggest. When Scarlett stares back in confusion, I clarify, "Carson's wife, Dakota, is a romance author. She's got a few books out now, I believe her pen name is Kota Lynn. Do you like to read?"

"Are you kidding me? How did I not know that? I've read all of her books and love them! She wrote a football series that I devoured. I honestly considered purchasing season tickets for the Voyagers after I read her first book."

"Wait a minute. Your family owns a professional hockey team and you considered purchasing season tickets to Minnesota's NFL team for what reason?"

"In hopes that one of the players would see me in the crowd and fall madly in love with me, obviously," she explains in a tone that hints it should've been obvious to me.

"Sorry, not sorry. You're stuck with hockey now," I grumble.

"Aw, no need to get your panties in a twist, Benny Boy. I just liked the way their butts looked in their uniforms."

I let out a grunt of acknowledgment before focusing back on the movie.

"Is it the pleather pants? Is that what does it for you, Little Red?" I question her a few moments later when Heath Ledger appears on the screen in what I'd call the most hideous outfit I've ever seen.

"You know, it just might be. If I got you a pair would you wear them for me?" The smirk she shoots my way is devious.

"Absolutely not."

"Your tree trunk thighs probably wouldn't fit in them anyways," she sighs in defeat.

A few scenes later, I don't take my eyes off the screen when I ask her, "Has Gemma pulled any of this on you yet?"

"What?"

"Lying about going to a party by saying she's studying? Or the boys?"

"No, thank god. I think homeschooling helped on the party and boy front. But I feel like she's been texting someone nonstop lately and I can't help but feel like she has a crush. Of course, she won't tell me anything, but I've got a feeling."

"Are you ready for that next phase?"

"The phase where she starts dating? No, I'm absolutely not ready. Is anyone ever ready for that?"

"The pregnant belly . . . oh shit, I forgot about this scene." I try to muffle my chuckle into my fist to avoid unwanted attention.

"I could see you doing this. The overprotective, embarrassing asshole act. What's the worst thing you did to scare off one of Walker's dates?" she asks me.

"Not much aside from threatening our teammates the few times she's come around. Thankfully I didn't have to do much since our father is a senator. Walker and I have a ten-year gap between us, so by the time she started dating, I was pretty busy with hockey and traveling too much to be as protective as I would've liked. Honestly, I think she scares off more guys than Jax or I would."

"A girl after my own heart," Scarlett hums.

The rest of the movie goes by in comfortable silence occasionally interrupted by a fit of laughter from Scarlett, and I commit to memory each reaction she has to various scenes.

Just as the end credits roll, the pilot announces we've made it to Chicago and requests the flight attendants prepare us for landing. Scarlett stiffens beside me so I take her hand in mine again and offer her a reassuring squeeze.

With her left hand in mine, I attempt to distract her. "Don't tell me you've lost your ring already," I tease, though I'm also curious to hear why she kept it off.

"No, I just thought since we hadn't shared our big news with our families yet that I probably shouldn't be flaunting my massive rock in front of your brother and my grandfather."

"Good call. Are you worried what they'll think of us sitting together?" I ask her, gesturing toward the front of the plane where her grandfather sits.

"Not at all. I think it's good for us to be seen together before we announce our engagement. We're already going to look like we rushed into things, but it'd be even more unbelievable, not to mention suspicious, if we went from not speaking for six years to engaged overnight."

"Valid point. So does that mean we're *courting*?"

Scarlett throws back her head and lets out a genuine laugh that nearly steals the breath from my lungs—the sound of it is mesmerizing. "I suppose so. How in the hell do you know that term?"

"My mom was a huge fan of *Downton Abbey* when I was growing up, and from time to time I'd be guilted into watching it with her."

"Ah, I love period dramas. I just started watching *Outlander* and I'm hooked."

"Haven't heard of it," I admit.

"I read the books first and just started the first season last week."

"Should we watch it together?" I ask and she just stares back at me in confusion.

"And why would you want to do that?"

"I don't know. Carson said he and Dakota watch *Bridgerton* together. Isn't that what couples do? Find a show and watch it together?"

"Sure, but shouldn't we find a show that you'd be interested in watching?"

"I like historical fiction. I'd be willing to give it a shot."

"It'd be quite the commitment, there's eight seasons. And you'd have to promise not to show-cheat on me."

"Show-cheat?" I question her with a quirked brow.

"Yeah, you know, like watch an episode without me there. That's a surefire way to break off our engagement."

"I didn't realize you were scared off so easily."

"I'm not." She chuckles and bumps her shoulder into mine. "Thank you, by the way."

"For what?"

"This," she says, gesturing at our joined hands. "For being just the distraction I needed to get through this flight without a mental breakdown. It took all the courage in me to put one foot in front of the other and board the plane. I'm not sure I could've gotten through the flight without you."

"You could've, but I guarantee you wouldn't have had as much fun. Besides, you not only got to fawn over Heath Ledger, but you also got to ogle your fiancé in a suit." I wink at her, and it's only then I notice the plane has landed and Jax has decided to turn from his seat in front of us with a shit-eating grin.

Fuck, this can't be good.

"Did I just hear you correctly or have my ears yet to pop?" he whisper-hisses, looking over his shoulder to ensure no one *else* is listening.

"That depends, what do you think you heard?" Scarlett asks with narrowed eyes.

"I thought I just heard my brother refer to himself as your fiancé, Little Red Riding Hood."

"Well, then you heard correctly. And you're going to keep that to yourself for the time being," I warn.

Clearly Jax didn't pick up on the warning. I shake my head as I read through the group chat with the guys once I've settled into my hotel room.

Pucking Legends:

Jackson:

Did you hear? Our Benny Boy is getting hitched.

Griffin:

Wait, what? I've got so many questions. To who? When? Where? Why? How?

Jackson:

Scarlett Carlisle. They've been having secret meetings at the office and he even goes to her house to give her sister guitar lessons.

Carson:

Congrats, Benny! When's the big day? I'd also just like to point out that she likely fell for you all those years ago because I agreed to sing karaoke with you.

Me:

WTF, J? I only told your nosy ass because we're family and you inserted yourself into our conversation.

Jackson:

I know. But you probably would've kept it a secret for weeks, and you're going to need our support so you don't fuck it up.

Me:

Shouldn't that have been my decision? And what makes you think I'm gonna fuck it up?

Jackson:

Oh, idk . . . probably the fact that you already messed things up with LRRH once.

Griffin:

LRRH??

Jackson:

FFS Little Red Riding Hood.

Carson:

FFS?

Jackson:

For fuck's sake.

Me:

You guys are exhausting.

Bennett has left the group chat.
Griffin has added Bennett to the group chat.

Griffin:

Are you going to answer my questions, Benny? When did this happen and how?

Me:

Last week. I asked and she said yes.

Carson:

Did you get down on one knee?

Me:

Obviously.

Griffin:

How is that obvious? None of us were there. And you conveniently haven't mentioned this all week. Also, why didn't you tell us the two of you were dating? When did that start?

Me:

The night of the family skate.

Jackson:

And then you went from perpetual bachelor to an engaged man in a month's time?

Carson:

What Jaxy means to say is we're happy for you, B. Sometimes your once in a lifetime love comes crashing into your life and knocks the wind outta your sails. From what I've seen, Scarlett can hold her own against you.

Jackson:

Yeah, and that's a hell of a lot more than most people can say when it comes to dealing with your stubborn ass.

Griffin:

Rally in Jax and Carse's room for some *Call of Duty* in a half hour. I'll bring the batch of chocolate chip cookies Kenna and Dakota made us. Bennett, get mentally prepared to indulge us with all the details.

Me:

Maybe I'll opt to stay in tonight.

Carson:

Not a chance. Take your post-flight shower and get your ass in here.

I sigh in defeat knowing I'm not getting out of this discussion. As I start the shower I can't help but wonder what Scarlett's up to right now. Should I go to her room to make sure she's settled in alright? I should probably check on her to see how she's feeling after the flight.

See how she's feeling? Chill the fuck out; she set up rules for this exact reason.

I take a deep breath as I lean into the spray and revel in the way the water pelts against my sore muscles. Instead of relaxing like I usually do in the shower, my mind is whirling with all the ways I can try to convince Scarlett over time that those rules were made to be broken.

She's allowed me back into her life with this arrangement, and I'm determined to make her mine—for real.

9

Scarlett

Benny:
What room are you in?
Me:
Who's asking?
Benny:
Me . . . obviously.
Me:
Room 707. Why?
Benny:
We're not on the same floor.
Me:
I think that was intentional.
Benny:
Yeah, they never have management on the same floor as the players.

Me:

> Right . . . well, as riveting as this conversation is, there's a bath calling my name.

Benny:

> The guys want to meet my fiancée.

> They are insistent they get to meet you before their women get their hands on you.

I stare at his text for so long that the text bubbles appear and disappear five times before a third text from him comes through and makes me freeze.

Benny:

> I'll be up to get you in five. Put some clothes on and join us.

> Or don't, and I'll have an excuse to help resurrect those memories you seem to have forgotten from years ago. Just kidding . . . we've got rules to follow ;)

Was that another attempt at Bennett flirting?

Me:

> When you say join us?

Benny:

> I mean join me and a few of the guys for drinks at the hotel bar. You've got four minutes, Little Red.

I scramble off the bed and sift through hangers in the hotel closet until I find the black halter-top cocktail dress I brought in case I needed a dressier outfit. The top is fitted with a skirt that somewhat flares at the bottom and has an eye-drawing slit up the front. I hope Bennett wishes he never asked me to leave this room when he sees me in it.

Why in the hell did I open my big mouth and put a "no crossing the line" rule in place? I'm blaming it on the panic and fear I had from flying for the first time. Am I pathetic for wanting to say fuck it and make an amendment? Perhaps, but there's just no way I'll be able to resist Bennett for three freaking years. Just the thought of that alone is like actual torture.

I've just clasped the eye fastener on my top when a knock sounds at the door. I quickly spray my Chanel No. 5 onto my wrist and dab it across my pulse points before grabbing my black Saint Laurent clutch off my bed and stepping into my black Christian Louboutin pumps.

A second later I open the door to find a devastatingly handsome Bennett standing with his shoulder leaned against the doorframe, the picture of casual sexiness. He looks like maybe he's showered and trimmed his beard since the flight. His hair is now pushed back and styled in a way that makes me crave to run my fingers through it and mess it up. My core clenches as I take in the way his sage cashmere sweater clings to his chest and biceps. He's got the damn sleeves pulled up, exposing his delicious forearms, with his hands in his pockets. He's still wearing his suit pants and dress shoes, and the sight of him looking effortlessly polished has me weak in the knees.

Damn him and his good looks; I wanted to be the one to knock him off his feet. And damn me for making that stupid rule.

"Red," he lets out in a low whisper, his eyes smoldering as he takes me in.

Well, I'll be damned. Warmth and longing I haven't felt in six years have me flexing my stomach to contain the butterflies threatening to break free. It takes everything in me not to shout the thoughts screaming in my head. *I take back the damn rule. Fuck me right here. Right now.*

"You don't clean up so bad yourself, Benny Boy." My cheeks burn under his aching gaze. "Shall we?" I ask him before stepping out into the hall and shutting the door behind me.

"After you," he gestures toward the elevators before placing his hand on the small of my back as we walk down the hallway. "I'm sorry about this. Apparently, Jax isn't affected by my threatening tone anymore."

"Was that what that was? Hmm," I hum in indifference.

"It was," he clarifies, clearly annoyed with Jax.

"Then I can see why we're headed to meet them for drinks. So, cat's outta the bag? Who all knows?"

"Just Jax, Carse, and Griff," he tells me as we step into the elevator and he presses the button for the rooftop where the hotel's restaurant and bar are located.

"Well that's not so bad," I tell him as I lean against the wall of the elevator farthest from him.

"Were you anticipating that we'd be walking into an engagement party with the entire team?" Bennett asks as he leans back against the opposite wall of the elevator and crosses one foot over the other with his hands in his pockets again.

God, my fiancé is stupid hot. Suddenly I remember the first time the two of us were alone in an elevator.

Bennett balances me against the wall as he hikes up the silk skirt of my dress before slamming his hips against mine once more. The feel of his erection through his suit pants rubs perfectly against my exposed clit.

"Stop," Bennett commands roughly.

"Stop what?" I ask, blinking out of the memory.

"Stop thinking about that night, or I'll be forced to stop this elevator and bring it all to the forefront of your memory. Rules be damned.

It's written all over your face, and even if it weren't, you're practically panting over there," he says in a gravelly tone, gesturing to my chest. "Tell me, Scar," he starts as he stalks across the elevator toward me, "if I were to drift my fingers up between those perfect legs, would I find your pussy wet and needy for me?"

"Bennett," I start as a whisper but end as a gasp when he reaches me and pauses with his hand on my thigh at the hem of the slit of my dress. My pussy throbs in anticipation of where this could go. "If you drift your fingers any higher, you'll be met with my soaking, bare pussy."

"Fuuuuck, Scar," he groans and rests his forehead against mine. "Let me guess, you didn't want panty lines again?"

"You're picking up on things quickly," I whisper to him, waiting with bated breath to see where this will go.

Disappointment floods me when Bennett drops his hand from my thigh as the elevator chimes and the doors open to the bar's entrance. My feet remain rooted in place as I try to calm my racing heart. Bennett steps back and walks out of the elevator but turns around and holds the door with his arm when he notices I haven't moved yet.

"Is that a hint of disappointment I see on your face, Little Red? Hmm." He pauses as if pondering something. "How about this, if you're a good little fiancée, perhaps we can pick up where we left off when I escort you back to your room. But only if you beg me to break the rules."

My pussy clenches at the promise in his tone and begs me to be on my best behavior, but my strong will won't let him get away with that bullshit.

"Thank you, *dear*, for reminding me what an arrogant man I'm engaged to," I purr as I brush past him. I'm about to dazzle the hell out of his friends so he can eat his words later. I don't plan on begging, he'll willingly drop to his knees.

Bennett

Scarlett Carlisle is the most frustratingly stubborn woman. If she didn't drive me so crazy with want, it'd almost be endearing.

She's currently making me pay for my comment in the elevator. I haven't quite figured out if it's because I teased us both and pulled away, if it's because I crossed the line of our no-touch rule, or if it's because I told her she had to earn picking up where we left off. Honestly, probably all of the above.

Her willingness to go to battle with me has my dick twitching behind my zipper each time she sends a witty retort my way. Or right now, for example, when we lock eyes from across the bar and she sends me a wink before turning back to listen to whatever Carson is talking about. Yeah, she knows exactly what she's doing to me.

Scar won the three of them over within a matter of minutes, not that she needed to earn their approval. But seeing her so easily interact with three of my closest friends has me smiling to myself like a fool.

"Look at you," Jax says, slapping me on the shoulder before sidling up next to me at the bar as I wait for our second round of drinks. "You're looking at Scarlett like she hung the moon."

"That doesn't sound like a bad thing, considering she's about to become my wife."

Fuck, I think I like the sound of that far too much for someone who hadn't really thought about marriage up until a few days ago.

"And how did that come about so quickly?" he asks, curiosity shining in his eyes.

"Why are you asking?"

"I'm happy for you, big bro, I really am. I just can't help but wonder if there's more to the story than you're letting on. I mean, when we got drinks about a month ago, you had just left her house after your first lesson with Gemma and you swore up and down things were platonic—that you were just doing her a favor. Now I hear you've been together since the family skate, but I thought she basically told you to go to hell after that."

"So?" I ask in a tone that borders on defensive.

"So, do you love her?"

My shoulders stiffen at his question. "People don't always marry for love, J. You and I know that better than anyone," I tell him.

"And that's exactly where my concern lies," he says, shaking his head. "Look, Scarlett seems like an amazing woman. I think she'd be a great match for you—she'd keep you on your toes and I doubt she'd let you get away with your typical moody bullshit. But you're right, you and I know better than anyone what happens in a loveless marriage. And it's not just the two of you from what you've told me, you've got to consider Gemma and Gunner as well," he points out and I'm not mad at him for it. Jackson's concerns are coming from a good place, and I'm glad that he's not just looking out for me, but the three people about to become my family as well.

He's my brother, and I'm not going to lie to him, but I also made a promise to Scarlett not to tell secrets that aren't mine to share. "I can't really share all of the details of our engagement, but the way I look at it, I'm getting another shot with the one woman who's knocked me on my ass and left me wanting more. Trust me, I didn't go into this without thinking about Gemma and Gunner. I'd like to be there for them in whatever capacity Scar is okay with, even if that's just being another role model to them."

And I mean that. Even if our agreement has an end date, I'll still treat them as my family every step of the way, and after if she'll let me. In the short amount of time I've spent around them, they've already taken up residence in my heart, just like their older sister.

Jax looks down and plays with the peel of his beer bottle, seemingly lost in thought. When he looks up, he holds my stare as he says, "I can't think of a better role model for any kid to have than you, B. Hell, you've been the best big brother and role model to me and Walker our whole lives so you've had plenty of practice."

The sincerity shining in his eyes has me clearing the emotion clogging my throat. "Thanks, Jax. That means a lot."

He brings me in for a hug, and once he's pulled away, he does what he does best—he completely ruins the sentimental moment between us with a snarky remark. "I can't wait to see what the ladies think of Daddy Bennett."

"Oh, I do like the sound of that," Scarlett hums in approval from where she stands behind us.

After I've given Jax a shove for his comment, I turn my attention to Scarlett to find her biting her bottom lip, her cheeks flushed.

"Do you?" I ask, trying to mask the humor in my tone because I think my fiancée may be slightly buzzed from only one drink.

"Yep. And here I thought I'd come see what was taking so long with my drink, but I wasn't expecting to come over here and hear you talking about how many babies you were planning to knock me up with." She punctuates her statement with a bop to my nose.

Okay so maybe a little more than slightly. "Jesus, I didn't realize I was marrying such a lightweight."

"Buckle up, Benny Boy, you've got so much to learn," she singsongs.

"Ah, hell, the two of you are adorable. She calls you Benny Boy and you call her Little Red," Jax points out, shaking his head. "I can't wait to add that into my best man speech. You're turning my brother into a simp. He might even give Griff and Carsey a run for their money soon," he tells Scarlett.

"Who said you were the best man?" I toss back.

"If you choose Griff over me, I'll never forgive you," Jax warns.

"No, I think maybe I'll ask Griff to get ordained as payback for him having me officiate their wedding."

"When is the big day?" Jax asks.

"We haven't gotten that far in the planning yet. We should probably tell our families before we set a date," Scarlett explains.

"Yeah, that makes sense. Which reminds me, I forgot to ask, what does your grandfather think of all this?"

Scarlett gives him a sheepish look. "I haven't exactly told him that I'm marrying the captain of his hockey team just yet."

"Oh, shit. This just keeps getting better. Between your grandfather and our old man, I'll be praying for the two of you," Jax says before grabbing his beer and heading back to the table where Griff and Carse are sitting. "It was good talking to ya, sis," he calls over his shoulder.

I notice the change in Scarlett's posture and demeanor almost immediately. Goddammit, Jackson.

Gently grabbing her chin, I look into her whiskey eyes and shake my head. "Hey, don't listen to him, he was only giving us a hard time."

"No, he's right. What will your dad think of this? He'll probably think I'm some gold digger only marrying you for your money and status." The words rush out of her in panic and I'm consumed with the urge to put her at ease.

"Scar, you're about to become the owner of the NHL team I play for. If anyone looks like they're marrying for money or status, it's me in this situation. And my father will gladly point that out, I'm sure," I say, but it doesn't seem to work because she goes on as if she hadn't heard a word.

"And my grandfather will probably scold me for fraternizing with a player. Oh my god, I wouldn't be surprised if he just sells the team once he forbids us from marrying each other."

I place my hands on each of her shoulders and meet her frazzled gaze. "Scarlett, take a deep breath with me," I tell her and watch as she deeply inhales and exhales along with me. "Good. Now, do you have your engagement ring with you?"

"Yes," she answers, her brow wrinkling in confusion.

I take one of my hands off her shoulders to look at my watch to see what time it is. "Do you think Joseph will still be awake? It's a quarter after nine."

"I'm not sure, probably."

"Alright, here's what we're going to do. We're going to go to your room to grab your engagement ring and a glass of water to sober you up a smidge, then go to your grandfather's room. There's no sense in delaying the inevitable; I think it's better to get it out of the way. Especially now that some of the team knows, I think it'd be worse if he heard the news from someone else."

Scarlett's expression sobers before she nods in agreement. "It's your funeral, Wilson," she says before turning toward the elevators. I fight back a groan at the extra swing in her hips as she walks away from me.

I don't follow her out of the bar right away, instead, I head back to the table and toss some cash on it. "We're headed in for the night," I tell the guys, grabbing a bun from the bread basket sitting in front of them to give to Scarlett.

"Have fun, Benny Boy," Carse teases.

"But not too much fun," Jax adds.

"Don't listen to him, have all the fun you want, B," Griff says before I turn and toss my middle finger up at them as I make my way to the elevators where Scar is waiting for me.

She turns and gives me a saccharine smile that has me rolling my eyes and tossing the bun to her. Like I said, my fiancée would probably be endearing if she didn't drive me wild.

10

Scarlett

October

"It's about time the two of you caught on to my matchmaking," my grandfather says with a mischievous smile.

I have to blink several times in rapid succession for my brain to process what I've just heard. Maybe that bread didn't soak up the alcohol as well as Bennett had hoped.

My grandfather thinks he played matchmaker?

"And how do you suppose you played matchmaker?" I ask a few moments later after my mouth can catch up to my brain.

He rolls his eyes at the pair of us sitting across from him in the small sitting room of his suite. "I may have heard whisperings of a past between the two of you. And the look on Bennett's face when he saw you in my office that first day was all the confirmation I needed. Tell me, Firefly, how many players have I suggested you take back to your office to talk to?" he questions.

I notice Bennett's posture stiffening and his fist flexing once, then twice, at my grandfather's question.

"One," I answer and watch Bennett's shoulders relax at my response.

"And when did I happen to inform you about the stipulation of ownership?"

"During that meeting, right before Bennett walked in," I reply, slowly putting the pieces of the puzzle together.

"Bennett, how many family and friends preseason skates have we done during your time with the organization?"

"None, sir," he responds.

"Exactly, none. It wasn't a coincidence. I decided to add a few more opportunities for the two of you to run into each other in hopes that you'd figure it out. And enough of that 'sir' business. Call me Joseph as you always have. Besides, we'll be family shortly," he tells him in an amused tone.

"And you're okay with that—with the two of us getting married?" I ask him, slightly bewildered at his plotting. If I'm being honest, I'm impressed he was able to pull this off with his health slowly declining.

"Of course. I've known Bennett since he was a teenager just entering the league. I couldn't think of a more stand-up gentleman for my little Firefly to marry. But it doesn't matter what I think, Scarlett, the only opinions that matter are the two of yours. I'm not the one entering into this marriage." My grandfather pauses, looking back and forth between the two of us before finally looking down to where Bennett's hand is wrapped around mine. "Do you want to know what your grandmother's father told me when I asked for his blessing?"

The two of us nod, and he continues. "Her father told me that the key to a successful marriage is friendship. That first and foremost, the two of us be friends. And that if we put that friendship before anything else, if we always remained each other's best friend, we could get through any curve or challenge that came our way. Do you consider yourselves friends?"

Bennett's gaze meets mine and he gently squeezes my hand in his before turning to answer my grandfather. "Yes, Scarlett is my friend."

It's a simple statement—not a romantic declaration of love—so it shouldn't have my chest squeezing, but I think being Bennett's friend means more to him than most. From what I've seen, he keeps his circle small. I'm not quite sure why that is, but I know opening himself to me in this way is major for him.

I turn to my grandfather and nod in response, unable to find any words at the moment.

"Good, I'm glad to hear it. Bennett, will you be joining us for Sunday dinners now when you're available?" my grandfather asks him.

"Uh—" Bennett looks over at me in question.

"Gemma, Gunner, and I try to have dinner with my grandparents every Sunday. It's a tradition we've had since I was a little girl, and it was important to me that we continued it after my dad passed away. You're more than welcome to join us when you're in town if you'd like," I offer, but I don't expect him to spend more time with my family than he needs to.

"I'd love that, thank you for including me," Bennett says, surprising me.

"Of course, my wife will be so excited to hear the big news. Why don't we celebrate when we get back to town since you'll be back on the road this Sunday?"

"Just tell us when and we'll be there," he answers for the two of us, and I'm oddly okay with it.

Moments later, Bennett is escorting me back to my room when I stop in the hallway. He halts his steps, turning to face me. "Thank you for that," I blurt.

"For what? You have nothing to thank me for," he replies.

I train my gaze on my shoes, unwilling to meet his eyes. "For agreeing to come to Sunday dinners. They've always meant a lot to me, but after losing my dad, and now, with my grandfather's diagnosis, they've become sacred. It will mean a lot to my grandparents to have you there, and to Gemma and Gunner. And, well, me too."

Bennett softly grips my chin and lifts my face until our eyes meet. "Don't thank me, it's not a favor. It'll be my pleasure to join you for Sunday dinners whenever I'm in town."

I stare up at him and my breath hitches when I catch his gaze retreating to my lips. Bennett eliminates the space between us, and my heart slams in my chest in anticipation.

"We didn't finish what we started earlier," he rasps.

"We didn't," I agree in a whisper.

Instead of pulling me in for a kiss like I had hoped, Bennett takes a step back and runs a hand through his hair. "I believe I suggested we play twenty questions to get to know one another better, but we didn't finish before the movie started."

I almost whine in frustration, but quickly mask my disappointment. Friends, we're supposed to be friends first and foremost. Even if this is temporary, I should probably get to know my future husband better than I do now.

"When's your birthday?" he asks, starting off the questions.

I play along and answer him. "May twenty-first. And yours?"

"December twenty-third."

"Oh, you and Gemma have the same birthday!" I point out.

"It'll be her sweet sixteen, right? I know Gunner said he was five, but I kind of assumed Gemma was fifteen when I saw her driving with you. She does have her permit, right?"

"Yes, she'll be sixteen and she has her learner's permit." I roll my eyes at him.

"And how do you feel about her getting her license?"

I wince at the thought of my baby sister behind the wheel, and in the dead of winter, no less.

"I'm hoping I can convince her to hold off until she's eighteen to take her driver's test."

He chuckles as he presses the button for the elevator. "Good luck with that. The day I turned sixteen I took my driver's test and couldn't wait to get that bit of freedom."

"That's exactly what I'm afraid of. She's at the height of her hormonal spiral and some days it feels like I'm doing everything wrong," I admit to him, shifting my weight in my heels before deciding to forego them altogether. I place my hand on his shoulder for balance, but before I can bend my leg to take off my heels, Bennett lowers to his knees.

Bennett fucking Wilson is on his knees before me. *What in the actual hell is going on right now?*

With my hand still resting on his shoulder, he looks up at me from his knees. "I'm not a parent, but I think that means you're doing everything right. From what I've seen and heard so far, I'd say you're doing a hell of a job raising them on your own."

My cheeks heat from his compliment and the sincerity in his tone.

"And I'm not sure what you'd like my role to be with them, but if we're doing this, I'd like to be involved," he tells me as he grabs the back of my ankle, lifting my foot off the ground so he can slip my heel off. Goosebumps erupt on my skin from his heated touch. "You'll quickly learn that I'm the all-in kind of guy. Once I set my mind on something, there's no half-assing it on my part."

I stare into his hazel eyes and try to find the hesitation or unease hidden beneath them, but come up short in my attempts. Instead, Bennett looks genuinely interested in being involved with my siblings.

God, what would that be like? To have someone to share in the good and bad with? To have a partner to lean on when things feel too heavy to fall solely on my shoulders. Gemma and Gunner have never been a burden to me, but I have to admit that raising them on my own the past five years has weighed on me.

I love them immensely, truly I do. They've been my entire world. So letting someone in and trusting them to be a part of their lives is no small ask of me. Can I really trust someone I've only known such a short time to be around them?

"They've already lost so much. I can't ask you to make that commitment to them. We know the deal, three years and then we part ways. Where will that leave the two of them?"

"I understand where you're coming from, I do, Scar. But keeping people at arm's length to avoid hurt may just cause more hurt and loneliness in the long run. I'd like to be a role model to them—a male presence in their lives. I want to be the best partner to you, and being there for them is the only way I can do that."

He's not wrong. After experiencing so much loss, I've pushed people away and built walls around my heart as barriers to protect myself. It's only natural that I'd also want to protect Gemma and Gunner, who are an extension of my heart beating outside my chest, from any hurt and pain that I could.

But I've also seen how great he has been with them in such a short time. And he's the one asking me if it's okay if he's a role model to them. How can I deny my siblings the opportunity to have someone as special as Bennett in their lives? I shouldn't. Although I think it'll take time for me to get there.

Bennett lowers my foot to the ground and I shift my weight as he grabs the back of my other ankle, lifting my foot so he can take off my other heel. When he sets my other foot down, he maintains eye contact with me as he slowly grazes his hand from my ankle to my knee. My breathing becomes stuttered, and when I don't stop him, instead nodding down at him, his hand continues up my inner thigh at a torturously slow rate until he pauses at my uppermost thigh. If he moves his fingers mere centimeters, he'll touch me exactly where my pussy is throbbing with need.

Instead, the elevator doors open and Bennett lowers his hand to gather my heels before turning his back to me in a squat. "Hop on," he commands.

"What? No. I can't in this dress." Even with the slit, I'd probably rip the tight fabric of the skirt if I got on his back for a piggyback ride.

"Fine. Have it your way," he says as he stands to his full height and faces me again.

"I'm perfectly capable of—" I'm cut off when Bennett scoops me into his arms full-on bridal style and I let out a yelp instead. "What are you doing? Put me down you barbarian!"

"Consider this practice for our wedding night, wifey," he says with a chuckle, clearly delighted with himself.

"I haven't signed my life away yet—it's not too late," I protest.

"Yes, it is. And do you wanna know why?"

"Sure, I'll humor you," I tell him as he steps into the elevator and presses the button for my floor, still refusing to set me down.

"Because you're wearing *my* ring on your finger. And it's *me* your needy pussy is weeping for right now," he rasps, and holy fucking hell, he's right.

"You're wrong," I start and he smirks at my pathetic attempt at a lie.

"Then why did I feel how soaked she is without even touching her?"

She? Her?

"You didn't," I try again, but he just shakes his head and lets out a low, menacing chuckle.

"I did, because she remembers. Your tight, aching pussy *remembers* what it's like to stretch around my thick cock. She's been deprived for far too long, Scar. It's a shame we agreed to those rules."

Ohmyfuckinggod. Fuck the rules!

"She's gotten plenty of attention in the years since," I double down on my lie, feeling slightly lightheaded from how breathless his words are making me.

"If I recall correctly, I believe I warned you what happens when you bring up other men, Scarlett."

"Hmm, did you?" I feign ignorance, hoping like hell he'll remind me.

"You're playing with fire, Little Red."

And yet, I'm begging to be burned.

11

Scarlett

I'm not sure when the change happened, but last night my husband-to-be decided to be a perfect rule-following gentleman after he walked me to my room and left me there aching and needy as hell.

I've come to the conclusion that edging me like that and depriving me of the pleasure he is no doubt capable of giving me was his punishment for bringing up other men.

Little does he know, he left me so thoroughly corrupted all those years ago that no man or toy has been able to do the trick since.

I'm interrupted from my packing when my phone buzzes with an incoming call. I glance at it and smile when I see Gemma's name scroll across the screen.

"Hey, Gems—" I greet her but she cuts me off.

"Don't 'Gems' me, are you freaking engaged?"

My stomach sinks at the accusation in her tone. Shit, this is not how I wanted to tell her.

"Yes—" I start again but she interrupts once more.

"When did you and Bennett have time to get engaged? On the plane to Chicago? I don't understand."

"No, not on the plane. He-he proposed the other night at our house before your guitar lesson," I tell her.

"So you got engaged at our house and didn't tell me? I can understand waiting to tell Gunner, but you didn't want to tell me?" The hurt in her voice cuts me like a knife.

"We were going to tell you together tomorrow when we got back."

"Yeah, and instead, I find out at school in journalism class because Grandma published an engagement announcement in the freaking newspaper."

"She what?!" I shout, unable to compose myself.

"Yeah, and now there are about a dozen online articles claiming to break the news that Minnesota's captain is engaged to the team owner's granddaughter. Some of the stuff they're saying about you is awful, I don't get how people can be so cruel."

Shit. Shit, shit, shit.

This isn't good. Not only did we not get the chance to tell Gemma and Gunner about the engagement, but I know for a fact Jackson is the only one in Bennett's family who knows. Well, knew. His father is probably going to flip a lid when he's briefed by his press secretary that his oldest son is not only seeing someone, but he's engaged to her.

"Don't read them, Gems. I'm not going to. People will always have an opinion, and honestly, they can think whatever they want, but we know the truth," I tell her.

"But, I didn't. I didn't know the truth and I still don't. Why didn't you trust me to know? I wouldn't have told anyone."

My heart sinks as her words register. "Gemma, I trust you implicitly. I'm so sorry that I wasn't able to tell you myself in person. This is the last way I wanted you to find out."

Her sniffles on the other line have me spiraling. "I know. I'm sorry, I was just surprised."

"Don't ever apologize for how you're feeling, Gems. Look, I'll be home really late tonight because we're flying back after the game. I wasn't planning to get you guys from Grandma's until the morning for school, but how about I come tonight instead?"

"Really?" she questions.

"Really," I promise.

"Will Bennett be with you?" she asks and my forehead wrinkles in confusion.

"No. Why would Bennett be with me so late, Gems?"

"Oh, are you waiting until you're married to move in together? I just figured most engaged couples move in together at some point, don't they?"

Shoot, she's not wrong.

"Um, we haven't quite figured out the timeline for when that will happen," I tell her truthfully, though I don't tell her it's because we've yet to discuss the fine details of our arrangement, including living accommodations.

"Well if Bennett doesn't want to move into our house, would we get a new one or would we move in with him?"

"We just got Gunner settled in at his new school, and we live pretty close to your school, so I would say we likely wouldn't be moving out of our house," I explain.

"Okay, I don't care either way. It's just that I finally got my room set up how I wanted."

"I know, and I love how you've transformed the space."

"Thanks, Scar. Lunch is almost done, so I've got to go. We'll see you later tonight, right?" she asks.

"Tonight," I assure her. "I love you, Gems. Tell Gunner I love him too, please."

"Will do. Love you too, sis. And don't worry, I'll make sure Gunner doesn't hear about your big news until you tell him."

"I'm not sure what I did to get such an amazing sister. Thank you," I tell her before she tells me goodbye and hangs up.

Tossing my phone on the bed, I drop my head back and curse at the ceiling before letting out a defeated sigh.

I'm not sure why my grandmother thought it was a good idea to publish an engagement announcement before she had talked to the two of us.

I hesitantly pick up my phone from the bed and search my name online. Grimacing at the dozens of article headlines that come up, I don't give in to the temptation to read them. Instead, I pull up my contacts and call Bennett.

"Miss me already, Red?" he asks when he picks up.

"As if. Considering the way you left me last night, you're lucky I'm even speaking to you," I reply with an air of disdain.

"I believe I warned you," Bennett tuts in response.

"Right, well I thought the punishment would be something served with a side of *pleasure* like it had been in the past. My mistake."

"Jesus, I'm just getting back from morning skate," he tells me in a hushed voice.

"And that matters why?" I ask in a tone as innocent as I can muster behind the cheeky smile spreading across my face.

"You know why," he growls, and my panties dampen from the deep bass of his voice alone.

"Do share, darling," I taunt.

"Because I very clearly remember the way your body responded to said pleasure, *sweetheart*," he hisses in reply. "And that is not the image I want to recall while I'm in front of all the guys."

Got him! I smile like the cat that ate the canary.

"Oh, I'm sorry, Benny Boy, I won't mention the time you turned the creamy skin of my ass red as a punishment for bringing up the men who came before you. Literally—" I cut myself off with a peel of laughter I can't contain.

When I've finally got some semblance of control a few minutes later, he asks, "Are you sure this is how you wanna play things, Scar?"

My laughter subsides, quickly shifting into sheer desire at the promise in his question. I had been laughing so hard, I'd honestly thought he'd hung up.

Before I can respond, someone knocks—more like pounds—on my door.

"Hang on a minute, someone's at my door," I tell him.

"You'd better get that," he says and then hangs up.

Shit, why'd he hang up? I hadn't got around to telling him the reason I'd called him in the first place.

When I open the door, my eyes widen at the sight of a heaving Bennett bracing himself with both arms reaching up to where he has a death grip on the top of the doorframe.

"Bennett—" I start but am cut off when he lifts me with one arm around my waist, and slams the door shut with his other. My legs wrap around his waist on instinct, and when my clit rubs against his thick erection, I have to bite back a moan that threatens to escape.

"Now do you see what you've done to me, Red?" he asks as he braces me against the wall of my hotel room and grinds his length against my aching core, still holding me up with only one arm under my ass and the other bracketing my head.

My pebbled nipples brush against his still-heaving chest, and I feel as though I could combust right here right now with clothing between us and not so much as a kiss.

His gaze is intense—his eyes wild with desire—as he stares into my eyes. When he peers at my mouth and frees my bottom lip from my teeth with this thumb, I can't help the whimper that slips free.

"Tell me to stop, Little Red."

I stay silent, which only makes his body tremble against mine in response.

"Remind me of our rules. Tell me this is a bad idea. That I don't know what's good for me—good for us."

Screw any rule I put in place saying this was wrong. I don't utter a single word, the only sounds escaping me are my ragged breaths. His eyes search mine for hesitation, which he won't find. I want this. God, do I want this. Him. Here. Now.

"Fuck it," he rushes out before claiming my mouth in a kiss so intoxicating, it leaves me heady at the feel of his plush lips fighting for dominance against mine.

Bennett kisses me and it feels like my life has been at a standstill all this time up until the moment I could feel his lips on mine again. He kisses me with such ferocity and hunger, it feels like he'll never be sated. And I'm not sure I'll ever be able to get enough of him either now that I've tasted him once again.

It's been *so long* since a man kissed me, though I've never been kissed like this. It's possessive. *Claiming.* Bennett isn't just kissing me—he's altering my brain chemistry.

We kiss in a clash of lips, teeth, and tongues until we're both gasping for breath. Bennett moves across the room and lays me on my bed before standing to his full height at the edge of the bed.

"I should go," he says as he sinks to his knees.

I shake my head in response, unable to form even a simple "no."

His hands glide up my thighs until his fingers rest just inside the waistband of my satin sleep shorts that are doing nothing to hide the mess he's making of me.

"I really should walk out that door right now," he brings his forehead to rest against my lower stomach, almost as if he's about to beg me for mercy. If he does, there's no chance I'll willingly give it. I've never been so turned on in my life.

"Tell me to leave," he pleads and I shake my head fervently in silent reply. "Is this what you want?" he asks.

I nod my head but he shakes his head at me. "Words, Scar."

"Yes. Yes, of course, this is what I want. Now stop torturing the both of us and fuck your fiancée," I demand.

"But what about the no-touch rule?" he questions.

"Fuck the rules," I pant, desperate to feel his touch anywhere and everywhere.

An impish grin spreads across his face as he slowly slides my sleep shorts off, letting out a low groan when he finds me pantiless once again.

He peppers whisper-soft kisses up and down my slit and I somehow whimper in both satisfaction and frustration.

"I need—" I start but he lifts his head, cutting me off.

"I know exactly what you need, Scarlett. The only question is whether or not you've earned it," he rasps, each syllable vibrating against my clit.

"Not this again," I groan in frustration.

His hazel eyes lock with mine. "Will you relinquish control to me, baby girl?"

I keen at the sound of the nickname he used for me that night rolling off his tongue. "Yes," I half-whisper, half-moan when he flattens his tongue and lazily strokes my clit before sliding one finger inside me, and then adding a second shortly after.

"Such a good little wife you'll be," he hums to himself as he paves a path of kisses up my stomach, lifting my sleep tank as he goes until he takes one nipple in his mouth, his fingers still working in and out of me at a feverish rate.

In the back of my mind, the feminist in me is screaming *fuck the patriarchy*, but goddammit, I *want* to be a good little wife for him, even if only in this capacity.

Squirming with the need for more, I buck my hips in a silent plea for him to grind against me, fuck me, just something more, *anything more.*

Rather than giving me what I'm seeking, Bennett places a knee on the bed and gestures for me to sit up. When I comply, he lifts my tank over my head and slides me up the bed until my head rests against the pillows. Then he stands to his full height and reaches behind his head to slip off his Wolverines Hockey shirt.

"Do you have any toys with you, Red?"

"What?" I question, unsure if I heard him correctly.

"Did you bring any of your toys along?"

"Yes," I admit, completely unashamed.

"And did you bring any lube for your toys?"

"Yes?" I answer as more of a question, wondering where he's going with this.

"Tell me where."

"In the lavender toiletry bag in my suitcase," I tell him, gesturing to the corner where my suitcase sits open.

Without another word, Bennett stalks over to my suitcase and grabs the small bottle of lube before making his way back to the edge of my bed. He tosses the bottle onto the bed beside me, and then I watch with rapt attention as he slides his athletic shorts and boxers down his thighs, revealing his throbbing cock that is now even more mouthwatering than it was before.

My eyes widen as I take in the changes. "Is that?"

"Jacob's ladder piercings? Yeah," he says with a wicked grin.

"What made you decide to do that?" I question, suddenly overcome with irrational jealousy at the thought of him getting it for another woman.

"If I'm being honest, it was either this or a dick tattoo, and I didn't really have anything I wanted to permanently etch across my manhood. I figured a piercing was temporary, though I've become quite attached to them over the past nine months."

"What do you mean it was either a pierced dick or a tattooed dick?"

"I was the biggest loser for our fantasy football league again, and that was the winner of the league's chosen punishment. I probably could've gotten out of it, but I was curious to see what it'd be like."

My brows furrow. "Who was the winner of the league?"

"Griffin, that sadistic bastard," he answers.

"And has your curiosity been quelled?"

"Honestly, I'm not sure. I haven't given them a test drive yet," he admits to my disbelief, and the shock must be written all over my face.

"You haven't—"

"Nope."

"Not even with yourself?"

"Come on, Scar. I can't even count how many times I've fucked my hand over the past two months since you came waltzing back into my life."

"So I'd be the first?"

"The only," he clarifies, and fuck if that doesn't reignite the flame that was burning only minutes ago.

"Is that what the lube is for?" I question as I take in the two barbells on the underside of his cock. My mouth waters at the thought of running my tongue over them.

"No, this is my self-restraint," he tells me as he holds up the bottle.

"Restraint?" I ask.

"Yes," he answers as he kneels on the bed and fists his cock in one hand while pouring lube over his length with the other. I watch as he pumps his fist, working the lube up and down his shaft. Once he's thoroughly lubed, he crawls up the bed until he's kneeling between my spread thighs.

"Tell me to get lost, Scar."

"I wouldn't dare."

"Famous last words," he mutters as he leans down and spits on my pussy.

Holy fucking hell. Why is that one of the hottest things anyone has ever done to me? What is wrong with me?

Bennett braces himself on his elbows, his biceps bracketing my head as he lowers his hips until his cock grazes my clit. When he works his hips forward, his piercings brush against my clit and my hips buck from the stimulation.

As Bennett continues to glide the head of his cock over my entrance, to my clit, and back, over and over again, my moans must get louder, because he silences me with a searing kiss.

When he pulls his lips from mine, he looks down at where our bodies fervently move against each other.

"I need more," I tell him.

"No," he growls.

"Fuck me," I demand but he just shakes his head, unwilling to meet my gaze. "Why?" I ask.

"I haven't earned it yet," he answers as if that isn't the most vague thing I've ever heard.

Unable to put much thought into his bizarre answer, I mirror his fixed gaze and marvel at the sight of his cock sliding against my clit repeatedly. The depravity I feel in this moment from the way this man makes me feel without so much as entering me has my pussy clenching and my clit throbbing, rearing me toward release.

"Oh, fuck. Bennett, please. Please don't stop," I beg and I'm far too desperate to think of the consequences of my actions right now.

"Never, not until you get what you need," he promises through gritted teeth. I throw my head back and turn my face to muffle my moans into the pillow.

His thrusts become frenzied then, his length moving through my soaked slit without abandon until the head of his cock slips inside of me and I can feel the euphoric stretch of my pussy around his piercings.

I. Come. Completely. Undone.

White hot pleasure blazes its way down my spine and explodes in my core with lethal sensation.

Never before. Nothing has ever felt this good. Forget thinking about our previous night together all those years ago, this man has just shamelessly ruined me.

My clit continues to throb as Bennett pulls out and glides his length through my slit once more. He closes his eyes and his muscles quiver as he struggles with his restraint. With his teeth gritted, I watch in fascination as Bennett relinquishes control and comes undone right along with me.

His hot cum coats my stomach, and in an act so obscene I can barely wrap my head around it, he leans his weight against one forearm and uses his other to drag his fingers through his release and trace the word "mine" across my lower abdomen.

"Such debauchery," I tell him, left otherwise stunned by everything that just happened in the last several minutes.

"It's the truth. Don't act like you don't love it, baby girl," he says as he hovers above me, lowering his head for a tease of a kiss. "I'll be right back."

As he hops off the bed, I'm left bewildered and boneless from my release. Bennett returns moments later with a wet washcloth and a dry towel to clean me up.

"They say character is what makes a man, but I say it's the aftercare."

"I guess I'm not sure what to say to that," he replies with a chuckle and my eyes widen in horror when I realize I said that aloud.

"Is there any chance you'll forget I said that?"

"Nope. I've got it stored for later reference. What other kinds of aftercare should a man give?" he asks.

"Oh, I wouldn't know," I lie, thinking about the dozens of books I've read where I swooned over the main characters doing simple acts of service for their partners.

"How about I run you a bath?" I practically purr at his suggestion, earning me a laugh. "I'll take that as a yes." He moves to sit up, but I drape my arm over his waist and pull him back toward me.

"Not yet. I've got to talk to you about something," I tell him and my stomach sinks.

Bennett lifts my head before tucking his arm beneath it and pulls me in so my body is draped over his. "What is it?"

"My grandmother may or may not have spilled the beans of our engagement," I blurt out.

His chest rumbles with laughter. "That's not a big deal, Little Red. Who did she spill the beans to? Let me guess, a bunch of her girlfriends at brunch this morning?"

"I wish, but not exactly . . . more like the entire Twin Cities and surrounding area," I confess, afraid to meet his gaze now that I can feel his posture stiffen beneath me.

"Wait, what? How did she manage that?"

"She published an engagement announcement in the *Twin Cities Tribune*, and now dozens of online publications have picked up on it and the story is running wild. I'm so sorry, Bennett, I know you haven't had a chance to tell your family yet."

"Forget about them. Do Gemma and Gunner know?" His question and the concerned look I'm met with when I finally have the nerve to peek up at him leave me awestruck for a moment.

"Gemma found out at school and was actually the one who broke the news to me."

"Was she upset we didn't tell her?"

How is he even real? Instead of worrying about the fallout he'll face, his first questions are surrounding his concern for my siblings?

Clearing my throat, I tell him, "She was at first, but I explained that we had planned to tell them tomorrow when we get back. She promised she'd do her best to make sure Gunner doesn't find out until I pick them up tonight."

Tucking a stray piece of hair behind my ear, he looks down at me. "We get back really late, I thought you said you weren't picking them up from your grandparents until the morning for school."

"I wasn't going to, but Gemma sounded so hurt that I hadn't told her, I decided to pick them up tonight so they can sleep in their own beds."

"Okay, do you want me to drive you over there and bring you guys home?"

A soft chuckle escapes me, and Bennett knits his brows in confusion. "It's funny, Gemma asked if you'd be with me when I pick them up. She assumed now that we're engaged, that you'd be moving in with us."

Bennett doesn't respond at first, he just uses his free hand to trace mindless patterns along my spine. "Is that what you want? For me to move in with the three of you?"

"We haven't really discussed living arrangements yet. I don't even know where you live." My cheeks heat from my admission.

"I live in a three-bedroom condo in the heart of the city. It's got shit closet space, and it's not in Gunner's school district, so my place isn't an option. I know you're just getting settled into your place, and from what I've seen of it, I like the layout and would prefer we don't uproot the kids in the middle of the school year—"

I don't let him finish before I crash my lips against his, hoping that through this kiss I can express even a fraction of the gratitude I'm feeling for him in this moment.

Bennett didn't fight me on it. He didn't demand we move in with him. He put Gemma and Gunner first. He offered to move into our home so they wouldn't have to give up the space they've only just settled into. Never in my life has a kind gesture been so thoroughly sexy.

Lacing his fingers through my hair, Bennett cups my neck and breaks our kiss.

"So when should I tell the movers to pack up my stuff? Do you want me to wait until my realtor lists my place?"

"Are you sure you don't want to keep it still? You know, in case you get sick of me and need your own space?"

Bennett lets out a sigh and shakes his head. "I'm on the road for a better part of the year, Scar. If we get sick of each other, then we're doing a shit job of being each other's best friend. Not only that, but it doesn't make sense to keep a separate residence under my name when we're married. Someone might look into that and use it against us."

"That's a good point, I didn't think of that," I admit. After a moment of hesitation I say, "We should probably address the elephant in the room, too, while we're at it."

He quirks a brow. "And what would that be?"

"The fact that we just broke one of the rules I put in place for us yesterday," I point out.

Rolling me onto my back, he kisses me softly. When he pulls his lips from mine he asks, "Do you wanna know what I think? I think you knew that rule was made to be broken."

My heart picks up speed again. "Oh yeah?"

He rolls his hips over mine, and I whimper from the contact. "Mhmm. In fact, I think you regretted making it the second I came to pick you up from your room last night."

That's the god's honest truth.

"What if we strike that first rule from the record?" I ask on bated breath.

"That's fine by me, baby girl."

I worry my bottom lip between my teeth. "But the other rule still stands. Absolutely no catching feelings—no falling in love."

Except for with his bejeweled cock, because I'm pretty sure it's too late for that.

"I'll play by whatever rules you put in place for us, Scar. You run the show. If you want to keep things between us strictly physical, then I'll be willing and eager to fulfill your every desire. But if you decide you want more, I'd happily give you everything."

My heart stutters to a stop as butterflies break free like a riot in my chest.

Before I can try to respond, he changes the subject. "If you're okay with it, I'd like to go with you tonight to pick up Gemma and Gunner. I know it will be late, so maybe I can stay so we can talk to them together in the morning? If you're not comfortable taking that step yet, I can go back to my place tonight and bring breakfast in the morning before school."

"Is this what it's going to be like?" I ask, my voice pinched from the emotion clogging it.

"What do you mean?"

"How it'll be to have a partner to discuss plans with? To figure out the schedule together and bounce ideas off one another?" Tears swell in my eyes at the thought of having a teammate to lean on, even temporarily, through the chaos that is raising my siblings.

"Of course, we're a team now, Red. The four of us are all in this together."

His words flood my chest with warmth, and if I'm not careful, I might actually break my own rule and fall head over heels in love with my future temporary husband.

12

Bennett

October

Well, this is going horribly.

As I sit across from my father in his study in my childhood home, I can't help but wish it were yesterday again. It was such a great day, and I'd rather be anywhere but here right now.

Yesterday was my rest day, so Scarlett decided to take the day off and let the kids play hooky from school. We spent the morning making breakfast and sharing the news of our engagement with Gunner, and Gemma was a good sport by acting surprised to hear the news. After breakfast, we took the kids to the pumpkin patch and a craft store to get supplies for the front porch decoration contest. Scarlett didn't hesitate to use my muscles and put me to work. She even asked if I'd call to get Jackson's help. He brought Alexa with him, though he swears they're not serious and she's in agreement with not putting a label on things. After we finished the porch decorations, we ordered pizza for dinner and I stayed to help put the kids to bed and pack their lunches for school the next day.

"This all feels very domesticated, I bet your skin is crawling right now," *Scarlett sighs as she puts apple slices into Gunner's Spiderman lunchbox.*

"Today has actually been one of the best days I've had in a long time," *I tell her, feeling my neck heat from my admission.*

Gripping the edge of the kitchen island, she tilts her head to the side and takes me in. "You keep surprising me, Cap."

"Only in good ways, I hope."

"In the best of ways." She breaks eye contact, looking down at the counter and shakes her head to herself. "Do you want to hang around for a bit longer? Maybe we could talk about when you'll move in and then watch an episode of Outlander *or something. I mean, only if you don't have other plans already."*

Just as Scarlett and I had sat down to talk about the timeline for me moving in, my father called for the fifth time in a row, so I reluctantly left to take his call.

Which is how the four of us ended up at my parents' house for an early dinner this evening. I'd barely gotten through introductions when my father demanded "a word" and brought me into his study.

He offers me a glass of gin and I decline, just like I always do, because I can't stomach the taste.

"So, do you want to tell me what the hell is going on?" he asks me once he's sat down with his glass of gin.

"If you would've let me finish introductions, you would've heard that Scarlett and I got engaged a few days ago and we were excited to share the news with our families, but unfortunately word got out before we could tell everyone in person," I explain, bracing my elbows on my knees, anxious to get out of this room I've grown to hate over the years.

Even if it weren't for the cold, rigidity of the room, I would still hate it for all the memories these four walls hold. Dozens of scoldings. Meetings with coaches my dad had no business talking to. Shouting matches between our father and Jax that I had to break up. The list goes on and on.

"What's with the entourage?" he questions.

"What do you mean?"

"The kid and the teenager. Why are they here? Don't tell me the kid is yours. Haven't I taught you anything?" he asks, his tone laced with disgust.

"Their names are Gemma and Gunner, and they're her younger siblings."

"Couldn't her parents have found a different babysitter for the evening? This dinner is important to your mother. She was devastated to find out her oldest child had run off and got engaged without telling us."

"Like I said, we just got engaged earlier this week—we didn't run off. Scarlett is Gemma and Gunner's guardian; their parents passed away in a plane crash five years ago. I'm sure you remember their father, Charles Carlisle."

That bit of information catches his attention. "So is this guardianship temporary until another family member can adopt them? Five years seems like a long time."

My shoulders stiffen at his implication.

"No, Scarlett is the sole guardian of her siblings, and will remain as such until they're eighteen years old. She's in the process of adopting them, but that hasn't been finalized yet."

He moves in his chair, sitting forward. "If you marry her, what does that make you?"

"I would become their co-guardian once we're married."

"Christ, Bennett. We're Wilsons for god's sake. We don't become guardians to bastards." My father slams his free hand down on the arm of his chair.

I clench my jaw so tight I fear my teeth may crack. "They're not bastards. They were orphans and their sister became their guardian. Show some damn respect for my future family."

"Respect? Future family?" he questions, his voice raising so loud I fear they'll overhear. "I don't give a damn if her family comes from old money and is respected, you will not play daddy to two children who are not your own. End of discussion."

"Good, I'm glad this discussion is over because I'm not sure where you got the impression that you have any say in what goes on in my life. Scarlett will be my wife. And I will be the best co-guardian to those two children in spite of what you showed me growing up. If I can't do that as a Wilson, I'd gladly take her last name instead. Bennett Carlisle has a nice ring to it, don't you think?" Without another breath, I stand up and clasp the button of my suit jacket before leaving and slamming his study door behind me.

Fuck him for thinking he can tell me who I'll marry. It took everything in me not to knock him on his ass when he had the audacity to talk that way about Scar, Gemma, and Gunner.

When I get to the sitting room where the three of them are talking to my mother, I stand beside Scarlett and place my hand on her shoulder.

"I apologize for the interruption, Mom, but we unfortunately won't be staying for dinner."

The look of hurt she looks back at me with isn't easily masked. "Are you sure I can't change your mind, sweetie?"

"I'm sorry, Mom. Something came up," I lie, but after thirty years, she knows the truth. Something with my father came up, and I refuse to take his shit as an adult.

"Is everything alright?" Scarlett asks, concern etched across her features as she stands and moves closer to me.

Placing my hand on the small of her back, I lean in so she can hear me speak under my breath. "Yeah, I'll tell you about it later," I promise, though I know I won't be telling her all of the sordid details.

"Well, I'm sorry we didn't get a chance to talk more. It was lovely to meet you, Scarlett, Gemma, and Gunner. I hope we will have the opportunity to get to know one another more in the near future," my mother says before pulling each of them into a warm embrace.

When she gets to me, my mom wraps me in the biggest hug and does what she does best, apologizes on behalf of my father. "It's not your responsibility to clean up his messes, Ma," I whisper into her ear.

She pulls back and holds my arms. "I know that. But it doesn't mean I'm any less sorry for whatever he's done or said this time. I love you, sweetie."

"I love you too, Ma."

Turning to face Scar, she says, "Perhaps the five of us can get lunch when you're back in town next week. Your father is traveling for work over the next few weeks," she points out, telling me without blatantly telling me that he won't be joining us.

"We'd love that, Mrs. Wilson," Scarlett answers.

"Please, call me Kathy, I insist," my mother tells her, and Scar simply nods in response. "How about we leave the restaurant selection up to these two," my mom says pointing to Gemma and Gunner.

"Oh, I don't know. If we did that, they might choose a fast food chain," Scarlett replies.

"I'm not picky," my mom informs her. "Let them pick wherever, and you have my son send me the time and place and I'll be there. I can't wait to hear all about your schools and hobbies," my mom says to Gemma and Gunner.

Scarlett places her arms around the two of them, guiding them toward the foyer after she's thanked my mom for having them and I hang back for a second before following the three of them out.

"Thank you for bringing them to meet me, sweetie. I hope to get to know them more soon," my mom says in a hushed voice as I turn to face her. "Congratulations. I'm excited to have them be a part of the family."

"Thanks, Ma. At least one of my parents is happy for me."

She pats my arm. "He'll come around."

"Doubt it. But I don't care if he does or doesn't. Either way, they'll become my family. If he wants to be a part of my life, he better get on board."

I give my mom one more hug and place a kiss on the top of her head the way she used to do to me when I was little.

Once we've pulled up to Scarlett's house, I turn off the ignition and walk them inside. Thankfully, Scar accepts my offer to cook dinner now that our plans have changed.

I'm just pulling the steaks off the grill when Gunner joins me outside on the back patio. Setting the steaks aside, I squat down so I'm just about eye level with him.

"Hey there, Champ. How was school today? I'm sorry I didn't get a chance to ask you about it yet."

Gunner scuffs his shoe across the ground, avoiding eye contact with me. "It was fine."

My brows furrow at his change in demeanor. "Just fine? I thought today was your pajama party with your class."

"Yeah, it was fun."

"That's good to hear. Did you guys get to watch a movie or have popcorn?"

"Did I do something wrong?" Gunner throws me off with his question, still not meeting my eye.

"What do you mean?"

"Did I do something bad at your mommy's house?"

"No, buddy—" I start but he asks another question, cutting me off.

"Why did we leave? I like your mom."

"We left because of some grown up stuff with my dad," I answer him as honestly as I can, given the circumstances. "You didn't do anything wrong, I promise."

"I don't have a dad anymore. He's in heaven with my mama," Gunner tells me and his words cause a fissure to crack down my chest, especially when he finally looks up at me with tears in his eyes.

"Scarlett told me, I'm sorry to hear that," I tell him.

Gunner wrings his hands together. "Scar goes with me to my mom days at school. Are you going to go with me to my dad days?"

Unsure of how I'm supposed to answer that, considering Scar and I haven't discussed situations like these, I give it my best shot at sharing the truth with him. "As long as I'm not out of town for work, and Scar is okay with me joining you, I'd be honored to be at your dad days."

"What does hono-ed mean?"

"Honored. It means I'd be so happy."

And I would be, because not only does this kid have me wrapped around his finger already, but I also made a promise to Scar that I plan to keep—I'll be there for the three of them, not just her.

13

Scarlett

Tonight is the first home game of the season, and my grandmother insisted I watch the game with the other players' partners in the significant other's suite instead of in the owner's suite with my grandparents, Gemma, and Gunner. It's an early evening game, so I agreed to let Gemma and Gunner come, even though it's a school night. They're going to go home with my grandparents to stay the night at their place while I stay at the rink for post-game press interviews. News of our engagement has been kind of a PR nightmare since we weren't ahead of the announcement. The good news is, my grandfather thinks my grandmother's surprise announcement was hilarious. She didn't think anything of it, aside from her happiness that her granddaughter was engaged. I didn't have it in me to tell her it's an engagement of convenience, just like my marriage will be.

After finishing up a few work tasks, I'm just packing up my bag in my office, hoping I can run a few errands before I pick the kids up when there's a knock at my door.

"Come in," I call out without looking up from where I'm hopelessly trying to fit all the things in my black Kate Spade tote.

The door opens and then I hear the *click* of it closing followed by the turn of the lock.

Looking up, I find a devastatingly handsome Bennett dressed to the nines. A deep maroon suit that is so immaculately tailored, it fits him like a second skin, enhancing his chiseled physique down to his thick thighs. The pants are tapered down to his bare ankles where he completes the look with black velvet loafers, leaving his ankles exposed.

"Bennett," I gasp in surprise.

A sharp-dressed man is my kryptonite, and Bennett Wilson coming into my office wearing a game-day suit should be illegal.

"Little Red," he says, amusement lacing his tone.

"What are you doing here?"

Bennett takes a look at his watch before reaching up to adjust his black tie that looks very demure the way he's paired it with a black dress shirt. "I was hoping to catch you before you left to pick up the kids."

"You've got impeccable timing, I was just packing up to head out."

He saunters toward where I'm still sitting at my desk and rests his hip against the edge of my desk, effectively caging me in.

"Even better, we've got about a half hour before you need to leave," he rasps, moving to adjust his tie again.

Or not—he loosens his tie, lifts it over his head, and then I watch with rapt attention as his deft fingers work to untie the satin fabric.

Before I can question what he means by that, Bennett leans over me and begins kissing me with such ferocity I don't notice he's backed my desk chair up against the bookshelves. He breaks the kiss and kneels before me to hike up the skirt of my camel pencil skirt. Placing delicate, torturous kisses along my lace-covered pussy, he slowly tugs my panties off before pressing my shoulders back against my chair.

"Hands on the arms of the chair, Scar," he commands and my pussy clenches in anticipation, already knowing where he's going with this.

I do as he says and he hums his approval as he uses his tie to secure my left wrist to the chair before placing a quick kiss over my engagement ring. When he uses my lace thong to secure my right wrist, I squirm in anticipation.

"Look at you—tied up like my own personal plaything." He tucks a loose strand of my hair behind my ear, dragging his hand over my jaw before pulling my bottom lip down with his thumb. "Now, be a good fiancée and spread your legs for me. As you pointed out, I'm very superstitious, and eating your pussy has become my new favorite pregame ritual."

"How can it be a ritual if you've never tried it before?" I snark through bated breath.

"Do you recall what we did in Chicago before my last game?"

How could I forget?

His knowing smirk means he's practically read my thoughts. "In case you weren't paying attention, I had two assists and three blocked shots against Chicago. Oh, and we got a shutout that game. If you won't do it for me, Little Red, do it for the team."

"Don't try to disguise this as being selfless or that it's in the team's best interest," I sass back.

"Careful, Scar. I already used your panties to tie you up, so if I want to shut you up, the only solution will be to quiet you with my cock down your throat."

I whimper in response. God, it's pathetic how much I'm dying to suck his cock. And the worst part is he knows I'm desperate for it, which is why he chuckles when I lick my lips in response to his dirty threat.

Without further hesitation, I spread my legs open. Bennett grabs one of my heeled feet and throws it over his shoulder, moving my other leg to spread over the arm of my chair and my tied up hand.

"Can you keep quiet, baby girl?" he murmurs the question against my pussy, and the brush of his stubble against my clit has me squirming.

"Yes!" I squeak, desperately panting to catch my breath.

"Shhh," he hushes and the vibrations cause my hips to buck against his mouth. "I'd hate for the entire office to know the wicked sounds their future boss makes when she comes on her fiancé's face."

Nodding in agreement, I think I manage to promise I'll be quiet.

I do a pretty good job of keeping that promise until Bennett's tongue quickly flicks my clit while he works two fingers in and out of me. When he hooks his fingers, he hits a spot inside of me that makes me clench impossibly harder around him.

"Even when I thought you used me all those years ago, I still fucked my fist to thoughts of you time and time again. Each time that I'd imagine your tight, pink pussy gripping my cock instead of my fist, I'd come harder than anytime before."

Bennett leans back down and takes my clit in his mouth. He sucks while eagerly flicking his tongue over my sensitive bud.

The visual of my fiancé savoring my pussy, worshipping me on his knees, has me coming so hard my eyes roll back in my head as black dots spot my vision.

"Oh, god," I whimper as my pussy clenches around his fingers, and my clit throbs to the rhythm of his sinful tongue.

Once I've come down from my orgasm, Bennett looks up at me and begins to untie my wrists. "Not god. Your future husband, Little Red. Imagine all the filthy things I'll get to do to you on our wedding night. Will you let me fuck this pretty cunt before our big day?"

"Yes! Now, please," I beg.

He snickers at my pleading. "Not yet, baby girl." Once he's freed my wrists, he rubs soothing circles over the pinkened skin before peppering soft kisses over each one.

"Why?" I whine in protest.

"For starters, my pregame ritual consists of eating your pussy, not fucking it."

"Wait a minute, does that mean you'll refuse to fuck me before every game?" I ask as he moves to stand and I follow him. "The regular season is over eighty games alone."

"Eight-two. And I'm not sure, but I'm not willing to find out tonight. It's our first regular season home game," he explains as if his reasoning has any rationality.

"But you came last time we messed around before a game," I point out as I watch him dust off his suit pants before adjusting his cufflinks.

God, why is that simple act so sexy?

"Circumstances were different," he simply states as I stand and adjust my own clothes. When I move to grab my thong from my desk, it's snatched up and Bennett pockets it. I give him a shrug and a saccharine smile.

"What if your bride-to-be begs you from her knees to suck your cock before your big game?"

Bennett doesn't answer, he just backs me up, and when my ass bumps against my desk, he grips me by my hips, lifting me onto the glass surface. "You want to suck my cock for good luck, Red?"

"Yes," I whisper.

"Then lean your head off the edge of your desk and take your fiancé's cock to the back of your throat. I can't think of a better way to wish me luck, baby girl," he rasps with an edge to his tone, almost as if he's on the verge of losing control.

I eagerly obey, gathering my hair in my hand as I position my head on the desk before letting my hair drape over the edge.

Bennett fists my hair in his hand and softly tugs so my chin tilts farther back. "Have I ever told you how much I love your hair? That first night we were together, I couldn't get enough of the sight of your red locks wrapped around my fist while I fucked you from behind."

My nipples pebble to two insanely hard peaks from his words. And when he unbuckles his belt and slides his suit pants and briefs down, I lick my lips in anticipation.

"Open," he commands as he hinges my jaw open and slowly enters my mouth a few inches before pulling out and fisting his cock, working my spit over his length and his piercings.

I realize he's toying with me and my impatience gets the best of me when I demand, "I want to see if I can take all of you, Cap. Be a good boy and fuck my throat."

And so he does. Mercilessly. And I revel in his loss of control as I suck him into my mouth, flick his piercings with my tongue, and rake my teeth over the underside of his cock. At the feel of my teeth, Bennett's cock thickens and he lets out a guttural noise that I want to hear more of everyday for the rest of my life.

"Oh, fuck, Scarlett. I'm gonna come, baby girl," he groans as he coats the back of my throat with his release. I swallow every last drop, desperate to drag out his pleasure. "That's my girl. You took me so well."

Holy shit. I practically purr from his praise.

Bennett helps me sit up before tucking himself back into his boxers and pants. When he goes to grab his tie, I shake my head and tsk at him. "Nah, I don't think so. If you get to keep a memento, then so do I."

I grab the satin tie and drop it into my bag. "Besides, I think I prefer your outfit without the tie. You don't look quite as polished, and I like the slightly-out-of-control version of you," I admit.

"Only you could make me lose control," he confesses, and my heart works overtime to settle my racing pulse.

Bennett looks at his watch again and says, "Speaking of my impeccable timing, looks like you'll be right on time to pick up Gems and Gunner. Are they excited to come to the game?"

"Yeah, they can't wait. I'm embarrassed to admit this will be Gunner's first Wolverines game," I confess and feel my cheeks heat.

"Gunner may have mentioned that to me last night, so I thought I'd bring supplies," he says as he holds up three lime green gift bags. I'm not sure how I missed those, I guess I was a bit distracted by all that is Bennett in his maroon suit.

"What do you have there?" I ask as I admire his suddenly bashful smile.

"Here, this one's for you," he tells me as he hands me a bag with my name written on the tag. I open it to find a black Minnesota Wolverines jersey with lime green lettering on the back that reads WILSON and a green number seven stitched across the back and each sleeve. "I got one for Gemma and Gunner in each of their sizes as well," he says, setting the other two bags on my desk.

"I love it, thank you, BB. They're going to love theirs too," I tell him before wrapping my arms around his neck and placing a quick kiss on his cheek.

"BB?" he questions, wrapping his arms around my waist but pulling his face back to quirk his brow.

I playfully roll my eyes. "Benny Boy, obviously."

"Oh yeah, *obviously*," he mocks, rolling his eyes right back but gripping my waist tighter to press me firmly against him. "So what's with the cheek?"

"What do you mean?"

"Are you really going to cheek me after all . . . *that?*" he asks, gesturing to my desk and chair.

My cheeks heat, and I don't have time to respond before he continues. "I think I've got another new pregame superstition—no cheek kisses on game days, only passionate ones where you leave me wanting more."

"Mmm," I pause, pretending to ponder his little demand. "I feel like a cheek kiss leaves you wanting more, therefore you'll play harder to earn the passionate, toe-curling kisses after the game."

"Goddammit, why'd I have to go and get engaged to such a woman who's so much smarter than me? You're right, I will play harder if you leave me wanting more."

"Oh, my," I gasp. "Did Bennett Wilson not only admit that his fiancée was right, but that she's also smarter than him? Holy, shit. The world is ending!"

My theatrics earn me a swat on my ass and I have to bite back the moan that threatens to escape. Bennett's splayed palms rub over the fabric covering my ass as he hums to himself. "I think visiting you in your office is my new favorite pregame ritual for home games."

"Yeah?"

"Yeah," he echoes, dropping a quick kiss on my forehead. When he steps out of my embrace, he holds my hands out in front of me and looks me up from head to toe. "You look beautiful today, Scar. Have I told you that?"

"No, but compliments will get you everything," I tell him.

"I'll make note of that."

"You do that. Alright, you better get out of here before I'm late to pick the kids up. I'll see you after the game?"

"I'll see you in the press room," he agrees, placing one last kiss on top of my engagement ring.

When he drops my left hand, I lift it up and wiggle my fingers at him. "I'll be the one in a Wilson jersey with this massive rock on my finger."

He just shakes his head as he turns to open my office door, but before he turns the handle, I give him one last pregame pep talk. "The kids are staying with my grandparents tonight." That causes him to freeze, so I continue, "If you play well, I thought maybe we could have a sleepover in your condo before you put it on the market. What do you say, Cap?"

"I say it's going to be one hell of a night, Red. Pack a bag. Or don't—I'd love to see you in nothing but my jersey."

"Possessive much?"

"You have no idea," he murmurs before he leaves my office.

14

Scarlett

October

Most of the guys on the team warm up by juggling a soccer ball together in groups. Not Bennett, though. No, the captain warms up by riding the stationary bike for ten minutes before jumping rope for another five minutes. Today, he's aiming to be extra torturous. In the corner of the concourse, our captain—my fiancé—is jump roping with his shirt off.

Shamelessly, I watch the sweat droplets trail down his chest, over each rivet of his abs, before disappearing beneath the waistband of his black athletic shorts. I can't take my eyes off the way his muscular pecs bounce up and down as he jumps in a steady rhythm. And his thick thighs are showcased beautifully in his six-inch inseam athletic shorts that are hiked up, stuck on his quads.

My stare is brazen, and I don't even care when Jax walks up to me and wolf whistles, calling me out for ogling my man.

Shit. Not my man—my fiancé. My *fake* fiancé, for all intents and purposes.

Is it really fake if you've become part of his pregame rituals in the most salacious way?

Shoving my devious inner thoughts aside, I turn and roll my eyes at Jax's teasing.

"With the way you're watching my big bro, I feel indecent even as a bystander, Little Red Riding Hood," he pokes fun at me.

"I didn't realize you were such a prude, Jax," I give him right back.

"I can see why he's been so beside himself over you all these years. Keep giving him hell, yeah?" he suggests as he goes back to juggling the soccer ball with Carson and Griffin. Effectively leaving me to reel over what he just said. Bennett was beside himself over me? For years?

No. Jax must be mistaken. There must be another woman Bennett was hung up on.

Even when I thought you used me all those years ago, I still fucked my fist to thoughts of you time and time again.

Okay, so maybe he got himself off to thoughts of me a few times. So what? It's not like I didn't. On the darkest nights, in the far recesses of my mind, he's never strayed, and the reminder of our one night together often filled me with warmth when I'd realize how lonely I'd otherwise been.

Before Bennett has a chance to spot me, I sneak past the guys warming up and make my way into the locker room. I pull the laminated photo and crystal from my purse and set them in his locker cubby and then slip back out into the hallway before crashing into a solid chest that smells like sweat mixed with hints of campfire and cedarwood. Bennett.

"Whoa, where you headed in such a hurry, Red?" he asks as he catches me around the shoulders.

"I was just headed to the suites to make sure Gunner and Gemma have everything they need," I tell him honestly.

"Well you can't sneak away without at least giving me a peck on the cheek," he suggests.

Rolling my eyes, I place a quick kiss over the stubble spotting his jaw, but he holds me in a tight embrace.

"Careful, Scar. You know how I feel about that sassy attitude of yours," he warns, and heat immediately pools low in my belly.

"And here I thought you liked when I was a brat."

"Later," he growls and I squeeze my thighs at the promise in just that one word.

"Only if you play well so you earn more, Cap," I toss back over my shoulder as I walk away.

I feel so dazed making my way up to the suite level of the arena, that I don't recognize McKenna Turner until she's walking toward me with wide open arms asking for a hug.

Kenna and I have chatted quite a bit over the past few weeks since we caught up at the family and friends skate. She mostly stuck to the stands with their infant son, Rowen, while Griff chased after Cadence on the ice that day, but we exchanged numbers and are hoping to have a playdate for Cadence and Gunner. It's hard to believe how big Cadence has grown since I saw her briefly at their wedding.

"Scarlett! Was Griff teasing me or do I really get to watch the game with you tonight?"

"You do! Gunner and Gemma are going to sit with my grandparents during the game and then go home with them tonight."

Kenna loops her arm through mine and walks me the rest of the way to the suite. Not every organization has a dedicated suite for significant others, but I'm happier now more than ever that we do.

When we walk in, Kenna reintroduces me to Dakota, a petite brunette who I briefly met when Carson introduced me to his family at the family and friend's skate before he swept her away for hot chocolate. Next to Dakota is Alexa, who I met the other day with Jackson.

We make small talk for a few minutes before I excuse myself to go down the hall to my grandparents' suite to check on Gunner and Gemma.

"Woah, look at all the lights, Papa!" Gunner squeals to my grandfather.

"I'm glad you like them, Sport," he tells Gunner before he notices me enter the suite. "Ah, there she is! How's my Firefly?"

"I'm good, I was just coming to check on the kiddos."

"Scar! Did you give Bennett our presents?" Gunner asks me.

"I left them in his cubby for him to find before his game," I answer.

"Do you think he's gonna like them?"

"I know he is, buddy," I placate him while sending up a silent prayer that we didn't throw off his superstitions too badly.

"And what did you get Bennett for a present?" our grandmother asks him.

"We printed a picture of all of us and I gave him my most specialest good luck crystal!" Gunner's excitement warms my chest like it always does.

"The picture is from when we went to the pumpkin patch the other day—it's the only picture I had of the four of us. And then we all wrote him a little note on the back and I laminated it. The crystal was a great addition that Gunner thought of," I add, pulling Gunner to me and wrapping my arms around his shoulders in an embrace.

"Oh, that reminds me. I was talking to Sally the other day and she said her granddaughter is a wedding photographer. Have you already booked one? Maybe you could hire her to take your engagement photos and if you like them, you could hire her for the big day," my grandmother suggests.

My skin feels tight thinking about wedding planning. Not because I haven't always dreamt about what my wedding would look like, but because I'm not sure if this particular arrangement calls for planning it down to every last detail I've always envisioned. But I don't want to upset my grandmother so I ask her, "Could you have Sally send her granddaughter's contact information to my assistant? I'll go over it with Bennett, but I think that sounds like a great idea. Thank you for thinking of us."

She sends me a soft smile. "Always, sweet girl."

"Where's Gemma?" I ask, looking around the suite and not seeing her.

"She ran into a few friends from school so I said she could spend the first period in their suite," my grandfather cuts in.

"You what? Who? She never mentioned she'd have friends she knew here tonight. Did she get something to eat before she went off? Where is their suite?"

"Ease up, Firefly. Don't forget we've raised kids before," he says with a practiced patience I only hope to develop over time. "Gemma ate before she left, and we'll all get her Dexcom notifications if her sugar levels need attention. She said their names are Colton and Eva, and they're two suites down with the rest of the Connelly family. Take a look for yourself." He gestures toward the right and I peek my head around the corner of the open seating of our suite to find Gemma standing next to a tall girl with light brown hair next to an even taller boy about Gemma's age.

"Are those Nathan Connelly's younger siblings?"

"Yes, his younger brother is a senior at St. Christopher Academy and his sister is in Gemma's class," my grandmother explains.

"Wait, isn't that the captain's suite?" I ask my grandfather.

"Yeah, but Bennett wanted to make sure Connelly's family could make it to as many games as possible since they moved across the country to be closer to him."

My eyebrows lift a moment later when the boy—young man—wraps his arm around Gemma's shoulder and gives her a side hug.

You've got to be kidding me. Now I'm going to need to run interference in her love life when my own is in utter chaos?

My grandmother must see my worries written all over my face because she chuckles at me and shakes her head. "Want some sage advice from an old bat who raised a couple of teenagers?"

"Yes," I answer with a whine.

"Don't forget you were once a teenager too."

"*That's* your sage advice?" I ask in disbelief. "Need I remind you that I was constantly pushing the boundaries my dad set?"

My hysterics earn me another round of laughter, this time my grandfather joins in. "What I mean to say is, don't forget what it felt like to be a teenager when you're having the big discussions with her. I've found it's best to let them make their own informed choices while giving them guidance and the tools for success."

"Great, so basically I'm supposed to try to guide her to make the right choices, but ultimately trust her to take the safest path? That sounds like a recipe for disaster, not success."

"Nobody said parenting a teenager was easy," my grandfather murmurs before taking a swig of his fountain soda.

"If you're too hard on her, she'll rebel further, trust us," my gran says in a sorrowful tone, and I can't help but think of my Aunt Becky who moved out when she was eighteen and didn't look back.

"These are going to be the longest three years of my life, aren't they?"

My grandmother looks at me with both sympathy and humor. "Three? Oh, darling, we still worry about you all the time. The worry doesn't go away once they've left the nest."

I shake my head in disbelief as my gaze catches on Gemma once again. This time she's standing next to Eva while the two stare down at the players taking the ice for warmups.

"Speaking of flying the nest, aren't you supposed to be making new friends tonight? Go on, Firefly. We've got Gunner and Gemma. If they need anything, you know we'll call right away," my grandfather says as he practically shoos me out of the suite.

Before I leave, I wrap Gunner up in a big hug and smack a kiss on his head. "Be good, Bug. Love you," I tell him as I set him down.

"Love you too. My crystal is gonna make Benny score!" he squeals.

That'd make his whole week, so here's to hoping.

Making my way back down the hall, I run into Alexa and we decide to grab seltzers before we head into the suite. A tiny bit of liquid courage will help ease my nerves for the interviews Bennett and I have after the game.

Once we're back with Dakota and Kenna, they introduce me to the other women in the suite, and we find a few seats together at the front, watching as the guys finish their warmups.

"Do any of your men have specific pregame rituals?" I ask, turning to face the three of them.

Kenna's the first to answer. "Of course. I feel like all the players are superstitious when it comes to their game-day routines. Like Griff, for example, always wants a bag of Hot Tamales because I call him Hotshot and he knows I love everything cinnamon-flavored. Oh, and he adds custom-stitched symbols to each pair of gloves he wears. He has a kitten in remembrance of his sister Katie, a sun for me, "Ray" for Cadence, and a little oar for our son Rowen. Griff calls him "Rook" so he wanted to get a rook chess piece, but Carson freaked out for some reason and said he should do an oar instead." I watch as Kenna shrugs next to a blushing Dakota and wonder what that's about.

"Aw, that's super cute," Alexa tells her as the guys exit the ice and the zamboni starts its rounds before the first period.

Alexa is drop-dead gorgeous. She's tall—it was no surprise to learn she played college volleyball with Kenna—with long platinum blonde hair and a bronzed glow that I can only dream of having. She's a sportscaster, but had the night off. I can't quite get a read on her relationship status with Jackson. According to Bennett, the two of them aren't putting a label on things, but she's such a catch, I can't imagine why Jax wouldn't want to make things official.

Dakota clears her throat. "Carson wears a bracelet I made for him in Italy when we went to Taylor Swift's Era's Tour together. That, and he sneaks a FaceTime call in right before warmups. When he's on the West Coast for late games, it gets pretty hard to stay up while pregnant, but so far I've managed. We'll see how that goes later on in the season when I'm super pregnant."

"Ugh, I was so much more tired in the third trimester during my second pregnancy," Kenna says. "I'm not sure how, considering I was put on Griff-mandated bedrest any time he could get away with it."

Dakota laughs at that. "I thought Carson was overly protective when I was pregnant with the twins; that is, until I saw how Griffin was this past year when you were pregnant with Rowen. I mean, I get where he was coming from after the complications you had with Cadence and not having been there, but he was borderline insane."

McKenna and Griffin have been together so long, it's hard to forget the tragedy and heartbreak the two of them endured before they found their way back to each other. I briefly remember hearing about it since we went to the same college, though it was mostly secondhand gossip.

Kenna scoffs and rolls her eyes. "Yeah, I told him he more than made up for missing the first pregnancy, to which he said, 'You're supposed to wait until the fifth or sixth before you tell me that,' and I could've killed him right then and there."

"Wait, are you guys planning to have *six kids*?" Alexa's eyes widen in shock.

Kenna nearly spits out the sip of Diet Coke she just took. "No! That's why I could've killed him. Rowen is only four months old, and Griff's already begging me to try again. I told him it's all fun and games until we've got two under two that we're toting to his games, not to mention Cadence's hockey games," Kenna explains as if she needs to justify her decision to wait.

"I'm sure he just figures if he's going to get you knocked up six times, he has to get to work," Alexa mutters through muffled snickers, winking at Kenna.

"Ha, ha, very funny. Laugh all you want at my insatiable husband, but I've heard Jax on multiple drunken nights declare that he wants three or four kids to run around the countryside," Kenna throws back at Alexa.

Alexa rolls her eyes at her friend. "That's a good one, Mack Attack. But I've got this thing called an IUD so my situationship with Jax doesn't turn into more than I can handle. I'm honestly not sure I see motherhood in my future. And I know that's something Jax wants, hence the friends-with-benefits arrangement we've got. We both know we're not long-term, but that doesn't mean we can't have fun in the meantime." Turning her gaze to me, Alexa adds, "The only pregame ritual I know of is that Jax and Carse do this strange stick-handling thing where they get really close on the ice and pass the puck quickly back and forth before they smack each other on the butts with their sticks. It's honestly the cutest thing I think I've ever seen two grown men do."

Dakota nods in agreement. "Oh, I love when they do that!"

"Griff says Bennett's the most superstitious player he's ever played with. I remember in high school Carse said Bennett wore the same pair of socks the whole season and refused to wash them. They won the state championship that year," Kenna tells us, bringing her fist to cover her mouth as if she's holding back a gag.

I scrunch my face in disgust. "Oh my god, that's disgusting."

Dakota's face pales and she looks like she's going to actually be sick. "Please, no," she drawls.

"Ew, you should ask him if that was worth the terrible case of athlete's foot he probably got." Alexa fake gags. "You really gotta wonder who you're hitching yourself to, huh Little Red Riding Hood?"

"Not you too," I groan.

Alexa chuckles. "Alright, alright, I'll just stick to calling you Scar."

"Thank you," I mutter before taking a sip of my seltzer.

"So, is this your first game wearing Bennett's jersey?" Dakota asks me just as the lights in the arena dim and a video plays on the jumbotron to hype up the crowd.

Looking over them, I realize that both Kenna and Dakota are wearing Griffin and Carson's jerseys, but Alexa is wearing black, pleather skinny pants with a white long-sleeve bodysuit and a cropped black puffer vest.

"It is," I admit, shyly.

"You know what that means, right?" Kenna asks, waggling her eyebrows.

I give her a look that I hope portrays how clueless I am as to whatever she's asking.

Dakota winks at Kenna and then asks me, "Do you two have plans after the game?"

"Yeah, my grandparents are taking the kids tonight so Bennett and I were planning to stay the night at his condo before he puts it on the market." My cheeks heat thinking of what said sleepover could lead to.

"Well, I hope you got plenty of sleep last night because once he sees you, he won't be letting you do much sleeping tonight. The guys go feral seeing their women in their jerseys," Kenna explains before sending a wink my way.

"When he dropped by my office to give it to me earlier, he did mention I didn't need to pack a bag." If it's even possible, my cheeks heat further thinking back on what we did in my office before the game.

"He gifted the jersey to you? And he brought it to your office before the game? Did you guys eat together? You know that's going to become part of his game-day routine if he plays well tonight," Kenna points out.

We ate together, alright. And I hope he has a stellar game for so many reasons.

"Yeah, he brought a jersey for me, Gemma, and Gunner," I tell them.

Dakota chuckles. "Well, he's probably going to visit you at your office before every home game from here on out."

Alexa gasps, startling us all. "Oh my gosh, speaking of eating . . . Dakota, when are you finishing the next book in your football series?"

Kenna gapes at her friend before closing her eyes and shaking her head. "Your mind works in the strangest ways, my friend."

Dakota blushes and becomes suddenly bashful. "It's almost finished. I had to pump the brakes with how sick I got in the first trimester, but now that I'm feeling better and have more energy, the words have been flowing out of me."

"I've been telling her for years that we should start a book club, but it made us feel lame when it was just the two of us. Do you read, Scar?" Kenna asks me.

"I do—pretty much just romance novels, YA, and kids books, but I read well over one hundred books a year," I answer as the players take the ice.

"That's amazing! What do you say to the four of us starting a monthly book club? Oh, we could even try to all get together when the guys are out of town for away games."

"I'm in!" Dakota says, followed by an excited squeal from Alexa, which I think means yes.

"Me too!" I mimic their agreements.

"Let me grab your number and I'll start a group thread between the four of us. What should we call this book club group chat?"

"How about the Smutty Stickhandlers," Alexa suggests before continuing, "You know, because we handle their sticks."

This earns her a round of laughter.

"You're brilliant," Kenna agrees. "All in favor?"

The four of us all raise our hands and then Kenna's typing away on her phone just as they announce the starting lineups.

The Smutty Stickhandlers:

Kenna:

> I feel like T-Swift should write a song about us on her next album.

I can't help my excitement or the smile that spreads across my face when I think of how nice it'll be to have some female friends my age. This is a perk of our marriage I won't allow myself to feel guilty over—I realize I'm far too eager to feel bad about it.

15

Bennett

OCTOBER

After tapping the laminated photo I found in my locker earlier three times and rubbing the crystal next to it, I put my helmet and gloves back on for the third period, grab my stick from the rack outside the locker room, and head down the player tunnel.

"Come on boys, let's go!" Griff shouts as the team makes their way down the tunnel to the ice. They each tap gloves with me and Griff who stand just outside the ice.

"Let's get this done and finish strong!" I holler, giving a stick tap to the back of their legs just before they step out onto the ice.

Once the last of our teammates walks by, Griff and I stand just outside our team bench and do our handshake-stick-tap routine before he turns, kisses his glove, points up to heaven, and steps onto the ice.

I close my eyes and take a deep breath before finally charging onto the ice, doing one circle around our zone and then lining up at our blue line for the face-off. We're starting the period off on a power play due to a cheap slashing penalty one of Dallas's defensemen took at the end of the second.

Griff wins the face-off back to me and I cradle the puck as my legs skate on muscle memory, carving the ice with backward crossovers. Keeping my head up, I scan the rink and find Carson open up the ice and send a pass that hits the tape of my winger's stick.

Carson possesses the puck into the zone, drops a pass back to Griff—the exchange a freaky, silent thing the pair of them do often—before G sends a saucer pass to Jax, who sits just above their crease, tipping the puck up and over their goalie's right shoulder.

The goal horn sounds as Jax jumps against the boards in the corner of the rink. The five of us come together in a group hug before skating along our bench and giving glove touches to our teammates.

I leap over the boards for a shift change and look up at the jumbotron hanging above center ice to watch the replay of the goal. It was a beauty, clean with practiced passes our powerplay unit has perfected over the years.

We're now up three to one against a team I can't stand to lose to. Between Dallas and Colorado, we've been kicked out of playoffs in the first-round season after fucking season. This needs to be the year that comes to an end. I can't explain why, but this season feels pivotal. Like if we don't win it all, or at least go deep into playoffs, then everything will change.

After another grueling twenty minutes of game play, the third period comes to an end and we beat the Dallas Rangers four to one.

I'm stopped just outside the locker room by a reporter asking for a few minutes. I knew this was coming since our team publicist, Paytin, told me I was the lucky one for the sweaty post-game interview tonight. These ones immediately after a game when I'm still in my full gear and dying for a shower always have me grumpier than I'd like.

And instead of Jax's . . . whatever he and Alexa are . . . I've got to chat with Jim, who is a complete shit-stirrer when it comes to the questions he asks when I'm still full of adrenaline.

"Joining me postgame is Minnesota's captain, Bennett Wilson," Jim tells the camera before turning to face me.

"Tonight was a big win for the Wolverines. What does beating the team who took you out in the first round of the playoffs last season mean to you?"

Turning the mic to me, I run my fingers through my sweat-slicked hair before bracing my hands on my hips. "Winning our first home game of the regular season is a good start for our team. We've got some new players on our second and third lines who have already made significant impacts to our game. I'm looking forward to continuing to build upon what we did here tonight," I huff, straining to catch my breath after the strain a full game puts on my body.

"And how do you think being engaged to the owner's granddaughter has affected your game?"

There it is. The question I was expecting and have been prepping for with Paytin and Scarlett all week. I'm secretly thankful her grandma spilled the secret about our engagement. Not only did it mean I got to spend more time with Scar this week, but it also means the world knows she's mine.

"As you know, Miss Carlisle and I will be answering questions in the press room shortly. Now, if you're done asking questions specifically about tonight's game, I'd like to hit the showers so I don't make my fiancée pass out before our interview."

Unwilling to give him the chance to ask any further questions, I nod at the camera and turn my back on the jackass to do just that.

After rushing through my shower and putting my suit back on, I pack my personal belongings—including my new good luck charms—away in my trusty duffle bag. Even though I'll leave it here for the postgame press, I don't want to chance them being misplaced if the equipment staff comes in to do their thing.

"Is everyone decent?" I hear Joseph ask, which is unlike him since he's the owner and has never announced his presence in the locker room before.

"Yeah, as decent as we'll get, Joey," Jax tells him and I reach over to smack him in the back of the head.

"You've got to quit calling him that, J," I hiss under my breath.

"Why? We're about to become family." Jax shrugs and looks at me as if I'm the one who's being unreasonable.

"Good to know," I hear a feminine voice that belongs to my future bride.

When our eyes connect across the locker room, my chest tightens as I take in the sight of her, Gemma, and Gunner each in my jersey. The three of them standing there together look like everything I want to fight to hold onto—and for a hell of a lot longer than three years.

That sounds an awful lot like forever kind of talk.

"I hope you don't mind, they wanted to see you before they go with our grandparents—" Scar starts, but stops when she sees me squat down and open my arms.

"There he is, come here, Champ." I wave to Gunner before he takes off and runs into my arms. Scooping him up, he gives me a big squeeze. "How did you like your first game?"

"That. Was. Awesome!" Gunner squeals, throwing his fists above his head.

When he throws his arms around my neck again, I squeeze him to my chest as I look over his little head to find Gemma and a stunned Scarlett watching us.

"Hey, Gems. How'd you like the game?" I ask her once I've shortened the distance between us.

"It was great. I was able to meet up with a few friends of mine from school," she tells me as she takes in the locker room atmosphere.

"Really? Small world."

"Yeah, they're actually the younger siblings of your rookie." Gemma's cheeks heat when she tells me that tidbit, and as if summoned, Connelly walks over to pat me on the back.

"We still on for tomorrow?" he asks me.

"Yeah, but I moved back our ice time a bit. Let me know if that doesn't work for you," I tell him, though I don't mention that it's because Scar told me she'd be staying the night tonight.

"Sounds good," he nods before locking his gaze on Gemma. "Wait a minute, I know you," Connelly says, snapping his fingers before pointing at her.

Gemma's eyes widen and I think I see a slight shake of her head.

"No?" he questions her with a quirk of his brow.

"Not unless you've seen me hanging out with your brother and sister," she tells him in a shaky voice.

"Hmm," he hums, though a wide grin spreads across his face. "I don't think that's it," he pauses to scratch at his jaw. "Ah, I remember, you're the twirl girl I saw on the ice."

If I didn't know better, I'd think Gemma's expression was briefly panic-stricken before she schools her features.

My eyes bounce back and forth between the two of them. "You're probably thinking of the family and friends skate. Gemma, this is Nathan Connelly. Connelly, this is Gemma *Carlisle*." I emphasize her last name as a bit of a warning, but it doesn't seem to register with him.

"Not sure if that was it, but I guess that's what we're going with," he says, eyes alight with something I can't read as he smirks at Gemma's narrowed eyes.

"I'll see you tomorrow, *rookie*," I say, dismissing him. This time, he takes the not-so-subtle hint and leaves the locker room with an impish grin I'd like to smack right off of him.

"What's his deal?" Scar asks as she wraps an arm around Gemma's shoulder.

Gemma shrugs out of her grasp, and a look of hurt spreads across Scar's face. "Not sure. Seems to me like he'd benefit from a few of those etiquette classes we were forced to take."

"I'll look into that," I quip, smirking at her quick wit that reminds me of Scar.

"Did you like my presents?" Gunner thankfully interrupts.

That turns my smirk into a full-blown grin. "Of course I did. Why do you think we won?"

"My good luck crystal!" he bellows in a voice I've never heard from him that has the three of us chuckling.

"The crystal, and don't forget the awesome picture. Thanks for writing that note on the back, Champ." He nods at me like a bobble-head before squeezing my neck again, causing my chest to tighten and my throat to swell with emotion. This kid—he's turning me into a fucking softy.

"I hope we didn't mess with your rituals too much," Scar remarks.

"Not at all. We just won, and I happened to score, so that means everything I did today will now become part of my home game routine," I announce, winking at her.

Scar's brows rise briefly before she gives me a wicked smirk. "I'll be sure to clear my game day schedule."

"Alright you two, it's time to head out," her grandmother cuts in.

Gunner gives me another squeeze before I set him down, and Gemma surprises me by giving me a brief side hug.

"Have a good night and be good. Love you both," Scar tells them as she gives Gunner a big hug and Gemma gives her an even briefer hug than she gave me.

I wonder what that's all about.

Once the kids have exited the locker room with their grandparents, Scarlett turns to me and I ask, "Are you ready for this?"

"Not in the slightest," she replies as she worries her bottom lip between her teeth.

"Well, the quicker we can get this over with, the sooner we can head to my condo," I point out, tossing my arm around her shoulders.

"Is that so? What gave you the impression that you earned my company for the evening?"

"Oh, I don't know. Besides the fact that we won"—I pause, leaning down to whisper in her ear as we walk—"I believe I also had a goal, an assist, and blocked five shots, two of which left gnarly bruises that you're going to have to come over later and rub."

"So this is what I signed up for? Don't we employ a very qualified massage therapist around here?" she tosses back, giving me a playful hip check.

"See, with that personality and wit, you're sure to charm the pants off these reporters. Come on, Little Red, I've got plans for you later," I tell her as I fist the hem of my jersey around her hips and yank her into my chest.

Scarlett was a natural with the press, which should've come as no surprise. She charmed the room with every eloquent answer, looking like a pro and causing my chest to swell with pride.

I'm walking down the hallway toward the players' entrance when Scarlett's laughter echoes off the walls.

"You've got to be kidding me," she tells me, shaking her head. "You can afford the ring of my dreams no problem, yet you willingly walk around with *that* slung over your shoulder?"

I mock gasp. "Ah, don't talk about my Duffy that way."

"Your what? You named your dilapidated duffle bag?"

"You bet your sweet ass I did, Red. Duffy's been such a good girl to me over the years—she's stuck by my side and carried me through good games and bad," I explain.

Scarlett's bark of laughter rings through the cavernous space, and I'm dying to hear more. "And suddenly, I'm jealous of a duffle bag. She's been a *good girl*, huh?"

"*Such* a good girl . . . but you're not jealous of me sharing my praise, are you baby girl?"

I think I hear her faintly whimper at my use of her nickname I typically reserve for the bedroom, so I decide to test my luck and see if I can push her a bit further. Eliminating the remaining distance between us, I back her up until she's pressed against the concrete wall, sliding my bag off my shoulder before grabbing hers out of her hand and placing them on the ground.

My fingers drift up her thigh until I'm met by the hem of my jersey which I fist in my hand again.

"Bennett," my full name leaves her lips on a gasp that sounds more like a prayer, and I realize in this moment I've never wanted to see a woman on her knees for me more than I do right now.

"Yes, Scarlett?"

"Take me back to your place—now," she demands.

"Patience, baby girl," I preach to her.

"You've tested my patience enough tonight."

Without another word, I bend down to pick up our bags before hurling Scarlett over my shoulder. Her shrieks echo through the parking garage and that only urges me on as I grip her ass and squeeze with my hand that's holding her over my shoulder.

"Bennett Wilson, put me down right this instant!" she shouts.

I just chuckle in place of a reply.

Once we're to my car, I drop the bags at the back of my car before rounding to the passenger door and setting her inside. Her scoff is adorable when I buckle her in and shut the door.

Minutes later, we've arrived at my condo. The elevator doors open and I place my hand on the small of her back as I guide her to my front door, type in the code, and let us in. As interested as I am to see the space through her eyes, I'm too impatient to give her a grand tour right now. Slipping off our shoes in the entryway, I grab our bags in one hand and grab her hand with the other before taking off toward my bedroom.

"Here's the kitchen," I tell her, nodding to the left as we walk past. "The living room," I nod again. "Dining room is off that way," I say but don't make a gesture as to where, I'm too busy trying to walk her down the hallway. "Down this hall are the two spare bedrooms and a bathroom, and at the end of the hall here is my bedroom."

Opening the door, I guide her in, letting her hand go so I can set our bags down on the set of chairs in the corner of the room.

I try to take in the space through her eyes. My oversized bed was custom-made and takes up most of the space. The wooden frame is stained a dark oak with plush charcoal bedding and built-in shelves for nightstands that are an extension of the bed frame.

The exposed brick wall behind my bed was an accent I decided to keep from the previous owner.

In the corner, above the set of chairs, hangs my three favorite guitars as a make-shift accent wall, though I often sit in this corner to play them when I'm home.

"This is not at all what I was expecting," Scarlett trails off as she moves to the opposite wall that has the doors to my bathroom and walk-in closet.

"The door on the right is my bathroom, and the other is for the room I'm sure you're dying to see, though I'll warn you it's going to be underwhelming compared to your closet."

She opens the door to my closet and I reach over her shoulder to flip the lightswitch. My closet has dark oak shelves and organizers to match my bed frame.

"You've got an entire side dedicated to your suits, I'm impressed," she tells me as she runs her fingers over the sleeves of my suit jackets hanging in rows, color coordinated, as she once teased me about. "Do you prefer the dark wood and accents? My place has mostly light maple and white accents, but we could make the spare bedroom next to mine into a closet for you. If you prefer these finishes, we can do that in there."

"Isn't that room the craft room you and Gunner use?"

"Yeah, but we can move that to the basement," she suggests, and I immediately shut that down.

"And waste that natural light you love so much on a dark closet for me? No way, Red. Can't you make a little space in your closet for me? I mean it's as big as my entire bedroom."

She chuckles. "Well, yes, I don't use the far wall *yet*. But you'd be surprised by how much my wardrobe can grow in three years."

My stomach sinks as she points out our agreed-upon timeline for our expiration date.

Clearing my throat, I hesitate for a moment, questioning whether I should push her on that a bit more before thinking better of it. "Oh, I've got no doubt in your ability to utilize that space, but for convenience's sake, I'd prefer I borrow that space for now instead of taking away a space you and Gunner love so much."

Scar smiles softly at that. "I suppose you're right." It's her turn to clear her throat. "Do you mind if I use your bathroom?"

"Not at all," I tell her as I make my way across my room to grab her overnight bag. "Here you go."

"Thank you, I'll be right out," she assures me as she backs into the bathroom and shuts the door behind her.

I take off my suit jacket and toss it on one of the chairs before unclasping my cufflinks and setting them on top of my dresser. I've just finished untucking my dress shirt and am working on making my way down the buttons when the bathroom door opens.

Scar looks positively breathtaking—heart-stopping, even—when she exits my bathroom. Her curled hair falls down her shoulders over the material of my home jersey, and long, bare legs trail down to her bare feet. I clasp my chest and rub my sternum to ease the ache that seeing her in just my jersey brings.

"I hear athletes go feral for a woman in their jersey." She does a little spin, holding up her hair to show off my last name splayed across her shoulders.

Unable to find words right now, I simply grunt in reply.

"What do you think, Cap?" she asks as she drops her hair and slowly lifts the hem of the jersey to reveal the globes of her tight ass.

"Let me guess, you didn't want any panty lines?" I finally manage to rasp in a tone that's gravelly with lust as I close the distance between us.

She turns and smiles up at me in amusement, and I can't help but feel a tightening in my chest at her carefree, teasing demeanor. When was the last time she was able to smile like that? Free from the weight of the world on her shoulders—the responsibilities she's handled alone while managing to make it look effortless? I want to make her smile like this as often as possible.

"What do I think?" I echo her question and she nods, biting down on her plush bottom lip. "I think I'm glad I got plenty of rest last night, because I plan to take my time with you tonight—all night. What do you think of that, Scarlett?"

Seeing her with my name across her back awakens a possessive side of me—has me wanting to do irrational things. Like hike up my jersey and fuck her until she's begging me not only to let her come, but to officially make her Mrs. Wilson. Only to wake up tomorrow morning and bring her to the courthouse to make that a reality.

Her breathing picks up speed the way it does when she's turned on, and I'm dying to see how wet she is for me without so much as touching her. Tonight I'd like to play with her—wind her up until she's pleading for my cock.

She drifts her fingers up the exposed skin of my chest before grabbing the fabric of my shirt and pulling it off. "I think I'd like you to finally fuck your fiancée so I can see if hitching myself to you is the right choice."

I unbuckle my dress belt and pants and slide them down my legs. Leaning in, I murmur against her lips, "Don't act like you've forgotten what it's like to have me buried inside of you, baby girl."

In nothing but my black boxer briefs, Scarlett backs me up and pushes down on my shoulders once the back of my knees meets the mattress. As I sit on the edge of the bed, Scarlett goes to her bag and pulls out my black satin tie from earlier.

"I think I rather liked when you used this on me earlier, Cap."

"Mmm. Is that so? Does my fiancée like being tied up like my own personal plaything?" Grabbing the backs of her thighs, I pull her on top of my lap so she's straddling me.

"Yes," she whimpers as she rubs herself against me. I grip her hips beneath my jersey and work her over my covered length, her breath hitching whenever her clit brushes against my shaft.

"You want me to fuck you, baby girl?"

"Please," she begs, and I chuckle because if she's already begging, she has no idea what I've got in store for her.

Standing to my full height with her still wrapped around my waist, I turn and walk to the side of my bed before lying her on her back in the middle of the mattress. I crawl to her and straddle her chest. When Scar licks her lips, my cock grows impossibly harder. Reaching above her head, I press on the headboard until the wood clicks and a secret panel opens to reveal a steel rod.

Scarlett's gasp has my dick twitching in anticipation. "Hands above your head, baby girl," I command, and when she complies, I make quick work of securing her hands to the rod with my tie. After tugging her wrists, I'm satisfied with my handiwork.

"Okay, that should definitely come with us in the move," she suggests.

I chuckle as I make my way down her body, reveling in the way she squirms beneath me.

"Hang tight," I tell her as I step off my bed and disappear into the hallway. When I return a moment later with a glass of ice water, I head into my closet to grab a second tie before setting both down on the bedside table.

"Thirsty?" she questions, her chuckles muffled by her breathlessness.

"You have no idea," I tell her as I slip off my briefs, my cock bobbing to attention as I fist it and roughly stroke it.

Scarlett writhes on the bed, rubbing her thighs together as she tries to find relief.

"What do you need?" I ask, my voice gravelled with lust.

"Your cock."

"How do you want it?"

"In my mouth," she admits, licking her lips again.

I grab my other tie from the bedside table and crawl back to her, repositioning myself above her.

"Do you trust me to make you feel good?" I ask her as I gently lift her head off the bed to slip the fabric of the tie under her head.

"Yes," she breathes.

"Are you okay with being blindfolded, Little Red?"

"Mmm. Yes," she murmurs.

I fasten my tie over her eyes and marvel at the sight beneath me. "Breathtaking," I muse as I place a chaste kiss on her lips.

Scarlett whines when I pull away, apparently too quickly for her liking. Unable to leave her unsatisfied, I give her what she wants, settling between her legs as I kiss her until she opens up for me and I deepen it until we're both gasping for air. I trail kisses along her jaw, down the column of her neck, and along each of her collarbones. When I suck the skin into my mouth, she whimpers, and it deepens my possessive urge to mark her. She doesn't protest as I pepper hickeys over her skin that will be a bitch for her to cover come tomorrow. All the while, I shamelessly grind against her, massaging her clit with my crown and piercings, withholding penetration, continuing her torture.

"I want your cock, Bennett," she wails impatiently.

"I'm not sure you've been patient enough yet. Have you earned my cock, baby girl?"

"Yes! I *need* it, please."

"Open up." Moving to straddle her once more, I hinge her jaw open further and trace the head of my cock along her lips, leaving a trail of my precum.

When her tongue glides over my crown, I barely resist the urge to push my cock to the back of her throat. Knowing her hands are bound, I have to remind myself to only give what she can take as I slowly feed her inch by inch of my length. Her mouth stretches around the thickness of my cock and I take a mental snapshot of her in this moment for nights when we're apart.

"Can you take more of me?" I ask and she nods, unable to respond with my cock down her throat. I piston my hips until she's nearly taking all of me. When my tip hits the back of her throat, I nearly come undone right then and there.

"Fuck, Scar. Your mouth is going to be my undoing, but not right now," I tell her as I pull out. "I refuse to come anywhere but inside your tight cunt tonight."

Her eager pleas for me to do just that have me craving the feel of her surrounding me as I sink inside her again after far too long, but instead I choose to prolong our torture.

"Not just yet, Red," I tell her and she growls in frustration.

"You're a fucking masochistic asshole, you know that?"

"I do. But I'm *your* masochist. If you can be patient, baby girl, I'll show you how good being mine feels."

16

Scarlett

I'm your *masochist.*

I'll show you how good being mine feels.

His words ring in my ears as he moves off me and I feel the bed dip beside me. The sound of ice clanking against glass pulls me from my reverie a moment later. Still blindfolded by his tie, my other senses are heightened, causing me to squirm in anticipation of what he has in store for me.

The bed dips again before Bennett settles between my thighs. I can feel the heat of his body atop mine, and I long for the press of his weight on me.

Then, his lips brush mine ever so slightly when he asks, "Tell me, have you ever tried temp play?" Instead of his breath feeling warm against my lips, I'm met with a cool chill.

"Never," I admit.

"And you trust me to make you feel good?"

"Always."

"That's what I like to hear," he hums against my abdomen as he pushes up my jersey and slowly kisses his way down my body. Goosebumps rise in the wake of his cool kisses. Not being able to see what he's doing or reach out and touch him—grab onto him—has me feeling needier than ever before.

As if he can read my thoughts, he asks, "Is my girl feeling needy?"

My girl. God, I really like the sound of that.

"Desperately so," I shamelessly admit.

My admission urges him on. I hear a suckling noise a moment before his chilled lips press a soft kiss on my clit. The frigid temperature of his lips against my most sensitive spot causes my hips to buck off the bed. Bennett's hand presses down on my stomach before he wraps my legs over his shoulders.

When his mouth clamps down on my clit and he pushes two freezing fingers inside of me, I'm overwhelmed by the sensation. My skin feels like it's been doused in flames, and the contrasted chill of his mouth and fingers has me feeling like I'll combust.

"Need your eyes on me, Red," he says before he removes the tie covering my eyes with one hand, while the other doesn't miss a beat as he continues to work his fingers inside of me.

Bennett reaches beside him and then there is a melting ice cube in his mouth, condensation dripping from his mouth and pooling at my entrance. He removes his fingers from my core only to replace them moments later with the spear of his tongue and what remains of the ice cube. The sharp bite of the cold elicits a moan from deep within me.

As his tongue latches onto my clit and his fingers push inside of me once more, I'm coming, shattering, only moments later.

Wave after wave hits me, just as I'm about to resurface from the most intense release of my life, the pleasure from his tongue pulls me back under.

"I-I can't." A deep shiver runs up my spine, and suddenly it's all too much and not enough at the same time. "Need you inside of me."

He finally lifts his head and the moment his eyes connect with mine, a devious smirk spreads over his soaked face. The combination of the melted ice and my release has his beard dripping, and the sight has me forgetting how to breathe properly.

Bennett reaches into the bedside drawer again before sitting back on his heels to roll on a condom. I didn't realize, but I must have let my groan of disappointment slip, because suddenly Bennett is hovering above me, bearing his weight on his elbows bracketing my head. His fingers comb through my hair before he curls them and softly tugs.

"What's the matter, baby girl?" He cocks his head to the side and then in a mocking tone says, "Did you want me to fuck you bare so I could fill this needy cunt?" He punctuates the question with a roll of his hips over mine.

Words have long escaped me, so I reluctantly nod in reply.

He tuts his tongue. "Patience, Red. Trust me, we'll get to that. But this is both of our first times with a piercing, and although I think it'll feel good for both of us, I also want to make sure the first time you take me again is as painless as possible."

"What if I like the pain?" I whisper as his hand tugs against the tie restraining my wrists, freeing them.

A deep grunt rumbles through his chest. "There are other, more pleasurable ways for me to inflict pain." He kisses each of my wrists before releasing them.

I don't answer, I simply hum in response. And because I can't take another moment of him prolonging this torture, I slide my hand between our bodies and grip his length guiding it toward my entrance.

When he slowly nudges the head of his cock inside me, I cup his face, curling the tips of my fingers through his hair. With our gazes locked, Bennett's jaw feathers for a moment before he plunges his full length inside of me. Bennett's deep groan is full of longing and relief. "I've missed you, baby girl—missed us."

I'd answer him if I could, but I can't because I'm too full. So unbelievably, magically full. And he was right, I needed to be able to adjust to the feel of him again without the full feel of his piercings, though I can still feel the ridge of them slightly through the condom.

His forehead rests against mine as he grinds his hips against my clit and my pussy clenches around his thick length, refusing to release him until I've adjusted. Our breaths are choppy as we pant in anticipation.

He pulls his hips back only to roughly thrust back into me. The combination of my whimper and the sound of our skin slapping together does something to Bennett—it's as if the last tether of his restraint snaps.

Pushing him over the edge, I plead, "More."

I catch one last glimpse at the wicked glare in his eyes before his lips are on mine. Bennett's kiss is animalistic, straight-up barbaric. He devours my lips, crashing his tongue against mine, our teeth clashing, before he roughly bites my lips, then my cheek, chin, and neck before clamping down on my collarbone, causing me to let out a moan so desperate I feel the flush down to my chest.

And all while he devours my mouth, he claims my body with both worship and punishment as his pace quickens and I relinquish control to him. Each punishing thrust moves us up the bed until my head is nearly touching the wooden headboard. Bennett cradles my head with his one hand and grips the metal rod in the headboard with the other. Flattening my palms over my head against the wood, I'm able to push myself down against his hips. As he continues to furiously piston his hips, I lose myself in this moment, in the way his hips grind against my clit each time he bottoms out. And when he hits a spot so deep I think I'll see stars, he ceases his movements, his muscles locked as he hovers above me. My body begins to tremble beneath him as he begins to circle his hips against mine, grinding deeper and deeper, the friction against my clit causes my orgasm to crest, and then the pleasure obliterates me.

Bennett continues to slowly grind his hips, remaining deeply plunged inside me, as I ride out my orgasm. Only as the last flames of pleasure lick at my spine does Bennett's pace quicken.

"You drive me crazy, Red," he growls.

When I hook my ankles around his waist, he slips a hand under my back and lifts onto his knees, pulling my body upright with him. Bennett pins my back against his headboard and widens his knees before he grips both fists around the rod that runs just below where my hips are pinned. And then, he begins ruthlessly bucking his hips against mine. The sounds we're making together only heighten the intensity to which he fucks me without abandon.

"Fuck, baby girl. What have you done to me? I'm there."

"Me too. Right there." Though I don't know where *there* is. He continues to thrust fervently into me. Once. Twice. Three times.

"Oh *fuuuck*," he groans, and the sound he makes as he finds his release has me clenching around him again and tumbling off the edge as I freefall into another orgasm.

Years worth of pent-up frustration, tension, and stress leave me with our mutual release, and I'm left a boneless mess, only held up by his body pressing me against the headboard. Sheer bliss spreads through my chest and consumes me when Bennett places soft kisses along my hairline.

I couldn't be more ecstatic that we agreed to keep things purely physical because it's red hot and *so good* it's off the charts. Three years of this explosive chemistry will be amazing.

17

Scarlett

"Are you sure about this? You don't have to watch them, I can tell the girls I can't come," I tell Bennett over my shoulder as he helps me into my jacket.

"Of course I'm sure. I've got this." He swats my butt and I turn to wrap my arms around his neck.

I stare up at him to see if he's placating me but am met with nothing but sincerity. Outside of my grandparents, I've had a hard time trusting anyone to watch Gunner and Gemma. Which is my own thing I've had to work through in therapy and probably why I've greatly lacked in a personal life. For the past five years I've been Scarlett Carlisle, guardian to my two younger siblings. It became my entire identity. These past couple of months with Bennett have quickly shown me I'm able to be so much more than that. Taking this leap of trust with him is another step in rediscovering myself.

Placing a kiss on my forehead, he reassures me. "*I've got this.* Where are you ladies going again?"

"We're just getting facials and then maybe pedicures if the kids are doing okay while we vote on what our first book will be."

"You know, Little Red, you don't have to leave the house to get a facial," he says with a lopsided smirk.

"Oh my god, stop!" I squeal before covering his mouth.

"What? The kids didn't hear me. They're upstairs—Gemma is in her room and Gunner is in the craft room." He brings me in for a kiss and I turn to give him my cheek.

"Did you just cheek me?" he asks as he begins tickling my sides.

"Mercy!" I gasp out. "Please! Mercy!"

Bennett stops his tickling but leaves his arms wrapped snugly around my waist as he leans down to whisper, "You know how much I love hearing you beg, Scar. If you keep that up, you're never going to be able to leave our house."

Our house.

He grasps my chin and brings his lips to mine.

God this feels so real—so effortless. The past few weeks together have left me so confused on where we currently stand. Some of the things he says, some of the things we do, don't feel like this is simply for convenience's sake anymore. Having him officially moved in has shifted things between us.

I don't travel with the team for every away trip, thankfully, so I've been able to keep the kids' routines steady, while also giving Bennett the space he swears he doesn't need.

And the time spent away from each other isn't anything I'll complain about. He's done a great job of making sure my needs are met even when he's not here, in multiple ways. He's ordered meals, arranged for groceries to be delivered, and given me more FaceTime orgasms than I can count.

The only bad part about his travel schedule is that it's made me realize how much I miss him. What's the saying? Distance makes the heart grow fonder? Well, I'm not sure if it's a good or bad thing yet if that's true.

I can't help but notice how things are straying away from just remaining physical with us. Bennett's caring and protective nature that he seems to reserve for only those closest to him has now included me and my siblings, and that feels somewhat unsettling yet all too *right* at the same time.

"Alright, you better get going. We'll see you later." Bennett peppers kisses along my cheeks and over the bridge of my nose, and I'm overcome with overwhelming gratitude for this man. He's taken my grandfather's advice and made our friendship a priority over the past two months. Not only that, but he's been so patient and great with Gemma and Gunner, and such a great partner to me, that I'm not sure how I'll ever be able to tell him how appreciative I am of him.

An hour and a glowing facial later, Kenna, Dakota, Alexa, and I are lined up with our feet soaking and massage chairs kneading away.

We've decided the first book club read will be the sequel to a novel that apparently each of us have already devoured: a friends-to-lovers romance called *Meet Me in the Valley*. I've been dying to read it. The coolest part is that Dakota has become close friends with the author, and she's going to see if she would join us virtually for our book club meeting.

"Have y'all decided what you're doing for Thanksgiving yet?" Dakota asks the group as she mindlessly rubs her growing bump. I've decided she's the cutest pregnant person ever.

"Well you and I are obviously spending the holiday together, and I'm so excited that you're hosting this year. Rowen is in the thick of a sleep regression, so I'd probably burn the turkey and put marshmallows in the corn instead of the sweet potatoes," Kenna quips with her eyes closed and her head thrown back into the massage chair as her feet soak in the pedicure tub.

Dakota reaches out and gives Kenna's hand a squeeze. "I figured we'd get the hosting out of the way this year so you can take on next year when we're in the thick of the newborn phase."

Kenna opens her eyes and they have a sheen to them. "I'm so thankful to have you as my sister," she tells Dakota before turning her head to me and Alexa. "So, what are you two doing for Thanksgiving?"

Alexa beams and does a little shoulder shimmy. "I'll be on the sidelines reporting for one of my favorite games of the year—the NFL Thanksgiving matchup."

That makes Dakota squeal and clap excitedly. "My brother is playing that game. I still can't believe that after spending nearly his entire career in Denver, he decided to sign a two-year contract with Minnesota."

"Tell me about it. It sent shockwaves throughout the league. But, off the record, of course, aren't you excited to have him so close?" Alexa leans forward and asks her.

"Of course, but I think with how close he is to retirement, it was shocking that he decided to make the deal he did in order to be closer to his niece and nephew," Dakota admits.

"Aw, that's sweet. Wait, who is your brother?" I ask, unaware as to who they're talking about.

Alexa turns in her oversized massage chair to face me with wide eyes. "You didn't know that the famous author has a famous future hall-of-fame quarterback brother?"

When I shake my head, Alexa says, "Brody Meyer."

It's my turn to stare wide-eyed at Dakota. "I know nearly nothing about football, and even I know who Brody Meyer is. Holy shit!"

"Alexa, oh my gosh, do you think you'll get to interview him?" Kenna asks her.

Dakota and Alexa both shake their heads in unison and now I'm confused.

"No, my brother, unfortunately, doesn't do interviews during games. He's even added it to this contract that he can't be penalized for refusing an interview before or during games," Dakota explains. "He's weird about that after an interview gone wrong earlier in his career."

"Yeah, and I'm typically in charge of interviewing the visiting players post-game anyways," Alexa adds.

"Ah, bummer! Well, we'll be watching and wishing you luck," Kenna tells her.

"Do you go to a lot of your brother's home games?" I ask Dakota, biting back a moan that wants to slip free when the nail tech begins massaging my feet.

"As many as I'm able to, though I haven't been to any of his holiday games since the twins were born. They love going with us to watch uncle Brody whenever they can. What are y'all doing, Scar?"

I let a half-contented and half-frustrated sigh slip free. "Well, this has been a point of contention because Bennett's father refuses to celebrate the holiday on any day other than Thanksgiving. So we'll be spending the early afternoon with his family, and having a late dinner with my grandparents. Honestly, it's my first time bringing a significant other to a holiday, so juggling between families is new for me."

"For Bennett too, I'm sure. I don't think in all the years I've known him that he's had a serious relationship," Kenna tells me.

"What are y'all doing with your free Saturday next weekend?" Dakota asks. "The guys don't have a game, they won't be on the road, and they have a late home game Sunday so Coach said they could have the day off."

"Really? I guess I hadn't noticed. Some days I can barely remember what day of the week it is lately," Kenna admits, covering her mouth as she yawns.

"Well if you're all free, maybe we could do a Friendsgiving at our place," I suggest before I can think better of it.

"Wait, that would be amazing! We've never done that before. We could do a combination Friendsgiving slash engagement party slash housewarming party for you and Bennett!" Kenna sounds far too excited for someone who was just yawning, and now I'm immediately overwhelmed.

I'm also second-guessing if Bennett will think I've overstepped by inserting myself into his friend group. Becoming friends with the ladies is one thing, intruding on his friendships with his teammates is another.

Before I can think of a way out of it, Kenna's phone rings and Griff is on speaker telling her he hopes she's having fun and to take her time, but asks if she wants him to thaw milk for a bottle or if she'd prefer to nurse Rowen.

"I'll be home in probably fifteen minutes, we're just finishing up. If you can hold off the hangry little guy, I'd prefer to nurse him, but I get it if he's being a gremlin," Kenna says into the phone.

"My little man? He's never a gremlin," Griff says with a chuckle. "Oh, the guys are also over with the kids, and we just ordered food so tell the girls if they want to join us for lunch, they're more than welcome."

"Which guys are there?" she asks him.

"Carse, Jax, and Benny," he says simply.

His answer sends alarm bells ringing through my ears. Shit, I typically don't leave Gunner with Gemma alone for very long just because I worry she'll have sugar issues and Gunner is too little to know what to do.

I pull up my text thread with Gemma and send her a quick message.

Me:

Hey, how's everything going?

Gemma:

Great . . . just like the three other times you've asked.

Guilt floods me for not only assuming Bennett left them alone, but I also need to do a better job of trusting that he can take care of them if I'm not there. Easier said than done when I've been doing this alone for the most part over the past five years.

"I think I've got to talk to Benny and Scar, though. Gunner is far too enamored with Cadence for my liking," Griff says over the phone and my heart squeezes at the thought of Gunner making new friends, even if said friend's dad is clearly overbearing.

Kenna's laughter echoes in the space. "We've talked about this, Hotshot. She's eight. Boys and girls can be friends at any age, but it's especially common when they're in elementary school."

Griff scoffs. "Really? I seem to recall a time when you and I were simply *friends*."

"Alright, baby. We're going to pay and head over. Love you and see you soon," Kenna says before ending the call. She shakes her head and mutters, "Men. I tell ya."

When we walk into Kenna and Griff's house a few minutes later, we're met with the odd combination of men hollering over each other and children's laughter.

"They must be in the basement," Kenna tells us as we hang up our jackets in their front entryway.

"You've got a beautiful home," I compliment her, and as I take in each room we pass, I love all of the accents and decor they've chosen for each space.

We walk down the carpeted stairs of the basement to find quite the scene before us, causing the four of us to pause mid-step on the stairwell.

On their hands and knees are four grown men—professional athletes, mind you—with miniature hockey sticks in their hands playing with four kids.

They've moved the furniture into a corner of the large living room to create a makeshift hockey rink, complete with miniature plastic boards and nets.

It looks like Bennett, Gunner, Griff, and Cadence are on one team, leaving Carson, Leo, Lainey, and Jax on the other.

I look around the space to find an amused Gemma holding baby Rowen on a barstool in the far corner out of harm's way.

"I hope you boys are playing opposite-handed and you're going easy on them!" Kenna strains to be heard over the chaos ensuing below.

Jax shoots what I'm assured is a foam puck, whizzing across the room, and hitting Bennett square in the ear.

"Ah, you fudge nugget," Bennett groans as he bends his neck at an odd angle to rub his ear against his shoulder so he doesn't have to take his hands off his mini stick.

Bennett regains possession of the puck and sends a pass to Gunner, who is wide open in front of the net. Gunner takes a shot at Carse, who is playing goalie, and sends the puck under his elbow right into the back of the net.

"Flip yeah!" Bennett shouts, tossing his stick on the ground as he rushes over to Gunner and twirls him off the ground. "Atta boy! I knew you could do it, Champ!"

My heart melts to the floor, and I'm officially a big ball of mush as I take in their shared moment of glory. Bennett's happiness is only outshined by Gunner's look of pure joy. Meanwhile, my ovaries are over here doing their own happy dance.

"Holy shit. Daddy Bennett? I think my IUD just threw itself out. Did my ovaries just high five? My uterus just did a backflip."

"Okay, okay. We get it, Alexa . . . down girl. There are kids present," Kenna reminds her.

"But I don't think you understand. I don't even want kids and seeing that . . . whew. It was a religious experience. I think I need to go to confession."

"Are you even Catholic? And wait, couldn't Bennett be, like, your brother-in-law some day?" Kenna asks.

That earns her a round of laughter, Alexa's peeling into a hysterical sort, pausing the game of mini hockey below as the guys peer up at us. Alexa snorts. "That's never going to happen."

The doorbell rings and Griff hops to his feet. "Food is here," he announces before running past us up the steps, only stopping briefly to give Kenna a kiss. "You look gorgeous, Sunshine," he murmurs.

The rest of the group turns to follow him up the steps, but I make my way to where Bennett is taking a fussy Rowen from Gemma's arms.

"Hey, big guy. What's the matter? Are you hungry? Yeah, me too. Should we go upstairs and get us both fed? That way you and I won't be so grumpy," he rattles off to the infant as if they're having a complete conversation. I watch as Rowen gives Bennett a big smile, causing one of the biggest grins to eclipse Bennett's face, and the sight has butterflies taking off at warp speed in my stomach.

"Don't get too big of a head, I hear when babies smile like that it's probably because they just passed gas," Gemma tells Bennett, patting him on the shoulder as she goes upstairs. Gunner follows after her, leaving me alone with my fiancé. Well, and the adorable baby he's cradling in his big arms.

Bennett smirks when he catches me ogling him. "Careful, Little Red. You look like you're about one baby giggle away from having your way with me."

I gawk at him, shaking my head at his comment. "No, I'm just surprised you know how to hold a baby considering you don't have any nieces or nephews yet."

"I consider myself to be Cadence, Rowen, Leo, and Lainey's honorary uncle. I've known them all since they were babies and, believe it or not, have done my fair share of babysitting over the years."

I must do a poor job of concealing my surprise because he chuckles as he takes in my shocked expression.

Bennett crowds my space, reaching out to wipe my chin, all while holding Rowen like a football in one arm. "You had a little drool right there. Don't worry, I got it," he teases.

I playfully swat his hand away before turning my attention to Rowen. "Hey there, little guy. Aren't you a cutie?"

"Not as cute as me though, right?" Bennett questions with a huff.

"Jealous of a baby, Benny?"

"I mean, you don't use that sweet voice with me very often. In fact, I don't think you've ever been sweet with me at all."

"And here I thought you preferred me either snarky or submissive. I didn't realize you wanted a sweet girl," I mock-coo at him.

"You're right," he rasps as he wraps his free arm around my shoulder and pulls me in. "I much prefer you submissive. How about you let the snark out now and save the submissive side for when I have you on your hands and knees for me later?"

Damn, he's good.

"Well, I was planning to be sweet by coming over here and thanking you for today."

"You can thank me later, Red," he tells me, throwing a wink my way as we head upstairs.

I plan to thank him in kind over and over for today. Little does he know, he gave me so much more than a couple of hours with friends—he gave me peace of mind that the two people who mean most to me in this world were safe and cared for. By someone who I'm realizing has taken up residence in my heart.

18

Bennett

Never in my life did I ever think I'd spend a precious day off hosting a "Friendsgiving." But I've got to admit, Scarlett's idea to have everyone over at our place today has really grown on me.

Our place—god, I love the sound of that.

I've just wrapped a towel around my waist after my shower when a frantic Scarlett comes barreling into our bathroom. Clad in only a silk robe loosely secured around her waist with a towel twisted around her hair, she's bordering on hysteria as she storms into our closet.

"Why in the hell did we think this would be a good idea?" she asks, her voice laced in panic as I follow her and head to my designated side of the closet.

We? I'm smart enough not to voice my question aloud, but unfortunately I don't do a good enough job of stifling my chuckle.

Scarlett whirls on me, eyes wide before she quickly narrows them. "Did I say something funny, *dear?*"

"Yes, *darling.* This entire hysterical episode you're having is quite hilarious to me."

"*What* did you just say?" she asks in an icy tone that immediately raises my hackles.

Oh, fuck.

I'm in trouble.

"Come on, baby girl. You've got to admit that you're kinda freaking out right now." It's adorable and scary at the same time.

"Don't you 'baby girl' me right now, Bennett Benjamin Wilson."

"My middle name is not Benjamin."

"Do I look like I give a fuck what your real middle name is right now?"

"No, but it's probably something we should know about each other before we get married. It's James. What's your middle name?"

"God, even your freaking middle name is sexy. Bennett James . . . that's stupid hot. Mine is Elizabeth."

My cocky smirk at her comment doesn't hit the mark with my future bride, in fact, I think it enrages her more, if that's possible. "So our wedding invites will say Scarlett Elizabeth and Bennett James. It's cute, I like it."

"Ugh. That's beside the point, stop trying to distract me," she growls at me. "I'm freaking out because of you. Because for some reason I've started giving a shit about you, and that means I want your friends to like me. It means I want to impress them and make them feel welcome in our home."

I'm storing that whole liking me comment away for later. Meanwhile I'm smiling like an idiot.

"Our home. I was just thinking to myself in the shower that I love the sound of that." I eliminate the distance between us. "Tell me, Scar, if I got down on my knees right now to show you how appreciative I am for the hard work you've put into today, would that help settle your nerves? Would that earn your forgiveness for my big mouth getting the best of me?"

"Y-yes."

I press her back against the floor-to-ceiling shelves as I drop down to my knees, still wrapped in only my towel.

"Eyes on the mirror, baby girl. I want you to watch how good your future husband can make you feel."

I've barely tasted paradise when a shrilling sound rings throughout the house.

"You've got to be fucking kidding me! That's the smoke alarm!" Scarlett says as she adjusts her robe and then rushes out of the closet.

I throw on the first pair of sweatpants I can find and run down the stairs as fast as I can.

When I enter the kitchen, Gemma is standing beneath the fire alarm with a dish rag laughing hysterically and Scarlett is spraying something down in the sink that's billowing with smoke.

"This is too good—I just started home ec class and even I know you shouldn't step away from the oven if you set the timer on it. You should've at least set the timer on your phone, Scar."

"Yeah, Gems, I realize that now."

"Why were you making cookies anyways? It's Thanksgiving, shouldn't you be baking pies?"

"I wanted the house to smell like fresh baked cookies," Scar admits in defeat as she throws her hands in the air.

"Well, now it'll smell like burnt cookies and burnt parchment paper," Gemma tells her as she chuckles at her sister's expense.

"What can I do to help, love?" The moment the words leave my mouth, Scarlett freezes from my slip of tongue. I'm not even mad about calling her that, but when she turns to face me, she not only looks frazzled but also unsure of herself.

Scar closes her eyes and takes a deep, steadying breath. "Would you please open the patio door to air out the kitchen and living room? And Gemma, would you and Gunner please set up the kids' dining table with the coloring place mats Gunner picked out?"

I nod my head as Gemma says, "We're on it, sis!"

I'm thankful Gemma seems to be in a good mood today, she and Scar have been butting heads lately, which has been weighing heavily on Scarlett. The other day when the three of us went to pick out Gemma's guitar, she was short and snippy with Scar. Gems and I had a good chat later that evening when we were tuning her new guitar. When I asked her what was going on, she admitted that change is hard for her and she has been going through a lot of it lately, and not that they are necessarily bad changes, but any change overwhelms her. She agreed to try to take it easier on Scar and chat about it with her therapist at her next appointment. Whether it's my place or not, I'm crazy proud of her.

Once I've opened the patio door and noticed Gemma and Gunner have gone upstairs to grab the coloring place mats, I move to stand behind Scarlett, resting my chin on her shoulder and wrapping my arms around her waist.

Her shoulders relax from my touch, giving me a sense of pride knowing I can do that for her. "What's this thing in your hair? I thought it was a towel at first, but now I realize you slept in it."

She shakes with laughter at my question. "It's a silk bonnet that I sleep in to hold my heatless curls. I should probably be mortified that you're seeing me in this state, but I'm honestly too overstimulated to care right now. Sorry, the honeymoon phase of our marriage is over before it's even begun."

"I don't know, Red, I think I prefer you being comfortable and real around me to living in a fake honeymoon phase," I admit.

"Hmm, someone's earning brownie points."

"And what do I get if I earn enough of those?" I murmur the question against her skin before trailing my lips down the column of her neck.

"Whatever you want," she says breathlessly as I move the satin fabric of her robe off her shoulder, desperate to kiss every freckle glittering her skin.

Laughter rumbles in my chest. "Is that so? I'd be careful if I were you. Giving me free rein to do whatever I want to you might be a roll of the dice you're not ready for," I warn.

"Didn't you ask me to take a gamble on you when you proposed?" she questions as she spins in my hold, wrapping her arms around my neck.

"I did."

"Well, I'd like to see what happens when I give you full control. Something tells me there's more to that rail you had hidden in your headboard . . . and I'd like to find out," she admits.

Fuck me. She's exactly right; there is more, though, I'm not sure what she'd think of the more I'd have in store for her. But before I can respond, Gunner comes barreling back into the kitchen.

"Benny! Look at my turkey wobble!" he squeals as he does a weird strut across the floor that has the three of us cracking up before we're all joining him in our own versions of a "gobble wobble" as Gemma put it.

"This was not on my bingo card this year, but I'm not mad about it," I hear Jax say from over my shoulder before he barks out a laugh. "I knocked, but let myself in when you didn't answer." He holds up a pack of butter in one hand and a bag of marshmallows in the other. "I come bearing gifts."

"You mean the groceries I asked you to grab on your way over," I correct him.

"Sure, that," Jax says as he tosses the items onto the kitchen island before turning to Gunner. "What dance are we doing, little man?"

"Gemma calls it the gobble wobble, Uncle J."

Scarlett suddenly freezes, eyes wide from what Gunner just called Jax, and I imagine her shocked expression is mirrored on my face.

Jackson doesn't bat an eye at his new title, in fact, he's beaming with joy as he joins Gunner in the dance he's made up.

"I'm going to go get ready," Scar calls over her shoulder as she strides down the hall.

"Take your time, I'm on turkey basting duty," I assure her.

"Try not to burn the house down again," Gemma teases as she passes by us to go upstairs.

"Thought it smelled a little funny in here," Jax starts, but I jab him in the ribs before he can say anything else.

"Is Alexa with you?" I ask him.

"She had to finish some interview prep so she's driving over later," he explains.

I give him a nod before grabbing the oven mitts and pulling the turkey from one of the double ovens to baste it again. I'm pleased to say we haven't burnt it and it looks like it just might turn out perfectly. Not too shabby for two turkey first-timers.

"I'm so tempted to post a thirst trap video of you basting that turkey with your shirt off right now. Or maybe I should wait and post a video of it when you inevitably lose the fantasy league again."

"You're freaking hilarious, J," I deadpan.

"I know. So, what can I help with?" he asks and I'm thankful he does because I'm not ashamed to admit he's a far better cook than I am.

After I put Jax to work on prepping the sweet potatoes, I lift Gunner in the air. "Let's get you changed out of your PJs, Champ."

"Look at me, Uncle J! I'm an airplane!" he squeals in delight, and goddamnit, the combination of his laughter and hearing him call my brother his uncle has me feeling all the feels.

Never change, Champ.

Making exaggerated airplane noises with my mouth, I swerve side to side as we fly up the stairs and Gunner lands a spot in my heart as one of my favorite people to ever exist.

It's not long before our house is filled with our friends and too many kids to count.

The doorbell rings and I open the front door to find Connelly with his younger siblings Colton and Eva. I knew he was bringing Eva along because she's friends with Gemma and offered to help her watch the younger kids for a bit so the adults could have a game night after we eat, but I wasn't anticipating him bringing Colt. Scar thinks Gemma has a crush on him, and I can't help the overprotective side of me from coming out as I narrow my eyes at the boy.

"Welcome," I tell them as I gesture to the coat rack for them to hang their jackets on.

"Hey, Cap. Thanks for having us," Nathan says.

"Of course, thanks for coming. Are you helping the girls babysit, Colt?" I ask him in a gruff tone.

"Uh, yeah, I love kids and good food so it sounded like a no brainer. I appreciate the invite, sir," he says and I have to hold back a chuckle.

Sir? This little shit thinks he's so good.

Scarlett walks up beside me and I wrap my arm around her shoulders. "Hey, guys. Thanks for coming. Gemma is with the kids in the basement."

"Thank you for having us, Miss Carlisle," Colt says, sucking up to her. I close my eyes to avoid them seeing me roll them. When he opens his arms to give her a welcoming hug, I stiffen beside her and quirk a suspecting brow at him. The kid might actually be smart because he drops his arms and takes a step back beside his older brother, who is shaking with muffled laughter.

Eva grabs Colt by the arm and heads down the hallway to the basement stairway and Nathan follows behind them, but heads to the living room to join the guys.

Scar turns to face me, securing her arms around my waist. "Perhaps I should start calling you 'sir.' What do you think?"

I place a chaste kiss on her lips. "You can call me whatever you want, baby girl, but I refuse to call you Miss Carlisle ever again."

"Well, if you want me to be Mrs. Wilson before next season, we should probably start wedding planning," she points out.

Trailing my hands down her waist, I tuck my hands into the back pockets of her jeans before giving her butt a squeeze. "We're taking our engagement photos next week. That's at least one step in the right direction. And if we want all of our family and friends to be there, we'll need to get married in the summer. Do you prefer July or August?"

"July."

"Okay, what's your favorite number?"

"Twenty."

"July twentieth it is," I tell her.

She shakes her head before burying her face against my chest. "What day of the week is that even on?"

"Does it matter? We'll be in Paris—I doubt our friends and family will care what day of the week we get married when they're in the city of love."

"Paris?" she questions, looking adorably confused.

I shrug. "You told me your dream wedding would be in Paris. So, Paris."

Scarlett's nose wrinkles in that cute way I've become obsessed with. "We would need to secure a venue that happens to have that date open. Most venues around here book at least a year, if not two, in advance."

"Can we hire a wedding planner to help us with that?"

"Well, yes. But are you sure? We don't have to do a big wedding."

"Last week at Sunday dinner, your grandma showed me the dream boards you used to make when you were little. Do you know how many you dedicated to your dream wedding?"

"No," she admits sheepishly.

I hold up three fingers. "Three. And each one of them featured a big, classic wedding in Paris. We're doing this, Scar. Unless you truly don't want that anymore, that is." My eyes move back and forth between hers as I try to read her expression.

A shy smile spreads across her face before she nods in agreement, or maybe it's in resignation. Either way, I'll take it. "Okay. Paris in July." Scarlett cups my cheek and pulls me in for a deep kiss that is cut far too short when the doorbell rings again. I grunt in frustration at the interruption.

"That's probably Alexa. I'll get the door and we'll meet you in the living room," Scar says, and then she rises to her tiptoes to give me a quick kiss before getting the door.

As I walk down the hallway into the living room, I can't help the overwhelming sense of gratitude I feel in this moment. I'm surrounded by my best friends, their families, my new family, and the woman I'm falling for. It may be cheesy as hell considering the reason we're all gathered today, but I can't help but feel like the most thankful man in the world.

The meal is done and the games have just begun. The ladies are starting a game of Sequence while the men get the kids settled.

After we ate, Carson, Griff and I wrangled up the young ones, put them in jammies, and now we've got the kids in the basement theater about to watch a movie with Gemma and her friends.

"Gemma, have you thought about your summer plans at all?" Carson asks her.

"I mean, no. Not really," she admits with a slight shake of her head.

"Griffin, McKenna, Dakota and I run a summer camp each year for the month of August, and we're looking for some camp counselors to help run our new figure skating program. Bennett had mentioned you were a figure skater. If you're interested, let us know. You're great with kids, and it's a fun opportunity."

"Really? That sounds amazing. I'd love to hear more. What's the camp called?" Gemma asks him.

"Camp Katie. I'll have McKenna get in touch with you after the holidays, but if you have any questions about how being a camp counselor is, you can ask Nate. He went from being a camp attendee for years to becoming a counselor last summer for our hockey program," Carson explains.

"Ask away, Twirl Girl," Nathan says from the theater seat beside her.

Gemma tries to be subtle with her eye roll, but I don't miss it. Instead of asking Nathan, she turns behind her, facing Colt. "Have you attended any of the camps there before?"

"Yeah, I went for a few years. We'd fly up from Colorado so we could all go. Nate and I were there for the hockey camp and Eva attended the golf camp. I'm actually going to be a hockey counselor there this summer as well," Mr. Thinks-He's-Suave informs her.

When Gemma's eyes widen, he continues, "And lucky for us, the figure skating and hockey camps are held in the same first two weeks of August."

Over my dead body is she being a camp counselor if he is going to be there at the same time.

I practically drag Carson up the steps after ordering my rookie to keep an eye on everyone since he decided to watch the movie instead of participating in game night. When we're finally upstairs, I ask Carse, "How much supervision is there for camp counselors?"

Carson shakes his head at me. "Chill out, Benny. The male and female counselor cabins are kept separate; they're on either side of the campers' cabins. And there's always a senior counselor and camp director on-site."

"Have McKenna go over the details with Scarlett," I tell him.

"Yeah, of course," Carson assures me, clapping me on the back and pushing me into the living room where the rest of the group is. "Now, are you ready to stop being an overly protective papa bear?"

"Papa bear?" Scar questions.

"Yeah. Bennett is freaking out about the possibility of Gemma and Colton both being camp counselors at Camp Katie this summer," Carson explains, shaking his head at me as he takes a seat on the sectional next to Dakota.

Jax chuckles from across the room. "Why is that the least surprising thing I've heard?"

Taking a seat next to Scarlett, I scoop her legs up into my lap and grumble, "Can we just start a game or something?"

"I've got an idea," Jax says. "Let's have the ladies hit us with their best pickup lines and we'll vote whose is best," Jax suggests.

McKenna doesn't hesitate to go first, throwing her hair over her shoulder. "Relationships should be 50/50, you give me your last name and I'll scream out your first."

Her pickup line would clearly work on Griff, because he pulls her into his lap and says, "I already gave you my last name, Sunshine."

"I know, but that'd be my pickup line if I were trying to pick you up tonight," she tells him with a dopey smile that mirrors the one Griff's wearing.

Carson turns to Dakota. "Alright, Austen. Woo me," he says, waggling his eyebrows.

"You're just like a wine tasting. They say spit, but I prefer to swallow," Dakota says with a slight drawl and I think we can all hear Carson swallow his tongue as he stares back at her wide-eyed.

"Something I didn't need to know about my sister-in-law," Kenna groans.

Alexa stands up then and points to Jax's face before asking, "Is this seat taken?"

He chuckles and grins widely. "It's all yours."

"Is that how you picked him up, Lex?" Kenna asks her.

"No, it was more so we were both sick of being the singles of the group," she admits before turning to face Scarlett. "Alright, Scar, it's your turn."

"I've never been very good with pickup lines," Scar tells the group.

"Oh, come on, Red. Don't be a poor sport, all the other ladies did it," I point out.

Scar rolls her eyes at me and says, "I don't have any pickup lines because I don't like to be picked up." She lowers her voice and slides her hand along my thigh before she murmurs, "I much prefer to be pinned down."

Fuck. Me. That's exactly what I'd like to do to her.

Leaning into her space, I whisper into her ear, "Tonight, baby girl."

"Promises, promises," she taunts.

I've got so many promises I'd like to make to her, if she'll let me.

19

Scarlett

After weeks of behind-the-scenes planning, it's the morning of Gemma and Bennett's birthday. Having a birthday two days before Christmas can't be fun, but I intend to make the day special for each of them.

Starting with Gemma. It's her sixteenth birthday and I've been an emotional wreck just thinking about it, but now that the day is here, I'm excited for what I've got in store for her.

Bennett's been gone for the past five days for the team's away series in Canada and his flight lands back in Minnesota right about the time I drop the kids off at school. Although today, only Gunner will go to his last day of school before winter break, while I bring Gemma to her driver's test. If she passes, she'll be a licensed driver and I'm not sure how to feel about that.

Tonight, Gemma and Bennett think we're going to a team holiday party. Little do they know, our friends and family will all be gathered at the restaurant we rented out to surprise them.

Just as I flip the last low-carb pancake, Gemma comes into the kitchen and I use the spatula as a microphone. "Good morning birthday princess! In honor of your sweet sixteen, I've made a batch of your favorite pancakes!"

She rounds the island to give me a big hug, and I have to look up at the balloon-covered ceiling in order to blink back the tears threatening to break free. "I love you so much, Gems. I can't believe you're already sixteen. Stop making me feel so old!"

Her shoulders shake with laughter, but I don't let her go. "You are old, nothing I can do about that. I love you too, Scar. Thank you so much for making the pancakes and taking me to my test today."

This. This is the best feeling in the world. Being hugged by my little sister and hearing her laugh. Things were tense between us for a few months and I tried talking to her countless times, but she'd been shutting me out. I couldn't figure out if she was still upset about how she found out about the engagement, or if she was mad about the fact that I'm engaged in the first place. However, I doubt it's the latter, because she's told me how much she loves Bennett living with us. Since he moved in, they've been playing guitar almost every night he's home after she finishes her homework. It's become my favorite nightly routine to listen to them play by the fire together with the guitar Bennett helped us pick out a few weeks ago. Something has changed recently, though, because the past few weeks things between us have felt more settled and she's back to being my easygoing little sister. I'm not even sure what's changed.

"Absolutely," I tell her before turning her by her shoulders to face the birthday banner I made for her that hangs above the island with two gift bags beneath it.

"What are these?" she asks as she makes her way over to the bags. "You've already done so much, I didn't need anything."

"Gunner, Gems is about to open her presents!" I call to him before I hear loud footsteps stomp down the stairs.

"Happy birthday, Gemmy!" Gunner shouts, running to give her a hug.

"Thank you, Bug. I love you!"

"Love you mostest. Now open mine first," he tells her as he points to the rainbow paper bag he painted himself.

Gemma rips the rainbow tissue paper out of the bag and pulls out a painting Gunner did for her. It's of the two of them on the ice together. It's such a sweet moment that I know meant so much to him.

"This is so getting hung up in my room! Thank you so much," she says as she wraps her arms around him.

"You're welcome. Now open that one," he tells her.

Gemma opens the teal gift bag, her eyes widen before she looks up at me.

"No way." I nod back at her and tears swell in her eyes. "A Taevin Gray T-shirt?"

"And . . ."

"And a signed poster? How did you get this?" She does a happy dance and squeals in excitement.

"Bennett had a connection. Do you like them?"

"Like them? I love them! Thank you."

"It's my pleasure, Gems. Oh shoot, I forgot, there's one more on my phone." I pause to look through my phone before handing her the phone.

"Shut up! Are these tickets to see her when she's in town?"

"They are. And . . . Bennett was able to get you backstage passes for a meet and greet with her after the show."

"Shut. Up. Oh my god, I have to call him to say thank you," she says, pulling out her phone.

"He's still on the plane, Gems. You can thank him after you pass your driver's test."

A radiant smile lights up her face as she nods in agreement. "Alright. Shall we eat these pancakes, Gunner?"

"Are they cake batter flavored?" he asks.

"Would it be a birthday around here if they weren't? Of course they are, it's tradition," I assure him.

"Did you make enough for when Benny's home?" Gunner asks me as he hops up on his stool at the kitchen island.

"I did, I thought he could either have them when he gets home, or we could do a birthday morning do-over for him tomorrow. What do you think of that?"

Gunner nods excitedly in agreement, making his wild hair fall over his eyes. Gemma reaches over to sweep it off his forehead, and I sigh in contentment at the small gesture of endearment. These two are my entire world, and I wish I could freeze time in this moment so they wouldn't get any older. But even if I could, I know I wouldn't. I'm far too excited to see how they'll grow and all of the amazing things they'll do, the dreams they'll reach, the goals they'll crush.

"I love you both, you know that?" I tell them as I hand them their plates full of pancakes and eggs.

Gemma rolls her eyes at my mushy sentiment. "You always get like this on our birthdays. You're such a sap."

Gunner giggles. "But we love you too!"

"Yeah," Gems sighs in exasperation before continuing with a sincere tone. "We really do love you, Scar."

I swat at the tears threatening to break free. "And this is why I didn't do my makeup before breakfast." With a half-sniffle, half-chuckle, I tell them, "Alright, let's finish eating and then we've got to get ready. Gunner, today it's silly sweater day for your class so I put the sweater you and Benny picked out on your bed. And Gemma, we'll have about thirty minutes to finish getting ready before we've got to drop off Gunner so we have enough time to make it to your driver's test appointment."

"Is it the sweater with the skateboarding Santa?" Gunner questions.

"Was there another sweater you picked out with Bennett?" Gemma asks him.

"Yeah, he called the jerseys he got me sweaters," he explains.

That makes us both chuckle. "That's just a term they call jerseys sometimes. I meant the Santa sweater for today," I clarify.

We finished eating breakfast together and got ready, and before I knew it, I was parking my car outside the DMV for Gemma's road test. First, she had to complete the knowledge test, which she passed with flying colors, and then she had to take the road test. They've been gone for about a half hour, and I've been nervously tapping my foot in the waiting room when a deep voice I'd recognize anywhere says, "Is this seat taken, ma'am?"

I'm up and out of my seat so quickly, I hardly have time to take him in before I'm jumping into his arms. I'd be embarrassed by my needy display of affection if I wasn't so desperate for his embrace after nearly a week apart.

Bennett's arms wrap around my waist, and I inhale deeply, feeling comforted by his familiar scent that's come to feel like home to me.

His chest rumbles against mine, and it makes me want to squeeze him tighter to me. "Miss me, Little Red?"

"I missed you so much. Happy birthday, Cap," I whisper into his ear before cupping his cheeks and peppering kisses all over his face.

He sets me down when someone clears their throat beside us, and I bury my head in his chest, embarrassed at how wrapped up in our reunion I got. But even as we sit down together, Bennett keeps an arm wrapped around my shoulder and intertwines our fingers with his other hand.

"What are you doing here?" I finally ask him.

"I came right from the airport hoping I'd make it in time to see our girl pass her driver's test."

I don't miss the way he said "our girl," and my heart warms at the way he's embraced my siblings in such a short time. It means more than I'll ever be able to express to him.

"She was so nervous, but she passed the knowledge test with flying colors and has been gone now for a little over a half hour," I tell him,

He hums in acknowledgment. "She's got this."

"She does," I agree as I lean my head on his shoulder. "You guys had a great away series. And look at you with two power-play goals in three games."

Bennett lowers his head closer to my ear and tells me in a low voice, "Coach says I'm playing some of the best hockey of my life and to keep up whatever's gotten into me." His rough chuckle elicits goosebumps down my neck. "Looks like I've got to keep up the sexy pregame FaceTime calls with you while we're on the road and the visits to your office before home games."

"I suppose we could do that . . . if it's what's best for the team."

"Mmm. It's what's best for their captain, so that's got to count for something."

I run my hand through his rough stubble he hasn't shaved in the days he was away. "Is that a gray hair I spot in your beard?" I mock gasp.

His eyes widen slightly before narrowing on me. "What? No, you're mistaken."

"I'm not sure if I am. Wow, thirty-one. You're getting up there, old man. Maybe I should reconsider hitching myself to your station wagon."

"You're teasing again. And, might I point out, lying to yourself. You know I'd be a silver fox if I got any grays in my beard."

"You're right, you would be a silver fox," I hum in agreement, imagining what he'd look like. My stomach sinks at the realization that I may not be with him still when that time comes.

"It'll happen sooner rather than later, I'm sure, between Walker, you, and Gemma, the women in my life are causing me a lot of stress," he admits just as Gemma walks through the side door of the DMV holding a piece of paper in the air.

"I passed!" she squeals in excitement, and when she sees Bennett, her smile only widens further. "Benny! What are you doing here? Happy birthday, birthday twin!"

"Hey, Gems. Happy birthday," he tells her as she gives the two of us hugs. "I came right here after our flight landed hoping I'd be able to take the two of you to lunch to celebrate you passing your test. We knew you could do it."

She smiles at the two of us before her expression turns hesitant. "If you don't mind, I was hoping to maybe go to school for the last part of the day since we have early release anyway. Eva and I were going to celebrate at lunch hour if I passed, and, well—" She shrugs, holding up the paper halfheartedly.

"Of course, it's your birthday," I tell her.

"Besides, that way you two can go out to lunch just the two of you as a birthday date since we've got the holiday party tonight," she suggests.

Bennett pats her on the shoulder. "Hear that, Scar? We've got the smartest sixteen-year-old living under our roof."

Gemma rolls her eyes, feigning annoyance. "Yeah, and said sixteen-year-old has the most embarrassing guardians on the planet."

My throat swells with emotion hearing their back-and-forth exchange. I'd probably focus on the tiny voice in the back of my head warning me that this is too much too fast if it weren't for the way my heart is beating overtime from the joy I feel.

Later, I'll reflect on this and decide whether this is too much. Later, I'll try to decipher what it is we've turned into.

Bennett

After a lunch consisting of cake batter pancakes—apparently a birthday tradition in this house—I'm unpacking my suitcase while Scar finishes coordinating the logistics of Gemma's Christmas present.

"Knock, knock," Scar says as she walks into our closet.

"You know you don't have to knock, right? You've seen it all," I tell her and send a wink her way when I turn around. It's almost comical the way my eyes widen in surprise as my jaw drops to the floor.

"I thought I'd give you one of your birthday presents now, before the kids get home from school."

Scarlett stands before me in an oversized wool dress jacket that's unbuttoned, exposing her mouthwatering lingerie set that matches her light pink heels with satin ribbon that laces up her ankles and lower calves.

"Do you like it? I designed the entire outfit myself," she informs me as she closes the distance between us and does a spin so I can take in her ensemble.

"Scarlett," I rasp, pulling her in by the lapels of the charcoal jacket. That's when I notice that it's a men's jacket. "Is this for me?"

"Yes," she says shyly.

Shifting the jacket open, so it's hanging just off her shoulders, I drag my hand over the oversized pink satin bow that's containing her breasts. "And this? Is this for me?" My voice sounds like gravel.

"Only you, birthday boy."

"When you say you designed this?"

"The jacket, the lingerie, the shoes—all of it."

"When? How? How did I not know you were a designer?"

"I'm not—well, not really. Sometimes I'll get inspired and if the urge is strong enough, I'll materialize a sketch. I noticed you didn't have a nice dress jacket for game days, and I didn't want you to be cold. I'd hoped it would be finished before your Canada series, but no such luck."

I stare at her, dumbfounded by this discovery. "You're incredible, Scar."

She takes a step back and shrugs out of the jacket. "Here, try it on. I want to make sure it fits. I went off the measurements from a few of your suits."

The jacket dangles between us, but I can't take my eyes off Scarlett in her pale pink lingerie that is only a few shades darker than her creamy skin. The bra encases her breasts with a satin pink bow that I'm dying to untie. She's got a matching thong that rides up over her hip bones with the center a see-through mesh fabric. The whole look is topped off with a set of satin garters on her thighs and those damn fuck-me heels.

Her look is lethal and I'm regrettably going to die on my thirty-first birthday.

I'm snapped from my ogling when she shakes the jacket in front of me. "Benny, focus! Here, try on the jacket, and then you can unwrap the rest of your presents."

I turn my back to her and slide my arms into the sleeves of the jacket. It's soft and luxurious against my skin, which I wasn't expecting with a wool coat. "This is incredible," I tell her as I slip the fabric over my shoulders. "And it fits perfectly."

"Yeah?" she asks in a hopeful yet hesitant tone.

"It's amazing, Red. How didn't I know this about you?"

"Well, I told you I was planning to be a fashion merchandiser, but ever since I was a little girl I've loved spending hours on end sketching and designing clothing. It's a hidden passion of mine, sort of like playing guitar is for you."

"But I'm not nearly as talented as you are, clearly," I point out as I hold out my arms to gesture at not only my jacket but her entire ensemble. "You look breathtaking, baby girl. You always do, but especially so in something you used your talent to create."

She shyly accepts my praise. "Thank you, that means a lot."

"Is this what you want to do? Design?" I ask her.

She scoffs somewhat to herself. "Maybe when I'm in my forties. Though, I may be slightly out of touch with my key demographic at that age, considering I'd like to design lingerie and women's sleepwear."

"Then don't wait."

Her head snaps up to meet my gaze. "What?"

"Could you do a pop-up boutique type of storefront for now in the summer until you can do it full time?"

She shakes her head. "Bennett, you know better than anyone that there isn't an off-season for me. I've still got so much to do. Sure, some of the chaos slows down after the season, but I'll still be far too busy to take time off to make that a possibility."

She's not wrong. Owning a professional hockey team takes a lot of work, and there isn't really a break for her. But that doesn't mean I couldn't offer to help her when and where I'm able to. Sure, I wouldn't be able to do the bigger aspects of her job such as selecting team leadership or representing the Wolverines on the league's Board of Governors, but I could help her be more hands-off with some of the off-season day-to-day operations.

"Let me help you with the hockey side of things after the season ends," I suggest.

"How would you do that?"

"I went to school and got my master's in sports management and business. Let me help with some of the day-to-day to lessen the load on your shoulders." Avoiding her gaze, I slip the jacket off and hang it next to the outfit I set aside for tonight.

"I-I didn't know that about you. How didn't I know that?"

"It hasn't exactly come up, and I don't really advertise it."

"Is that what you're interested in after you retire from playing? Management?" she questions, and if I'm not mistaken, she sounds oddly hopeful.

"Well, yes. I hope to play for as many seasons as my body allows, but when planning for my future, I got the degree I did because I'm interested in becoming either a GM or a President of Hockey for an organization," I explain.

"You'd be incredible," she declares, though I'm not sure why she's looking at me the way she is. I'm met with warm, amber eyes so full of promise that they pull me in, leaving me mesmerized.

"I appreciate your vote of confidence, but it'd be many years down the road before I could gain the experience required to hold a position of that importance."

"Yeah, maybe. But I can still think you'd be amazing at it. You're so knowledgeable, and you've done such a great job with taking Nathan under your wing. You've worked not only with the coaching staff for years, but my grandfather speaks highly of you as well."

"You kind of have to think highly of me as my future bride," I point out, tossing a wink her way. "But I am pretty incredible, aren't I?"

"I'll let your cockiness slide, but only because it's your birthday."

"I'm sorry," I cup my hand over my ear. "Did you just say you want my cock to slide inside you for my birthday?"

She pushes my chest and shakes her head. "You're incorrigible."

I don't give her a chance to back away from me as I lift her over my shoulder with her ass in the air. "I believe it's time for me to unwrap my presents, Little Red," I tell her as I make my way into our bedroom.

She wiggles around and lets out a shriek as I swat her ass.

"But I haven't even given you all of your presents yet!" she protests as I toss her on the bed.

"You can give them to me later," I suggest, unbuckling my belt. "We don't have much time for me to unwrap you before we've got to get the kids from school. And I haven't had my birthday treat yet," I tell her, pulling my shirt over my head before crawling up the bed to place featherlight kisses up her legs.

"Who am I to deprive you of your birthday treat?"

"Exactly. Now, spread your legs, baby girl."

20

Scarlett

December

"Merry Christmas!" Gunner squeals as he throws open our bedroom door on Christmas morning. Faint light peeks through the shades, meaning it's still early.

"Merry Christmas, Champ," Bennett says, his voice gravely from sleep.

"Merry Christmas," I tell them, my eyes still heavy as I try to blink everything into focus.

Gunner runs up to Bennett's side of the bed and asks, "Do you think Santa came?"

"I sure hope so. But we won't know unless we go downstairs and find out. Why don't you go to the bathroom and wake your sister up so Scar and I can get ready real quick," Bennett suggests.

"Deal!" Gunner shoots out of the room and slams his bathroom door behind him.

"Gosh, I love his excitement on Christmas morning," I murmur through a big yawn as I stretch out my arms and legs.

"It'll be fun to get to experience our first Christmas together with just the four of us. Last night was also fun." Bennett winks as he pulls me to his chest for a good morning kiss that's over far too quickly for my liking.

223

"Last night was fun indeed," I hum in agreement as I think back on what will likely be a core memory for me. We started our Christmas Eve with spending time with his family for brunch, which was full of tension, and I was glad that was pretty swift. We then spent the afternoon baking Christmas cookies at our house, where I invited his mom, Jax, and his sister Walker to join us. Bennett looked relieved that his dad didn't show up, and I can't say I was upset by his absence. Then Gunner and I snuggled up by the fireplace in our jammies while Gemma and Bennett played us Christmas carols on their guitars. I'm a sucker for Bennett's voice—the deep bass does all the *things* to me.

But I don't think that's what Bennett was referring to. If I were a betting woman, I'd say he was referencing what he and I did after the kids went to bed. The two of us stayed up wrapping presents, drinking hot toddies, and filling stockings. That's when I begged Bennett to give me a private concert, which turned me on so badly, I ended up giving him one of his gifts that I couldn't give him when Gemma and Gunner were present.

I'm not sure I'll ever forget the way his eyes widened before they became hooded with lust as he opened the bed restraint kit I got him. My headboard may not have a hidden rail compartment, but it doesn't mean our little night of bondage had to be a one-time thing. I realized I quite like relinquishing full control to him.

Thankfully, after we tested out his present, we tucked the restraints back under the mattress so the kids wouldn't see this morning.

I'm pulled from my memories of last night when Bennett leans over and whispers, "As much as I wish we could stay tangled up in bed together, we should probably get up before we miss them opening their presents." With one last peck, he tosses the blankets off us and I rush to put on a pair of fuzzy socks. I can't help but chuckle at our ridiculous matching pajamas that Gunner insisted the four of us get. I wasn't expecting Bennett to go along with it, but he's been so good with them—better than I could've ever imagined. I've come to accept that that's just who Bennett is—the all-in kind of guy, and being there for Gunner, Gemma, and me is no exception.

By the time I'm back in our bedroom, an excited Gunner is joined by a sleepy Gemma.

"Are you two ready to open presents?" Bennett asks them. They answer by flying down the steps and running into the living room where we set up the Christmas tree.

Gunner does a happy dance followed by a fist pump as he screams, "Yes! Santa came!"

Once they've opened their presents and the living room is littered with scraps of wrapping paper and gift boxes, Bennett's gaze locks with mine from where he's helping Gunner put batteries in his new remote control car. My fiancé winks at me, and I just about melt on the spot. Having Bennett here feels *right*. This is the happiest I've felt on a holiday since our parents passed away.

I'm so caught up in my feelings that I don't notice Bennett has approached me. "We got a Christmas present for you, Little Red, but we'll have to go upstairs in order for you to open it."

I playfully swat at his chest as my cheeks heat. "Why wouldn't you give me my present last night?" I ask him as my eyes widen.

His deep chuckle has my stomach pulling taut. "I promise, this present is G-rated. It's from the three of us," he explains.

"Oh." My cheeks heat deeper from my incorrect assumption.

Bennett turns over his shoulder. "Gunner, Gems, do you guys want to show Scarlett her present now?"

"Yeah!" Gemma smiles at me as she and Gunner move past us up the steps. My brows knit in confusion when the three of them stand outside the door to Gunner's craft room.

"This was all Bennett's idea, but we helped set it up yesterday while you were getting ready," Gemma informs me.

Gunner nods his head. "Yeah, I even held the screwdriver. But Bennett wouldn't let me do the drill by myself," he huffs, which earns him a laugh from me and Bennett.

Gunner swings the door open, and at first glance the room looks the same. That is, until I turn toward the large window and see an oversized, adjustable drawing table and chair.

"Now you have a place to work on your designs," Bennett explains.

I gasp as I take in the sketch pads, pencils, and various art supplies in the drawers beneath the table. "Oh, you guys! I can't believe you did all of this for me." I turn to face them as tears threaten to spill onto my cheeks.

Gunner and Gemma close the distance between us as they wrap me in a big hug. I close my eyes as I absorb this moment and bask in their embrace.

"Come on, Benny." Gunner waves him over.

"Yeah, you're part of this family too," Gemma declares.

I watch with rapt attention as Bennett wraps the three of us in a big hug. This feels all too real, and I'm hit with the sudden realization that Gunner and Gemma will be devastated when the time comes for Bennett and I to part ways after this arrangement expires. The gravity of that has a cloak of melancholy hanging over me.

How will I ever let this go—let him go—now that we've found our way back to each other?

But I don't have long to sulk in my thoughts, because Bennett takes that moment to remind me of another present that needs to be opened when he slides it into the pocket of my pajama pants.

Clearing the emotion from my throat, I give them a smile I know doesn't quite meet my eyes before I say, "Gems, there's one other present we wanted to give you downstairs."

She looks between us, but Bennett just shrugs, feigning ignorance.

When we get downstairs, I tell them to follow me as I make my way out to the attached garage. Bennett must've already opened the garage door, because when we go outside, natural light floods the space, highlighting Gemma's gift.

Her piercing screams of surprise echo off the walls and concrete floor. "Shut up! Are you for real right now?" Gemma asks as she runs over to her brand new SUV. It's a white Lincoln Corsair with black rims and red interior. I was honestly tempted to get it for myself, but it wasn't my sweet sixteen.

"Happy birthday, Gems, and Merry Christmas. I love you," I tell her as she crashes into me for a hug.

"Scar, I can't believe you got me a car! *Ohmygod*! I love you so much. Have I told you you're the best sister ever?"

I shake my head at her and pull her in for another quick hug, before pushing her toward the car so she can check it out. Her elation and joy are contagious, and when I sneak a glance over at Bennett, I find him grinning from ear to ear behind his phone as he records Gemma's reaction.

Regardless of how this arrangement ends, I have a feeling he'd want to continue to play a role in their lives. The thought is both reassuring and unsettling. I just hope my heart can take it.

"What are you doing back there, Benny Boy?" I ask him later that night while we're snuggled up in bed with my back pressed snug to his chest.

"Tracing your freckles."

"You seem to like doing that before bed."

"It calms me. Do you know you have forty-seven freckles on your left shoulder and thirty-six on the bridge of your nose? I count them in the mornings sometimes before you wake up. Is that weird? That's weird, isn't it?"

"No, I don't think so," I answer honestly as butterflies erupt in my stomach.

"Good, because I'm quite obsessed with counting and tracing them."

"Did you ever play the trace and guess game when you were younger?"

"Can't say that I did," he muses. "What is that?"

"So one person traces a pattern on the other person's back and that person has to guess what the person was drawing. Gemma and I used to do categories, so sometimes we'd do numbers or letters or phrases or pictures."

"Sounds fun. Let's play." Bennett's tone is amused and I've come to love these little moments like this when it's just the two of us pillow talking before bed.

"Okay, turn around and I'll go first," I tell him as he unwraps his arms from around my waist and turns over so his back is turned to me. "The first category is letters so you can get an idea of how to play."

With the tip of my pointer finger, I trace the outline of an *E* across his back.

"Well that was easy, *E*," he guesses.

"Yep! You're a natural. Okay, now I'll turn around and you can give it a go."

Turning over to face away from him, I bring the down comforter up to my neck to cover the chill spreading across my skin from the winter air. Bennett likes it arctic cold when he sleeps, so I've added two blankets to our bedding. He says the lower the temp in the house, the more I'll have to use his body heat for warmth.

Bennett begins tracing a letter on my back, starting with his finger just above my ass at the very bottom of my back. He traces his finger clockwise in a circle on my back and it takes me longer than necessary to register the letter he's traced.

"What was that? Was that supposed to be an *O*?"

He scoffs. "What do you mean 'supposed to be'? It was obviously an *O*."

"But you went clockwise. And you started at the bottom. For an *O* you start at the top and go counterclockwise," I argue.

"No, you don't. And who made you the handwriting police? There's not a right way or wrong way to write a damn letter."

"There most certainly is. You're not allowed to do Gunner's handwriting homework with him anymore if you write like that."

His arms wrap around my waist and the deep rumble of his chuckle vibrates against my back. Bennett nuzzles his face into the curve of my neck before placing three delicate kisses over my pulse point. "You're something else, you know that?"

"But you wouldn't have me any other way; you and I both know you love my sass."

"I do," he simply states, giving my hip an assuring squeeze. "Alright, let's see if you can get a phrase since you're so good at this game."

"Bring it on, Cap."

He traces a big letter *I* across my back first and I guess correctly, obviously. Next, he writes a word across my shoulder blades that feels a lot like *L-O-V-E*, and when I guess correctly again, my breathing begins to shutter.

Bennett's fingers pause as he places three more delicate kisses on the back of my shoulder.

He finishes his phrase by tracing a simple *U* across my back. Breath completely escapes me and my throat goes dry with his confession.

Did he mean to do that?

Pulling me against his chest, he rests his chin on my shoulder before he murmurs, "You don't have to say it, Scar, but I do." He takes a deep breath. "I—"

But I don't give him the opportunity to voice his confession aloud. I turn in his arms and capture his lips in a kiss that pulls us both under, stopping our game and this discussion, and instead turning things into a passionate frenzy of lips, tongues, and skin on skin.

I'm not sure why giving myself to him wholly is so daunting. Actually, I do. If I give myself to him physically, and only physically, I can't lose another person I care for—someone I love. Another piece of my fragile heart can't be ripped from my chest. Though, I think Bennett has the capability to do far more than that.

If I allow myself to love him, only for fate to take him from me, I know it'd break not only my heart, but possibly shatter my soul entirely.

21

Scarlett

Snowflakes as big as cotton balls fall down around us as everyone skates around the outdoor rink where the Winter Classic game will be played tomorrow at the Minnesota Thunder's baseball stadium in St. Paul.

The family skate is a tradition they do for each team the day before the game. With this year's Winter Classic falling on New Year's Day, I couldn't think of a better way to spend our New Year's Eve than with our close friends and family.

"Are you ready for this, Scar?" Gunner asks me as Bennett takes off his skate guards and double checks the straps on Gunner's helmet.

"I'm ready," I tell him, aiming my phone at him and pressing record. Gunner steps onto the ice and instead of the unsteady steps he took in the fall, he glides across the ice with practiced strides. My cheers of surprise have him stopping, which has me cheering even louder. "Oh my goodness, when did you learn how to stop?"

Gunner takes off as fast as he can skating back toward me before stopping again. "Bennett teached me!" God, I love this kid so much.

Strong arms wrap around me from behind and I melt into Bennett's embrace as he kisses my temple. "I've been taking him skating with Griff, Cadence, Carson, Leo, and Lainey each week after I do school pick up when you have your late meetings. I'm sorry I didn't tell you, he wanted it to be a surprise."

Tugging his arms tighter around my waist, I reply, "Bennett, you don't need to apologize. This is the best surprise!"

We stay wrapped in each other's arms as we slowly trail behind Gunner. It's only then that I watch Gemma spin on the opposite side of the ice accompanied by Nathan Connelly. The rookie takes her hands in his briefly before grabbing her waist and lifting her in the air over his head. The move looks practiced—rehearsed—which is unsettling.

"That's weird. Each time I asked Gemma if she wanted to skate, she said she wasn't ready to be on the ice yet. But she looks . . . *familiar* with Connelly," Bennett points out.

"Didn't Nathan say that his mom used to teach figure skating classes and that's how he got so good at his edgework in an interview earlier this season?" I ask Bennett.

"Yeah, but he didn't say he was a pairs partner ever. I think I should go warn our rookie not to hurt himself with those dangerous moves right before a big game," Bennett suggests but I stop him before he can go intervene.

"Let's just watch to see what happens. It's not a terrible thing to see Gems skating again. I mean, look at the smile on her face. I've missed seeing that."

When Nathan sets Gemma back down on her skates, they stride in sync, and it's uncanny the way they mirror one another like that. Their movements are halted when Colton and Eva skate up to them.

I remove my prying eyes from them when Kenna skates up to me. "Scar, these jackets are amazing. How did I not know you were a designer?" She makes a show of pointing out her favorite parts of the jacket.

My cheeks heat from Kenna's compliment. "Oh, I'm not."

Kenna chuckles and shakes her head. "I'd beg to differ. The group picture I posted of the players' significant others in our jackets is blowing up with comments of people asking where they can get their hands on them. I've already had wives from three other teams asking if they can have the name of the designer so they can get custom jackets made for their teams."

Bennett unwraps his arms from around my waist. "Scar is being modest. She's most definitely a designer. And a talented one at that." His praise has me turning bashful. "Oh, I forgot to tell you, Red, the guys were asking about the jacket you designed for my birthday. They wanted to know if you'd make them one of their own."

The Classic jackets were something I came up with a few weeks ago when I was designing Bennett's birthday jacket. For the significant other's jackets, I went with a mid-length black puffer style with lime green, oversized zippers and matching patchwork. Each jacket is customized with lime green stitched last names on the lower back to accommodate for longer hair with their players' numbers above the last names. The team logo is on the front left panel of the jacket with Minnesota written down one sleeve and Wolverines down the other.

Griff comes over to us with Rowen in his arms and Cadence skating behind him.

"Where's Gunner?" Cadence asks me, and I point over to where he's now skating with Nathan. Cadence zooms across the ice to join them.

Griffin narrows his eyes at Bennett. "What are you going to do about that?"

"About what?" Bennett questions.

Griff scoffs. "About the fact that Gunner has heart-eyes for my daughter."

Bennett bends over in a fit of laughter. "G, get a grip. They're kids. Cadence is eight, you can't go all overprotective daddy-mode already or you're going to have high blood pressure by the time she's a teenager."

That makes Griff turn to Kenna and pout. "He's not listening to me, Sunshine. I can't handle our Little Ray having a crush already. It's too soon."

"She could have crushes on far worse kids than a good boy like Gunner, baby," Kenna informs Griff, and her use of the term of endearment seems to relax him completely.

"You're always right," Griff tells her.

"Such a simp," Bennett coughs out.

Griff winks at Kenna before wrapping his free arm around her and she swoons as she nuzzles into his side. "Proud member of the simp club for over a decade now. Let me know if you want a membership, Benny."

Carson chooses that moment to skate up to us with Leo and Lainey in tow. "G, what's the first rule of simp club?"

"You don't talk about simp club," Griff and Carson answer in synchrony.

"Exactly," Carson says as he shakes his head. "Anyway, Benny's already a member. Has been since he serenaded Scar at your bachelor party. Speaking of which, when are we having your bachelor party, Benny?"

Bennett shrugs. "I prefer not to make a big spectacle of it. Let's just grab a whiskey together once the season is over or something. We're not getting married until July."

"Yeah, no," Jackson says as he stops beside his brother. "There's no way I'm not throwing you a bachelor bash. As your best man and only brother, I am making it my personal mission to make your grouchy ass let loose and have some fun."

"Well then we better have Scar join us," Carson suggests. "She's the only reason Bennett smiles. I think she cancels out the grump in him."

"If that's what it takes for you to agree to let me throw you a party, Scar is more than welcome to join. I promise, no strippers or anything crazy. But you only get married once, we've got to do this right," Jackson points out and my stomach sinks. He's lying to all of his closest friends and family because of me. I can't stop the guilt from souring my mood.

"What do you say, Little Red? Maybe we could do a joint party and you can serenade me this time," Bennett suggests and I smile at him but he must notice how it doesn't reach my eyes. "We don't need to figure it out right now. We've got plenty of time."

I'm not sure if it's the guilt or something else, but there's a sudden sinking feeling in my gut that I can't seem to shake.

Bennett

Later that evening as we're getting ready for bed, Scarlett and I are brushing our teeth before she starts her elaborate skin care routine.

"Be honest, do you really think you need all of those elixirs in your twenties?"

She screws up her face at me. "Elixirs? I think you mean serums. And to answer your question, yes. If I take care of my skin in my twenties, my thirty and forty-year-old self will thank me. You know, now that you're thirty-one, you should have your own skin care routine that consists of more than just using your body wash in place of a face cleanser."

"I'm pretty sure it's all the same. You've just fallen victim to the beauty industry's marketing," I point out before tugging my shirt over my head and tossing it in the hamper.

"Ugh. How come you doing something as simple as putting your shirt in the hamper is so sexy?"

I waggle my brow at that. "Does my cleanliness turn you on, baby girl?"

"You know, it just might."

Propping my hip against the bathroom counter, I watch in fascination as Scarlett puts a third product on her skin. "Is that the moisturizer?"

"No, that's the last step," she explains.

"How many steps are there exactly?"

"Tonight, only five."

"Only five? As in some nights there are more? Like, how many more are we talking?"

"Some nights if I double cleanse because of a mask and then I still do my regular serums along with my night serum, then"—she pauses to count—"eight. Actually, no, nine."

I nod as if that's not completely ridiculous. She's a marketer's dream, having fallen right into their trap. "Wow. Well, what if I start out small with a cleanser and the moisturizer?"

"That would be a great first step," she replies as she uses a dropper to pour an amber liquid onto her fingers.

"Okay, hand me your cleanser," I tell her, holding my hand out. She squeezes a dime sized amount of product onto my hand and I stare down at it. "What am I supposed to do with that little of product?"

"A little goes a long way. Just wet your other hand and lather it into your skin," she explains.

I do as she says, pretending to face the mirror while stealing glimpses of her beside me at her own mirror. "So," I start but clear my throat. "It sounds like the jackets you designed were a hit. And Dakota mentioned you were already working on a design for when we make playoffs."

I'm not exactly sure where I'm going with this, but I want to let Scarlett know I'll support her in any way I can.

"I love how you say 'when' not 'if,'" she teases.

"Not making the playoffs is not an option," I tell her. "What are you thinking for the jackets?"

"Well, I was thinking of designing a more lightweight jacket since we'll be indoors instead of the puffer jackets for the cold outdoor weather," Scar explains.

"That's a great idea. I know Kenna had said a few wives from other teams messaged her. Would that be something you'd be interested in?"

"Sure, I'd love to design jackets for other teams, but I don't exactly have a lot of spare time on my hands. Not only am I learning how to take over for my grandfather, but I'm also trying to plan a wedding while raising my two siblings."

"I know. You wear so many hats, and yet you somehow manage to make it look easy." I pause to rinse my face. "My offer to help you during the off-season still stands," I remind her.

Scar turns to face me, propping her hip against the counter as I do the same. "It would be great experience for when you retire. You said you're thinking GM or VP, right?"

"Yeah, that'd be the ultimate dream. But it'll take time to work my way to one of those positions within an organization."

She winks at me. "Well, considering your wife will be the owner of the team you've played your entire career for, I'd say you have an in with upper management. And you'd be far more qualified for that role than I would be . . ." Her words trail off as she gets a faraway look in her eyes. "It's perfect," she gasps.

My brows pinch in confusion. "What's perfect?"

"We're already getting married so I can obtain ownership, but then once you retire, you could take over the day-to-day of ownership and I could pursue my passion for design or merchandising." A wide, radiant smile splits her face, and I'm temporarily stunned speechless at the sight.

When I finally manage to find my voice, I point out, "There's only one problem, Red. I don't plan on retiring in the next three years. I'd only be thirty-four, and if I'm able to still play at the level I am now, I would like to play until at least thirty-five."

She waves her hand dismissively at me as she closes the space between us. "So I wait it out another year, that's not a big deal in the scheme of things. It's much better than waiting until Gemma or Gunner would consider taking over ownership—a job I know Gemma has no interest in."

Wait, now I'm even more confused. Scarlett was the one who was so concerned about sticking to the three-year agreement. Now she's considering extending it, what, indefinitely? And not only that, but she's trusting me to take over for her?

I must do a shit job of hiding my confusion and frustration because before I know it, Scar is stepping away from me, slowly backpedaling until she's nearly out of the bathroom.

"Oh my gosh, I'm such an idiot. I didn't—I wasn't thinking. I'm going to go get a glass of water and head to bed." She stumbles back a few more steps. "Good night, Bennett."

"No. Scar, let's talk about this," I start but clamp my mouth shut, flexing my jaw in frustration as she hurries out of the room.

What the fuck was that? I can't seem to keep up with or get a read on Scarlett's stance on us. One minute I think she's falling for me as hard as I'm falling for her, and the next I'm sure she's dead-set on sticking to the originally agreed upon rules of no feelings and a three-year timeline.

22

Bennett

J ANUARY

T he elevator doors open, and just as I'm about to go downstairs in search of her, Scarlett steps out onto the floor of our suite. I got us a hotel room for the night even though the Winter Classic was just in St. Paul because I wanted us to have some alone time.

After the game got over, I was selected for the media panel to discuss our win so I'm arriving to the hotel later than I had planned. Scarlett has been distant since we talked last night after the family and friends skate, and now that we've got uninterrupted time together, I intend to clear the air and finally tell her how I feel.

She's got her head down, so she startles when I ask, "Scar, where have you been? I've been looking for you."

Her eyes widen as she takes me in, and she wobbles slightly in her heels before steadying herself. "I–I've been in the hotel bar. Taking some time to think. I did a lot of thinking." She nods her head exaggeratedly to herself.

My brows knit in confusion. "Okay. And what were you thinking about, Red?"

"Well, you see, I had an interesting conversation this evening with your father."

My breath hitches and my hackles raise. "My father?"

239

"The one and only. God, I really can't stand the guy, but he had important business to discuss so he took it upon himself to find me so we could chit chat after the game." She sways slightly again before quickly regaining her balance.

My fist flexes at my side in frustration. She's talking in circles and I want answers. Now. "And what is it he wanted to talk to you about?"

"He seems to think we're not a good fit. I believe he was distraught at the fact that if you marry me, you'd be, and I quote, 'stuck fathering two bastards.' I hope you don't mind, I threw my drink in his face. But apparently that wasn't enough of a hint for him."

I would be filled with pride at that fact if I wasn't internally freaking the fuck out right now. "What did he do?" I bite out the question, but only because I'm frustrated at the audacity of my father.

"He took the liberty of having his PI look into me. He must be good, too, because he not only found out about the stipulation for ownership, but he also found a way around it."

My stomach sinks as I process her words. "A way around it. What's that supposed to mean?"

She continues rambling on as if she hadn't heard me. "Or, rather, I should say he found out that before my father passed away, he got the majority vote to rule to have that stipulation removed. Though, I'm not sure why my grandfather wasn't made privy to that information. Perhaps he got confused because of his dementia, I'm not sure. But either way, it looks like you're a free man. Besides, your father came up with quite the list of reasons why this marriage was only in my favor. So you should probably listen to him and run before it's too late."

"I'm not running anywhere. You're not making any sense right now, Scar. Look, you've had a bit to drink tonight. Let's go to bed and we can talk in the morning with clear heads."

She laughs but her face is void of any emotion, it's almost as if she's going through the motions without feeling right now. "I'd hardly consider one drink 'a bit,' but I don't need a clear head to know that this marriage was never going to be a mutual convenience. I was the only person who was really benefiting, and now that I don't need to be married in order to take over ownership, there's no reason for you to waste three years of your life."

I try desperately to plead with her. "Scarlett. Look at me. Stop this nonsense. None of that matters to me."

"You're off the hook, Cap. Now, please, just go. I want to be alone."

Her words cut me like daggers to the chest and I find myself staggering backward. She reaches behind me to press the elevator call button, and my stomach sinks with dread.

She's really doing this. She's pushing me away.

When the doors open, she literally pushes my chest and I stumble back into the elevator and watch in shock as she turns her back on me.

I gaze longingly at her retreating form, cataloging the way my chest aches deeper with each step she takes. The final blow comes when she turns one last time, tears streaming down her face, my bleeding heart in her hand, just as the elevator doors shut.

Fuck this.

Scarlett

I'm walking away from him.

What am I doing? Turn around.

When I dare to take a glance back at Bennett, I'm met with his crestfallen face just as the elevator doors close, and every part of me shatters.

What have I done?

Stumbling, my back hits the wall and I slide down until I'm a pathetic mess on the floor. With my head in my hands, my shoulders shake as the sobs wrack my body.

I'm crying so hard that I don't notice the elevator doors have opened until Bennett is crouched down in front of me, his chest heaving and a determined glint in his eyes.

"No," he growls through gritted teeth.

"No?" I question.

"No, fuck that. You don't get to push me away, not now. Not after everything we've been through. And all because of, what, some piece of paper telling us we don't *need* to get married?"

I struggle to get to my feet, and he holds his hand out to steady me as he stands to his full height. "This is all too much, Bennett. You should be ecstatic that you no longer have to play pretend. You can move on with your life and find something real."

"You're wrong. I'm not ecstatic, if anything you're breaking my heart, Scarlett." His confession nearly has me toppling over, sobering my muddled brain that's been whirling since his father talked to me. "Maybe it started out as an obligation—that this is how it had to be between us—but I quickly realized that this is so much more." Bennett presses me up against the wall, caging me in with his one arm over my head while he grasps my waist with his other, grounding the two of us.

"My love for you is a real, tangible thing that I want to grasp and hold onto for dear life. So, no, maybe we are no longer legally forced to get married for you to take ownership, but that doesn't mean I want to be with you any less. For a while now I've seen this, this thing between us for what it could be—for what it *must* be. I want this, Scarlett. I want you, me, Gemma, and Gunner to be a real family. I stopped pretending a long time ago, and if you're honest with yourself, I think you did too. I love you, Scar, and there's nothing fake about the way I feel for you."

"Bennett," I gasp before a choked sob escapes as I process his words. He grasps my face in his hands and I hold on to his wrists for dear life. My eyes move back and forth as I absorb the sincerity of his declaration. He loves me. Even with no obligation, with nothing forcing us together, *he loves me.*

"Fuck, Scar. Stop being so damn scared. Tell me I'm not alone in this. Admit your feelings now that we're free of any obligations. Please, Red." His pleading tone breaks me all over again.

Hearing his declaration has me throwing caution to the wind. Loving Bennett doesn't feel scary anymore because with him I know my heart is safe. And even though I could still lose him, the thought of him never knowing how I feel about him is unfathomable at this point.

"Of course I love you, you big idiot. I've loved you silently for months, even when my tortured heart begged me to not be so reckless—to protect myself from this inevitable heartache," I choke out.

"Then let's quit the silence. Love me out loud, Scar. Because, fuck, I want to love you so loud the entire world knows how I feel about you. My feelings for you have never been fake, Scarlett."

My gaze dips to his lips before I train it back on his eyes, and when I do, I can feel the heat of his intense stare. "Okay. Out loud," I whisper my agreement.

Bennett wastes no time crashing his lips against mine. His kiss is as passionate as it is possessive. He's not just claiming my lips, but my mind, body and soul as well. I am his and he is mine. There's no going back after this for either of us.

Without breaking our kiss, he guides me back to our suite and opens the door. Our lips only part as we hastily tear our clothes off and toss them to the floor.

"Come here, baby girl." His tone is softer than I'm used to hearing him use in the bedroom. It's sobering and I wonder if I'm going to see a different side of Bennett tonight.

He lifts me onto the bed and gently lays me on my back before settling himself between my spread thighs. When his tongue lazily laps at my clit, I moan so loud it echoes off the walls.

"Shhh," he murmurs against my swollen clit and my hips shoot off the bed. "You've got to be quiet, Red, or we'll get a noise complaint."

Struggling to catch my breath, I say, "Let them kick us out. We'll just pick up where we leave off at home."

That earns me a chuckle which vibrates against my overly sensitive core. I curl my fingers through his hair, guiding him to where I want him. His tongue works me into a frenzy, and when he thrusts his tongue into my pussy while rubbing my clit in slow circles with his thumb, I become untethered from this world as my orgasm pulls me under.

Only after he helps me ride out the aftershocks of my orgasm does he line himself up, slowly thrusting his length inside of me. Bennett captures my lips, sliding his tongue along my bottom one before gently tugging it between his teeth. When he bottoms out, he waits for me to adjust, taking his time as he deliciously grinds his hips against mine, brushing my clit in the most mindmelting way. His piercings have never felt more deliciously pleasurable.

When he finally breaks the kiss, he says, "I love you so fucking much, Scarlett."

The feel of his full weight on top of me combined with his declaration and intense eye contact is more than I can take, my heart cracks wide open as his love drowns me.

"I love you too, Bennett."

He suddenly goes still above me. "Fuck, Scar, I got so caught up in the moment that I didn't put on a condom. I'm so sorry, I've never gone without before. I'll go grab one."

Bennett moves to pull out, but I hold his hips in place. "It's okay. I'm fine to go without if you are. I don't want anything between us. You already know I've got an IUD and we've both been tested."

"Are you sure?" he asks, his gaze searching mine for hesitation he won't find.

"I've never been more sure. Now make love to me, Benny," I plead.

His answering thrust has me sliding up the bed and there's nothing but devotion and need reflecting in his eyes. The feeling of his piercing without a barrier between us is unlike anything I've ever felt. I rock my hips to meet his, watching with rapt fascination as he slowly loses control.

Bennett cups my face, tangling the tips of his fingers in my hair as he rests his forehead against mine.

"Scarlett, baby, you feel so fucking good like this."

"So good," I pant. "I'm so close." Bennett picks up his pace, grinding against my clit in the perfect way. "Right there, don't stop!"

He continues his pace, only hitting me deeper and deeper until my stomach tightens as my pussy clenches around his length in a vice grip.

With one final thrust, Bennett shatters with me. Warmth fills me as he spills inside me, heightening my climax even further as I feel his cock throb.

My chest heaves as we come down from the high. When Bennett pulls out of me, he doesn't move at first, instead he places soft kisses along my jawline.

Eventually, he gets off the bed and grabs a towel to clean me up.

I nuzzle against his chest, feeling safe in his warm embrace. A satisfied sigh escapes my lips, and it's not long before sleep takes me.

I wake the next morning to find Bennett staring at me.

"Are you counting my freckles again?" I mumble, my voice laced with sleep.

"Am I that obvious?"

"You are. But it's too early for this. Go back to bed," I groan.

"No, I've been sitting here staring at you waiting for you to wake up."

"What do you need, Benny?" I mutter, peeking at him through one eye.

His serious gaze gives me pause. "Marry me for real."

"Are you ever going to ask me, or will you just demand it," I sass back.

"Fine. If it makes you feel better, I'll ask. Scarlett, will you marry me for real?"

I don't answer him right away, instead pulling him in for a kiss.

"Yes," I whisper against his lips. "I'll marry you for real."

His hazel eyes have me entranced, I'm completely captivated by my future husband. Bennett's smile momentarily lights up his face before his lips crash against mine.

He pushes me onto my back and groans when his cock glides against my drenched core. "Fuck, Scar. I'll never get enough of you."

"Well then I think it's a good thing we're getting married," I muse.

A devastating smile eclipses his face. "You're right, you'll be mine for the rest of our lives."

"And you'll be mine," I remind him.

"Forever." He leans down to kiss the tip of my nose, then my chin, then my jaw, and the column of my neck.

"Damn, forever sounds good falling from your lips."

"Come here and let me show you what else these lips can do for you, baby girl."

23

Scarlett

After Bennett's morning skate and team meeting, I decided to leave the office for the day and get lunch with him since tonight is a game night. We then went straight home hoping to get some alone time before the kids got home from school and completed his pregame routine.

Bennett hangs up our coats in the mudroom before scooping me into his arms, and then takes off in a mad dash for the steps to our bedroom.

"What's gotten into you?" I ask through my fit of laughter.

"I've got plans for you, Red."

"Is that so? Do share," I quip as he kicks the door shut behind him.

Setting me on the edge of our bed, he steps back to pull his shirt over his head just as my phone begins to vibrate in my back pocket. I fish my phone from my jeans and see Gemma's name flashing on my screen, which is weird because she should still be in school.

"Gemma's calling me, hold that thought," I tell Bennett and he freezes with his hands on the waistband of his sweats.

"Hello? Scarlett?" My stomach sinks when I hear a younger man's voice instead of Gemma's, and I'm immediately put on alert.

"Yes, this is Scarlett. Is this Colton? Are you with Gemma?"

"No." There's a clearing of a throat. "This is, uh, Nathan. Nathan Connelly."

"Oh, hi . . . What's going on? Where's Gemma?"

"I'm with her at Maven West Hospital. We—we were skating and she just had a diabetic emergency. The paramedics were calling it ketoacidosis. Her phone was dead and I didn't have your number, and Bennett's went straight to voicemail. I couldn't get a hold of you until they gave me a charger. We just got to the hospital. I'm so sorry—" he cuts off, frantic and clearly choked up.

"We're on our way. Can you please put my phone number in your phone? And then text me what room number she's in?"

"I will, but they won't let me back there with her now. I-I kind of lied when we were in the ambulance. They thought I was her brother and I didn't correct them—I was just too worried about her."

"We should be there in about fifteen minutes. Hang tight," I tell him as I gesture to Bennett to go start the car.

Minutes later, I sprint through the doors of the hospital and get a visitor's pass from security before making my way to the third floor. I don't bother waiting for the elevator, instead I sprint up the steps.

When I get to the third floor, the pediatric intermediate care unit, I find Nathan standing by the nurse's station asking for an update on Gemma that they're unable to give.

"Hi, I'm Gemma Carlisle's guardian, Scarlett Carlisle. She just arrived by ambulance for a diabetic emergency. Do you have any updates? Is she in a room yet?"

"Hello, Miss Carlisle. Yes, Gemma is in room 318. She's stable, but they're still running tests and waiting for her bloodwork to come back."

"Thank you. I'm sorry, I didn't catch your name," I tell her looking for her badge but it's backward.

"Jennie," she replies.

"Thank you, Jennie. Can you please add Nathan Connelly and Bennett Wilson to Gemma's approved visitor list when you get a moment?"

"Of course."

"Um, thanks," Nathan says to her before turning to face me. "Scarlett, I don't need to be on the list. I just wanted to stay with her until one of you got here. I didn't want her to be alone, even if they wouldn't let me in her room."

"I've got some questions for you first. Besides, you'll need a ride back to your vehicle."

Nathan drags his hand across his jaw and blows out a deep breath. "I can get an Uber."

I let out a tired sigh. "Still doesn't answer my questions."

"I'll answer anything I'm able to," he assures me, and sincerity shines in his eyes mixed with a hint of what might be regret.

Bennett comes rushing down the hallway where we're still standing beside the nurse's station.

"Any news? How is she?" It's just then that he notices who I'm talking to. I hadn't told him all the details on the way here, only that I got a call that Gemma was in the hospital.

"Connelly? What are you doing here?" Bennett questions, his brows scrunching in confusion.

"That was going to be my first question. What were the two of you doing, Nathan?" I ask him in a calm voice I'm surprised I'm able to keep, given the circumstances.

"Gems and I skate sometimes. Well, we kind of started out fighting over ice time before we realized we could share if we just kept to our own ends," he explains, and then takes a deep breath. "I'm not even sure what I was doing there today. Typically I don't skate with her on game days. But she seemed a little off when I saw her this morning before she and Eva left for school. She had mentioned she was going to skate after school since they had early release. I guess I just had this gut feeling I should be at the rink, and I'm glad I was because when I got there,

Gemma was already puking into a bucket on the bench and she looked pale as a ghost. She said she left her backpack in her car with her insulin, but her Dexcom was alerting her of a high reading. And it was super high. Like 600s. Her eyes started rolling back in her head and I didn't know what else to do besides call the ambulance. Thankfully we were at the rink and there was someone from the medical staff that came and helped her until the paramedics arrived. She just looked so . . . helpless. God, I'm so sorry, Scarlett."

My brows pinch together. "Why is this the first I'm hearing about her skating again? I mean, I knew she skated at the two family skates, but I had no idea she'd been skating regularly."

Nathan looks between the two of us, looking unsure of himself. "She started renting ice time a few days after the preseason family skate. She would sometimes take a bus there before she got her license. I'd drive her home sometimes when I was at the rink at the same time as her, but she's been skating multiple times a week for months. Do you think that's what made this happen?"

"No, skating is something she's able to do safely when she listens to her body and stays on top of managing her sugars. I don't get it, she'd been doing so good. That's the only reason I felt okay sending her to school," I tell them.

Bennett cuts in, "Why didn't you tell me anything, Connelly? It sounds like this has been going on for months."

"It wasn't my story to tell. And I honestly didn't realize she'd kept it from you," he admits. "I can't tell you how sorry I am, Cap." Nathan looks so remorseful, and it throws me off because this is nothing he should apologize for. If anything I should be thanking him.

"Mr. and Mrs. Carlisle?" A woman with light blonde hair in navy scrubs approaches us.

We look at each other, but neither of us corrects her. "Yes?"

"Hi, I'm Dr. Frederick, I'm the doctor overseeing Gemma's care. I'm working with our endocrinology team as well. Can we talk in here?" she asks, pointing to a small conference room."

"Sure," I respond before turning to Nathan. "Nathan, would you mind sitting in the room with Gemma while Bennett and I talk to the doctor?"

Looking uncomfortable, he nods reluctantly.

Once the door is shut behind us, the three of us take a seat at the small table. Bennett gives my hand a gentle, reassuring squeeze and I welcome his silent gesture of solidarity.

"I spoke with Gemma to try to see what caused her to go into ketoacidosis so quickly. After looking at her blood sugar readings over the past week, there was a very obvious shift a few days ago where Gemma had to adjust by taking more insulin due to higher readings. She stated there had been no dietary changes and that her lifestyle habits and physical activity had been the same as previous months. However, she did tell me about a new medication she is taking."

When I stare back blankly, not registering what she's meaning, I tell her, "I'm not aware of any new medications."

"I figured as much. Gemma gave me permission to discuss this with you, as she is protected by law in Minnesota to not have her medical history disclosed to you without her consent."

"Doesn't that law only pertain to things like mental health, STIs and birth control?" I question.

The doctor nods and my breath hitches. "Yes, which is why Gemma consented for me to inform you that she'd been prescribed and began taking birth control pills for the past two weeks."

"I don't understand," I start, but pause, trying to think of subtle changes to her moods the past few months. Things had started to get better, but now that I think about it, she started getting moodier the past week or so, which could've been due to her sugar levels fluctuating.

I should've known—should've been paying better attention.

"I think it's best if you talk to her. Starting any new medication can impact blood sugar levels, but there is a greater potential for her levels to be impacted from birth control. Typically for my diabetic patients, I recommend a non-hormonal birth control or condoms."

Bennett chokes out a cough beside me and he looks so uncomfortable but also like he might punch a hole through the wall.

"I think maybe we should go in there and you can talk to Gems while Connelly and I have a little chat," Bennett suggests as he chances a glance at me.

"Okay, but don't lose your temper," I warn him.

"No promises," he grunts in response.

When we walk into her hospital room, Nathan is sitting beside Gemma's hospital bed, running his fingers through his hair before placing his stocking cap back on his head. I place my hand across Bennett's chest to halt him from making our presence known, and when he looks at me in confusion I just shake my head. Placing my finger over my mouth, I signal for him to be quiet.

"I don't get it, Gems. Why take the risk if you knew that it could affect your blood sugars?" Nathan asks her in a gruff tone.

She scoffs. "You don't get it. Can you please just drop it? Thank you for saving me. Now, let it go and move on."

"Move on? You were being reckless with your life. And for what? Some high school boy who's trying to get in your pants?"

"I'm not talking to you about my sex life or lack thereof with your brother!" she shouts at him.

Bennett turns to look at me with wide eyes. *Well, that clears up a lot of the confusion, Colton.*

Nathan looks like he's going to be sick and like he's ready to punch a wall of his own at the same time.

Bennett leans in to whisper in my ear, "I knew I didn't like that little fucker the moment I saw him with her."

"There's such a thing as condoms for fuck's sake," Nathan tells her. "And unless you're allergic, they won't kill you."

"It wasn't for sex!" she nearly screams. "How many times do I have to explain myself? As I already told the doctor, I have acne and a few girls at school said it helped them. You don't understand."

"So? I've got acne too, it doesn't make you any less beautiful, Gems."

"Cut the shit and be real for once, Nathan."

"You want real? I'm pissed at you right now. In fact, I'm furious that you were so completely reckless and you drew me into your web of lies. Why didn't you tell anyone about your skating or your decision to go on freaking birth control?"

"It's none. Of. Your. Business."

He lets out a menacing chuckle as he shakes his head. "You're right. You've made that abundantly clear, and yet I can't seem to take the hint." He stands from the chair and grabs his jacket. "I should go."

That's when he notices the two of us standing by the door and his face falls. "I'm heading out. Sorry again, Scarlett. Bennett," he says and nods as he passes by us into the hallway where Bennett starts to follow him, but I grab onto his arm.

"You heard the same thing I did. He was just being a friend to her. Go easy on him. In fact, please thank him for me."

"I will, Red. I've got a favor to ask of him, but then I'll thank him for us." He leans in and kisses my forehead before he says in a hushed voice, "I'm not going to play the game tonight. I want to make sure both you and Gemma are okay and then I'll go pick up Gunner from your grandparents' house."

My eyes widen in shock. "Bennett, you don't need to do that. We'll be fine. You have to play."

"I know you're strong, Scar, but we're a family. And the moment you agreed to marry me, that meant you agreed to have me there to lean on in good times and bad too. Things might not be official yet, but Gemma and Gunner are mine just the same as you are mine." He pulls me in for a hug and when his lips touch my forehead again, my eyes well with unshed tears.

"Okay. I love you, I'll see you in a bit," I tell him before he turns and walks into the hallway.

Clearing my throat, I take the seat Nathan just occupied and grab Gemma's hand in mine.

"Hey, Gems."

Gemma's face falls the moment the greeting leaves my lips, and silent sobs wrack her body.

"So it sounds like it's time for the birds and the bees talk after all. With you being homeschooled, it kind of slipped my mind. But, here we are."

Her lip wobbles and she takes a deep breath. "Can we not? I've taken health class. Which is why I knew to be on the pill before doing anything with anyone."

"So you are being physical with someone?"

"What? No!"

"But, Nathan just said—" I start but she cuts me off.

"Let's just clear that up right now. Nathan Connelly doesn't know anything about me, and he never will. Colton is my friend—one of my best friends."

Right. Glad we got that cleared up.

"Gems, you know you can talk to me, right?"

She looks down at her fidgeting hands. "I didn't think you'd understand," she explains, her head down in defeat. "You've always had impeccable skin. And some of the girls at school have been mean."

"Gems, I had horrible acne when I first got my period. But that was in middle school and you were way too young to remember that. Eventually, my skin cleared up and that happened without me going on birth control. Tell me the truth, are you being bullied?"

"No, the comments just get to me more because I'm already insecure of my skin. As if being as pale as a ghost and having a million freckles wasn't boy-repellent enough, now I've been cursed with acne."

"This is going to sound cliché to you, I know, but one day you're going to find a guy who loves your fair skin, auburn hair, and freckles."

"Just like how Bennett loves you?" she asks, sounding somewhat hopeful.

"Exactly," I tell her as tears fall down my cheeks.

Because he does love me. Wholeheartedly. Despite my flaws and imperfections, my fiancé loves the hell out of me.

24

Bennett

"Scar, baby, we're going to be late!" I call up the stairs. "I've got Gemma and Gunner and the luggage in the car. I'll lock up the front door, come out through the garage."

When I shut the driver door, Gemma leans forward from the back seat. "Does she realize she's going to make us miss our flight?"

I look at her in the rearview mirror. "Gems, you know she gets nervous flying. And this is her first time flying with the two of you. Besides, private jets don't exactly take off without the people paying for the flight." I spin in my seat to watch Gunner. "You ready for a plane ride, Champ?"

"Yep! Gems said I'm gonna get my wings today," he says proudly, and my eyes widen for a second before I realize what he's saying.

"She's right. I'll make sure to request they give you your first time flyer pin when we get on the plane," I assure him.

"Hey, Bennett, do you ever get scared?" Gunner asks me.

"Sure do," I answer him. "Are you nervous for the plane ride?"

"A little bit. What are you scared of?" he presses.

"Snakes. I really really don't like snakes."

"Kinda like how Scar doesn't like clowns?"

"Exactly," I tell him.

Scarlett opens the car door and huffs out a breath which makes her bangs fly up for a second. "I swear, I'm making it my mission to be on time for at least one flight this year."

"Lofty goal," Gemma mumbles not so quietly under her breath.

Leaning over the center counsel, I place a quick kiss on Scar's cheek before taking her hand in mine. "It's only February, so you've got plenty of time to make it happen," I point out, tossing her a quick wink.

"I can't believe you're going to leave me with Grandma and Grandpa while you have your bachelorette party," Gemma complains for about the tenth time this week as I pull out of the driveway.

"We've been over this, Gems. A bachelorette party in Vegas is not a vibe for a sixteen-year-old."

"It's actually very much the vibe, Scar. Besides, Walker isn't twenty-one yet and she gets to go!"

I chuckle before pointing out, "Walker is going as the sober companion."

That makes Scarlett bend over in laughter. "You're hysterical thinking that Walker isn't going to try to drink while she's in Vegas. Her twenty-first birthday is only a week away."

"Scarlett, you've got to look out for my little sister. Especially because there will be a whole city full of the NHL's biggest All-Stars. The last thing I need is Walker having a run in with a player."

"Why would you care if she dated a hockey player?" Gemma asks.

I scoff. "Because none of them are good enough for her. Or you, Gems," I tell her, giving her a stern look in the rearview mirror. She sticks her tongue out at me and I just roll my eyes.

Gemma lifts a brow. "But you're a hockey player, so does that mean you're not good enough for my sister?"

"That's exactly what that means. I'm what's called the reacher and Scar is the settler in this relationship," I explain.

Scar lets out an adorable snort. "You did not just make a *How I Met Your Mother* reference."

"Yeah, I did. Because it's the truth. I outshot my coverage and managed to snag the most stunning woman. And to my surprise, she even fell in love with me." Smirking, I send a wink her way before bringing our joined hands to my lips and placing a kiss on each of her knuckles.

An exaggerated gagging noise comes from the backseat. "You two are disgusting. Also, Colton is a good guy and he's a hockey player," Gemma points out, and it takes everything in me not to curse his name in front of Gunner.

"He's yet to prove himself worthy of you in my eyes, Gems. Besides, he's too old for you, don't you think?" I ask her, and Scar gives me the side eye right as Gemma points out my hypocrisy.

"You're four years older than Scar and Colton isn't even two years older than me. And we're only friends, I was just pointing out that he's a good guy who also happens to play hockey." She sighs and mutters, "But what's the harm in crushing on someone older than you?"

I shift in my seat feeling slightly squeamish and as we stop at a light, I look over at Scar and send her a *help me* look.

Scar turns over her shoulder and tells Gemma, "There's nothing wrong with having a crush on an older boy. I had plenty of crushes on senior and junior boys when I was a freshman or sophomore." I give Scar's hand a light squeeze and she playfully elbows my arm. "Anyways, you've just got to vet them out to see what their intentions are. If you think Colt is a good guy then trust your gut."

I give her another look that I hope says, *What the actual fuck, I thought we didn't like him?*

"Enough boy talk. We can save that for a few years down the road, yeah?" I ask gingerly, hoping like hell we can change the topic. "Are you excited to watch me kick butt in the All-Star skills competition?"

"Which one are you gonna win, Cap?" Gunner asks me, causing me to smile.

"I'm hoping to win the hardest shot competition."

"You're gonna win for sure!"

"Appreciate your vote of confidence, Champ."

Scar and Gemma both let out a squeal when a song comes on the radio so I turn up the volume. The female singer's voice is one I'm familiar with. "Is this—"

"Taevin Gray's new song!" they shout in unison.

"Oh my god, Scar, can you imagine how great this is going to sound when she sings it live?!" Gems asks her.

"I cannot wait!" Scar tells her.

And I drive the rest of the way to the airport with a dumb grin on my face, completely content listening to our little family scream sing the words to a song they have no idea is likely written about my brother. Something to share with them at a later date.

"I just think it's the luckiest coincidence that you, Griffin, and Carson are all playing in the All-Star game," Scar says once we've settled into our hotel suite. Gemma and Gunner are staying in their grandparents' suite for the night because of our bachelor and bachelorette parties.

"We're having the best season we've had in years, but it's still crazy how it worked out," I agree, hanging up my suit and grabbing my toiletries bag from my suitcase to set it in the bathroom.

"And I'm glad Jax joined us even though he could've done anything on his break," she points out, kicking her legs up on the bed and crossing them at her ankles.

"Jax was practically foaming at the mouth when he realized he had the opportunity to throw me a Vegas bachelor party; I'm sure there's nowhere else he'd rather be."

We flew in a day early to have our parties tonight. I don't plan to get too crazy, but I'm thankful that tomorrow is only a media day.

"I'm not sure what the ladies have in store for us, but perhaps our paths will cross tonight." Her eyes sparkle with mischief. "Now, will you be a good boy and shower with me? I'm in desperate need to wash that flight off me."

She doesn't have to ask me twice. I scoop her off the bed and toss her over my shoulder. "How about I do you one better? I'll be your good boy and allow you to come multiple times before we need to head out. Does that sound good, baby girl?"

"*So* fucking good," she giggles as she swats at my back and ass. "Now make me come. Happy wife, happy life and all that."

"Ask and you shall receive, my love."

After we take our time showering and thoroughly washing each other, I leave Scar to get ready in the bathroom while I take a quick call with my agent Jared to finalize the media day schedule for tomorrow.

The call took longer than I anticipated so I've got to hurry and get dressed before we're supposed to meet up with the rest of the group.

Jax is a slut for throwing a themed party, and a bachelor party for his only brother was no exception. Tonight's theme is 007 High Rollers for the guys. He's got all of us guys dressed to the nines for a night of gambling and in return for me placating him, I'll have all the whiskey my heart could desire, according to J.

The ladies stuck with Jax's theme and are calling Scar the Bond Bride. We're supposed to meet everyone in Jax's penthouse suite any minute now. I'm just tying my dress shoes when I look up and see Scar step out of the bathroom.

"Scarlett," I say in amazement. She looks stunning in a strapless white mini dress that's covered in crystals and flares at the waist. And don't even get me started on the way I want to worship at her feet in those white sky-high heels with a sexy satin bow that ties at the back of her ankles.

"You like?" she asks as she does a cute little spin-shimmy combination, causing her skirt to flare just enough for me to get a peek of her cheeky lace panties.

"No, baby girl, I love it. So much so that I don't think I can let you leave this room. I want to strip you out of that dress and keep you all to myself," I rasp, my voice laced with desire. She must like that idea, because she strides toward me and practically melts into me when I wrap my arms around her.

"Later."

"Careful, Scar, I just might have to wife you up looking like that."

She raises a brow at me and bites her plush bottom lip as if she likes the sound of that.

"If you didn't want the big wedding, we'd already be married. But I'll be a patient man if it means you get everything you've dreamed of."

"Just because I dreamed of a big wedding when I was little doesn't mean I need it now. The real dream was marrying someone I love and can't live the rest of my life without. I'm already living out my dream, Benny Boy." She gives me a playful shove. "In fact, I'd marry you right here, right now."

Her words have me spreading my legs and tugging her closer. "You mean you'd elope?"

"You bet your sweet hockey ass I'd elope if it were with you. But only you," she clarifies.

I pull my head back in shock. "Scar, baby, don't fuck with me right now."

"I'm not—I'm being completely serious."

"Where?"

She does that adorable nose-scrunch thing that she does when she's thinking. "The Little White Wedding Chapel is pretty iconic."

"Paris is iconic, and your dream," I remind her, pulling her down into my lap.

"Like I said, you're my dream, Cap. Besides, they have an Eiffel Tower here. It's meant to be."

"But we've already booked everything for July in Paris."

"So we have an intimate wedding here and then celebrate with a big party in Paris. Where's the harm in that?" she asks, and I have to admit she has a point.

"I mean, it's kind of perfect. Both of our siblings are here and your grandparents. Our closest friends."

"We'd just be missing your parents," she points out.

"And they'll be in Paris," I remind her, shrugging because I don't mind one bit that my dad won't be here for this, especially not after how he talked to Scar at the Winter Classic.

"You're sure?" she questions.

I place a kiss on the tip of her nose and tell her, "I've never been more sure."

"You've got to admit, your wife is kind of a genius," she singsongs, standing before grabbing her license from her wallet. "Think I should just need this. Can you please put it in your wallet?"

"Gladly, what else is new?" I smirk as I put her license in my wallet before she takes my hand and leading me out of our suite to the elevators.

"Are you going to tell the group that instead of a bachelor and bachelorette party, they're about to be our witnesses for our elopement?" I ask her as we wait for the elevator.

"We could still spend the night celebrating with them. We'll just be doing it as husband and wife. That way their party planning efforts won't go completely to waste."

As we step into the elevator and I use Jax's spare keycard for the penthouse suite access I admit, "Fuck, Red. I love the sound of that."

"Of what?" she asks as the doors close and I wrap my arms around her waist once more.

Leaning down, my lips brush the shell of her ear as I whisper, "Of you being my wife. I can't wait to have the privilege of calling you mine for the rest of our lives, Little Red."

Scar grabs the lapels of my suit jacket and pulls me closer so our lips are breath away from touching. "I love you, Mr. Wilson," she purrs, and before I can tell her how much I love her right back, she presses her lips on mine and I forget the words, how to talk, fuck, how to breathe.

I know it's cheesy as fuck—because that's what she's turned me into, a sappy motherfucker—but I've hit the mother of all jackpots getting to marry this woman.

25

Scarlett

The elevator doors open in Jax's penthouse suite and as we step out, I'm stunned silent, frozen in place as I take in the space. I swear, Jackson Wilson could have a career in event planning after he retires from hockey.

The view from the suite is amazing, highlighting the lit up Vegas strip. Along one of the interior walls is a backdrop full of black, glittery streamers with big block letters that spell out LICENSE TO WED with balloons surrounding the phrase. Next to the backdrop is a table full of goodie bags that have AGENT 007 tags on them. An actual bar with a bartender is by the other wall with a mini marquee sign that says SHAKEN NOT STIRRED with martini glasses lined up beside it.

Jax comes out of the bedroom in a navy pinstripe suit with no shirt beneath the jacket, shooting us a wide grin when he notices us. "It's about time the guests of honor arrive. Come here, sis, bring it in," he says to me as he encases me in a tight embrace.

"Alright, that's enough," Bennett huffs out beside us, causing me to snort out a laugh.

"Down boy," I tell Bennett and he quirks a brow in response and the challenging look in his eyes is extremely sexy.

"You two," Jax says pointing to the two of us, "are so fucking perfect for each other. You're the kind of couple they write love songs about."

I can't be sure, but I think Bennett mutters, "You'd know a thing or two about that."

Jax must've heard him because he replies with a gruff, "I don't have nearly enough whiskey in me for that topic, B."

Before I can push Bennett for answers as to what the heck that was about, the elevator doors open and out struts a platinum blonde bombshell.

"Scar! Oh my gosh, it's so good to see you again!" Her curly blonde hair bounces with each step she takes toward me.

"Walker! I'm so glad you could make it," I tell her, wrapping her in a hug.

"I wouldn't miss this for the world. Besides, I hear there's a ton of tall and athletically gifted men in town this weekend." She shoots me a wink as she steps out of my arms.

"Absolutely not!" Bennett and Jax shout in unison.

Walker rolls her eyes. "You do realize I'm a grown ass woman and can do whomever I please."

I would say she meant whatever, not whomever, but from what little time we've spent together hanging out or chatting over FaceTime, I know Walker meant what she said.

Jax groans. "Come on, Dubs. Don't give me a heart attack this weekend. It's supposed to be my All-Star break, and having to protect you from assholes doesn't sound like my idea of relaxing."

I find it cute that they nicknamed her Dubs because her name is Walker Wilson. When Bennett told me about her and their childhood, I expected Walker to be a total tomboy, but that couldn't be further from the truth. She has that old money prep style—she wears mini dresses or skirts every time I see her and she's always got a bow in her hair. She calls it the "Hamptons grandmother aesthetic" and it totally works for her.

It's only as the three siblings continue to bicker about the boys being overbearing older brothers that I notice the rest of the group has also arrived.

Kenna rushes up to me and squeezes me into a big hug. Being five foot seven, I've always felt decently tall compared to my friends, but with Kenna being six foot, I feel small. Though, not as small as when I'm beside Bennett.

"Are you ready to celebrate?" Kenna asks.

"So ready," I tell her, though she doesn't know just what we're about to celebrate yet.

Dakota and Alexa both give me hugs next. "I'm so glad you were able to make it!"

"Me too! It helps that I'm covering the All-Star game this weekend and the skills competition," Alexa explains.

Dakota's hug is more of a back pat due to her growing bump being in the way. "How are you feeling after the flight?" I ask her. We all flew out here together and witnessed how sick she was on the plane. I felt so helpless the entire flight.

A soft smile spreads across her face. "Much better, thanks for asking. Carse got the twins settled with his parents while I took a nap so now I feel like a whole new woman."

As we're grabbing drinks, Jax tells Dakota and Kenna he had a special mocktail concocted for them. Bennett drinks his typical whiskey while I decide on a dirty martini. I'm sticking to just one for now so I have my wits about me for what's to come.

Leaning down to whisper in my ear, Bennett asks, "Should we tell them now?"

"Someone's in a hurry to tie me down," I quirk, playfully bumping my shoulder against his.

Bennett hums in my ear. "You have no idea, baby girl." He sets down his drink so he can wrap both of his arms around my waist. Standing behind me, I melt into his embrace.

"Scarlett and I would like to make an announcement." I give his arms a reassuring squeeze and he holds me just a little bit tighter. "We're getting married," Bennett declares.

"No shit, Captain Obvious. That's why we're here celebrating the last of your days as a bachelor," Jax says in an annoyed tone.

"Tonight." That one word leaving Bennett's mouth has everyone stunned silent.

Clearing my throat, I add, "And we'd love it if you would all join us for our ceremony and then celebrate with us after."

Griff just fist pumps and turns to Carse, holding out his hand. "Pay up."

Carse bats Griff's hand away and scoffs. "No way, they haven't actually signed a marriage certificate yet."

"Don't care. You said they wouldn't get married this weekend and what did I say?"

"*When in Vegas*," Carson mocks.

"Oh, come on. Don't be a sore loser, Carsey," Kenna scolds her twin brother. "My hubby won fair and square. Besides, you're taking away from their moment." She turns to face us, brimming with excitement. "I can't tell you how happy I am that you're getting married!"

"We're all so happy for you!" Dakota agrees, raising her mocktail toward us in cheers.

The group sends us a chorus of cheers as we celebrate and partake in a few of the party games Jax had planned.

"Should we go get Gunner and Gemma now?" Bennett leans in to ask me.

Running my fingers over his knuckles, I look up at him through a lust-filled haze and nod in reply. Being around him for hours on end and only getting to look at him in his suit without getting to touch him the way I'd like has been torture.

We tell the group where we're headed and where they should meet us in thirty. As we're making our way out, I see Jax and Walker whispering, and I definitely wouldn't put it past them to have something up their sleeves for later.

My grandmother opens the door to their hotel suite and asks, "Is everything okay? We weren't expecting to see you until morning."

My giddy smile must reassure her, but just in case, I tell her, "All is well. Perfect, actually. Where are Gemma and Gunner? We've got some news to share with you all."

"They're just eating dinner with us. Come on in." My grandmother waves us in and we follow her down the hall to their kitchen and dining room.

"Scar! Benny!" Gunner shouts as he tumbles off his chair and runs straight into Bennett's arms. "What are ya doing? Thought we were having a slumber party here tonight."

"You still are, Champ, but Scar and I have some news to share." As Bennett holds Gunner, I turn to face my grandparents and Gemma.

Clearing my throat, I announce, "Bennett and I have decided we'd like to elope tonight. We would love it if the four of you would join us as witnesses to our ceremony."

My grandmother gasps and claps her hands together. "Oh, Scarlett! That's lovely news. We'd be thrilled!" She stands from the table and wraps me in her arms.

"We're still planning to do a reception in Paris," I tell them. "We just didn't want to wait that long to be married."

"That sounds lovely, Firefly," my grandfather says, and hearing his approval nearly brings me to tears. I hadn't thought of it until just now, but I realize a huge benefit of us getting married is that he'll be in the right frame of mind. Who knows how much his dementia will steal from us by the time July comes around. He wraps me in his arms and I bask in his embrace, sending a silent prayer that he'll be able to join us in July.

"Love you, Pop Pop," I say through the emotion squeezing my throat.

He pulls back and takes my hands in his. "Love you more, Firefly. Now let's get you married."

Gemma comes barreling over to me and Bennett and wraps us in a group hug with Gunner still in Bennett's arms. "Family hugs for the win," Gemma says and my heart swells.

I pull Gemma in for a hug just the two of us and ask, "Will you be my maid of honor, Gems?"

She rolls her eyes at me. "As if I'd ever let you ask anyone else. Of course!"

While the four of them get changed, we tell them to meet us at the chapel so we have time to make a quick stop at a jewelry store down the strip.

"This place has to make a killing," Bennett murmurs as we walk into the jewelry store only a block away from the chapel.

"I'm sure it does. We're most definitely not the first to make a last minute decision to get married here and be in dire need of rings."

"So, what are your thoughts on me having two rings? One for everyday use and then a silicone one for when I'm on the ice?" Bennett asks me as we sit with a salesperson.

"I love that," I tell him as we browse through their selection of tungsten and then silicone rings for him. He decides on a charcoal tungsten ring and a black silicone one. I, on the other hand, have no clue what my wedding band should look like.

"How about this one?" Bennett asks, holding up a gold band with intricate marquise and round-cut diamonds in a half eternity band. "It kind of looks like a tiara a princess would wear but for your finger," he says as he holds it up for me to try on, which has me giggling at his description.

I slide it onto my finger, noting how it fits perfectly, and admire it next to my elongated cushion-cut engagement ring. "They look like they were made for each other," I admit.

"You're tossing me a beach ball with that one, aren't you?"

I wrinkle my brow in confusion. "What do you mean?"

"Come on, you can't say that and expect me not to say 'kinda like us.'"

"God, have you always been this cheesy?"

"Never in my life." He shakes his head in spite of himself.

"You're right—you're the perpetual grump turned down bad simp."

"Should I put that in my vows?" he muses.

My eyes widen at that. "I don't know, are we writing our own vows?"

"We can. Or if you'd prefer, we can save our written vows for Paris," he suggests.

"I think we save them for Paris. That way I have more time to come up with them."

"We'll take these three rings, please," Bennett tells the sales person. "I'm shocked that we were able to find bands that fit us both."

"It was meant to be, my love," I tell him before pulling him in for a kiss.

He cups my chin and his hazel eyes are intense as he searches mine. "Are you sure about this? Tonight? We can wait if you're not sure."

I nod and give him my most assuring smile. "Positive. I've never been more sure."

"No second thoughts or cold feet?"

That earns him a giggle. "Toasty warm feet and a clear mind." I pause, now internally freaking out. "Why, do you?" I question.

He smiles back at me with an effortless confidence. "I've never been more sure either. Let's do this."

"Shall we make this official then, Mr. Wilson?" I ask him, taking his hand in mine as we leave the store. Bennett's holding a shopping bag with our wedding bands in tow, and things are now beginning to feel real as we walk hand in hand down the strip to the chapel.

My soon-to-be husband brings my hand to his lips and peppers kisses along each of my knuckles. "I can hardly wait to make you Mrs. Wilson."

26

Bennett

February

"Like you said, technically we got married by the Eiffel Tower," I tell Scar as we walk by the Eiffel Tower Experience.

Scarlett chuckles at that because it's not wrong.

"I promise, we'll have the big wedding. This summer, just like you've always wanted."

Scar stops in her tracks and spins to face me, pushing my shoulders so I'm pressed against a brick wall. "And I promise that this is everything and more I could've dreamed of, Benny Boy. Now stop worrying and celebrate with your wife."

Wrapping my arms around her waist, I spread my legs apart and pull her in closer. "Fuck, Red. I think we should celebrate alone first."

Scar presses herself impossibly close to my body, surely feeling the proof of my arousal. Lowering her voice, she whispers, "You've got the rest of your life to go caveman over calling me your wife. For now, let's celebrate with our friends and family."

And celebrate we do. I'm pretty sure—no, I'm absolutely positive—I've never danced this much in my life. But you won't find me voicing any complaints with the way my wife grinds her ass against me in her tiny dress as we dance at whatever club Jax has us at.

273

Walker took Gemma under her wing for the night until Gemma decided it was time to turn in. Dakota and Carson walked her back to her grandparents' suite before they turned in for the night too.

"Who is that talking to Walker over there?" Scarlett asks McKenna once we've gone to the bar for some water. But before I can see who she's asking about, Jax pulls me aside rather aggressively for my liking.

"How come you didn't tell me Calvetti was going to be here?" Jax asks, his voice laced in frustration.

"I didn't think I'd have to considering he's one of the All-Star goalies for the weekend," I answer in an annoyed tone.

Jax scoffs before taking a pull of his beer. "But you do recall my history with that clown, right?"

I fight the urge to roll my eyes. "Honestly, J, not really. I mean he was the goalie for your college hockey team. You only played with him for a year before he signed with LA. I still don't really understand what made you hate him so much in one season."

"The fucker messed up my one chance at getting her back."

I sigh in understanding. "It always comes back to her."

"And it always will. How would you feel if you lost Scarlett? If she walked away from you to move on to bigger and better things without you?"

"I'd be devastated."

"Yeah, well I was—*am*. I'm sick and tired of people discounting my feelings for her just because we were teenagers at the time. Sometimes it doesn't matter how old you are, when you know you know. And I fucking *knew* beyond a shadow of a doubt, that Taevin Gray was the fucking one for me."

"I know that, Jackson. Believe me. I know. But I still don't understand how that has anything to do with Enzo Calvetti being here."

"Because she came back for me in Cambridge. And he fucked me over. And now I'm forced to live with the what ifs and what could've beens," Jax shouts in defeat.

Not sure what I can possibly say to make him feel better, I offer to take a shot with him, knowing it will not only distract him, but it will also give me the perfect excuse to make an escape after this with my bride.

Once we've got our shots of tequila—Jax's choice—we clink our shot glasses together and tip them back. I wince at the taste, having never been a fan of tequila, no matter what kind.

After giving Jax a smack on the shoulder, I tell him I need to go find my wife and whisk her away. To which Jax waggles his eyebrows and I think he's all but forgotten about Calvetti . . . for now, at least.

I make my way through the throngs of people crowding the dance floor and stop dead in my tracks to take her in.

My wife.

Scarlett has her head thrown back with her hands in the air as she shakes her hips side to side, making the short skirt of her dress whirl around her in a way that can only be described as ethereal. I'm not sure if there's an actual spotlight on her, or if I've just summoned one in my mind, but she looks angelic right now. Simply too good for this world. Too good for my grumpy ass. But she's mine now, and I think it's about time I take her back to our room so I can worship my wife.

With her arms still in the air, I wrap my arm snuggly around her waist from behind and use the other to grasp her chin, turning her head toward me.

"I've somehow managed to convince the most gorgeous woman in the world to marry me tonight, and now I'd like to show her my—what was it you called it?—caveman tendencies."

Bringing her one arm down around the back of my neck and her other around my arm on her waist, she tugs my neck closer to her. "Trying to claim me, Mr. Wilson?"

"Mark you. Claim you. I just fucking want you, Scar. Can we please go, baby girl?"

"Only because you asked so nicely like a good husband," she sasses, and I intend to fuck the snark right out of her.

I'm at a complete loss for words at the sight of my bride tugging me by my tie out of the elevator toward our hotel suite. When we're outside our door, Scar grabs the lapels of my suit jacket and pulls me closer. Her heated gaze stokes the flames that were mere embers moments ago. As she traces her hands down my chest to my abdomen, my skin erupts in goosebumps and a fire blazes to life inside me.

"Tell me, Mr. Wilson, have you ever fantasized about tying your wife up on your wedding day and fucking her until her voice goes hoarse?" Her eyes are so filled with lust that if I wasn't already rock hard, the look on her face alone would get me there.

Scarlett Carlisle was a hellish siren. But Mrs. Scarlett Wilson is a scorching inferno devouring me with her formidable flames.

Bending down, I sweep her into my arms bridal-style before tapping my keycard against the lock. When I step across the threshold, my chest swells with pride as this moment with my wife sinks in. "We've got the rest of our lives for me to tie you up. Tonight I want your hands all over me as I make love to you until the sun comes up."

I place her on her feet in front of our bed and turn her around, sweeping her hair over her shoulder so I can take off the dress that has tested and tempted me since she first walked out in it. Drawing her zipper down at a glacial pace, I intend to rile her up like she did to me this entire night.

"Bennett," she groans in frustration and I chuckle at her impatience.

"What's the matter, baby girl?" I ask as I bring her zipper down to the base of her spine. When I let go the fabric falls to her feet, leaving her in nothing but her cheeky, lace panties and her white-bowed heels.

"Ditch the panties if you don't want me to rip them but leave the heels on," I command, loving the way her jaw falls open and her eyes flare with lust.

My attention is solely hers as she strips the white fabric and tosses it at me. I catch them and tuck them in my pocket.

"On your knees, Scar," I rasp and have to bite back my grunt of approval when she immediately does as I request.

"Look at you," I say, awestruck at the sight of her naked body kneeling before me. My fascination is only amplified when she begins to rock her hips, effectively fucking the air in desperation for my touch.

Unbuckling my belt, I maintain eye contact with her as I strip out of my suit and shed my boxers. My cock twitches with need, begging me to sink inside her.

"Crawl to me, Mrs. Wilson," I command as I grip my cock and roughly stroke it from the base to the tip, spreading the precum leaking out over my piercings.

When Scar obeys, crawling to me in nothing but her bowed heels, the sight has me nearly falling to my knees before her. And when she's at my feet, looking up at me through her long lashes, I feel my balls draw up in anticipation.

Scarlett lifts to her knees and wraps her hand around the base of my cock. The first pass of her tongue over the head has me rocking my hips forward. And when she takes me to the back of her throat, I tangle my hands in her hair to steady myself, holding her in place for just a moment until I hear her gag and then I pull out of her mouth.

"You've teased me for far too long today. I need to be inside of you now," I tell her, lifting her to her feet before taking her in my arms and setting her on the bed.

I kneel on the bed and work my way between her spread thighs. Steadying myself above her, I take a moment to simply admire her beauty.

"You're magnificent. I honestly can't believe you're mine."

Burying my head in her neck, I deeply inhale and groan when her sweet scent floods my system. Flipping onto my back, I pull her up so she's straddling me. Lust and need consume me—I can't see anything but red as Scar's hair falls over me like a curtain of fire.

"Goddamn," I groan as she grips the base of my cock and sinks down over my piercings. Her breath hitches as she adjusts. "Fuck, Red. You're soaked for me. Are you going to be a good little wife and come on your husband's cock?"

Instead of answering, she just nods her head and moans as she slightly rocks her hips. My breath comes out in heavy pants, and she's so wet I can feel her arousal dripping down my thighs.

"I need to move," I grunt out. After a single nod from her, I cup the back of her neck with one hand and grasp her hip firmly in the other before ruthlessly bucking up into her.

"Y-yes," she pants through bated breaths. "You feel so good."

I simply grunt in response as I continue to work her up and down.

"You're such a good. Fucking. Wife. And you're so exquisitely *mine*." I punctuate each word with a thrust of my hips, and with each slam of her hips against mine, I feel another inch of my control slipping through my fingers. Instead of spiraling, the feeling is freeing as I relinquish myself completely to my beautiful bride.

It's as if she can't get enough, each thrust a brutal claim that has her screaming out for more.

"I'm yours, Scarlett. Only yours. For the rest of my life," I rasp, breathlessly.

"Only mine," she gasps as I plunge deeply into her over and over again, swiveling my hips each time I do. "Yes! *Bennett*," she moans.

"Oh, fuck! Baby, I'm gonna—" I choke for air as our orgasms hit us simultaneously. "Fuuuck," I groan into her neck as her pussy pulses around me and I fill my wife to the point I think it'll never stop. And I hope it never will—these feelings swirling in my chest, this fire burning between us.

I'm going to spend every waking moment for the rest of my life showing my wife how much she means to me.

27

Scarlett

My husband has found himself in the sin bin.

I'm not even sure how he found himself dropping gloves with the other team's goalie, no less, but he did. Even though he's a massive defenseman, Bennett isn't typically the enforcer on the ice. He's more of a skilled, offensive defenseman. So this is honestly the first fight I've seen him get in . . . and I'm not mad about it.

I'm also not mad about the seats that we've got for the game happening to be next to his team's penalty box. My seat is literally right next to it with only a pane of plexiglass separating the two of us.

Especially because once he takes a seat in the penalty box, he throws down his helmet and gloves that came off during the fight, and picks up a water bottle. What does he do with said water bottle? Well, he squirts his entire face, neck, and chest with it before wetting his hair and slicking it back. When he throws his head back once more to squirt water in his mouth, I can't help but squirm a little bit in my seat as I watch in fascination at the way his throat works and his Adam's apple bobs when he swallows.

Fuck, that is stupid hot.

And what's even hotter is that when he notices I'm sitting right beside him and catches me eye-fucking him, he sends me the most salacious wink, and holy hell I think I could spontaneously orgasm right here on the spot.

Somehow, in my lust-filled haze, I notice something different about him. Something I hadn't noticed until just this moment. He's holding the water bottle with his left hand and instead of the silicone ring we purchased three nights ago, there is now what looks like a black band tattooed on his ring finger with a clear adhesive bandage around it.

Tapping on the glass, I point to my own ring finger before pointing to his and mouthing to him, "What the hell is that?"

His face curls up with a panty-melting smirk and he mouths back, "A tattoo. You like that?"

My eyes widen in realization that he got his very first tattoo, a man who is secretly scared of needles, and I only know this because he went with me to donate blood last month and passed out just from the finger poke they do at the beginning to check your hemoglobin levels.

Bennett scoots closer to me and mouths, "We're forever, baby girl."

My heart rate picks up speed and I can't wait for the game to be over so I can ask him all about his decision to permanently mark his skin. And so I can show him just how much I love it.

Bennett

My phone buzzes in my pocket for the third consecutive time, and I decide I've delayed this conversation enough. Swiping to accept the call, I don't sugarcoat my greeting. "Why are you calling me?"

"Why? Because you haven't answered me for a damn month, that's why."

"That's because I have nothing to say to you."

"It doesn't matter. I've got things to discuss with you. Don't get smart with me, boy."

"I'm not a boy. I'm a man. And after this phone call ends, I will not be speaking to you again unless you learn from your mistakes and change."

"What the hell is that supposed to mean?"

"How dare you speak to my wife behind my back, attempting to scare her away."

"I think I heard you wrong. Your *what?*" he shouts through the other end of the line so loudly it echoes off the cinderblock walls of the hallway. Huh, I guess my mom didn't share our good news with him. I'm happy to hear that.

"You heard me just fine. I said *my wife.* You will never speak to her again without me there, do you hear me? You won't look her way unless I give you permission. Matter of fact, don't even think about my wife. From this day forward, for now and forever, Scarlett, Gemma, and Gunner are my family. If you ever want to consider yourself a part of that, you better figure it the fuck out. Until then, only mom, J, and Walker are invited to our wedding in Paris. I sincerely hope you can pull your head out of your ass before you lose all three of your kids."

I hang up the phone without waiting for his response. Part of me wishes I were in person for that conversation, but the better part of me knows I wouldn't have been able to hold back my frustration and grievances with my father. Fuck him for not only talking to Scarlett, but thinking he has a say in anything that goes on in my life. He controlled the game for far too long, and I refuse to let him hold the power any longer.

I'm pulled from my spiraling thoughts and my stomach swoops in anticipation when I hear the clicking of heels coming down the hallway.

"Are you ready for this, Benny Boy?" Scarlett asks when she reaches me. I take my time with my response because I'm honestly at a loss for words. My wife is a fucking bombshell every day of the week, but today, she's dressed to kill. Her outfit is all black—black leather pencil skirt, black blouse, black strappy heels. But what really steals my breath away are the two pieces of jewelry adorning her left ring finger.

I grab her hands in mine and rub said finger with my thumb. "Ready as I'll ever be, Red."

"Aw, you've got to liven up a bit, Cap. I've been dying to kick your ass when we play this game together."

Narrowing my eyes at her, I point out, "I thought this was just a fun little social media sketch they were filming. Why do you look so excited?"

When she doesn't answer, I go to tug on her wrist, but Morgan from the social media team joins us in the hallway and says she's ready for us.

She leads us down the players' hallway just in front of the lockerroom where she has two chairs set up for us with a table and a phone on a tripod.

Once we've assured her we're ready to go, she clears her throat before giving us a nod that she's begun filming.

"Good morning Wolverine fans! I'm here with newlyweds Bennett Wilson and Scarlett Carlisle—" Morgan starts, but Scarlett interrupts her.

"It's Mrs. Wilson now," she informs her before taking my hand in hers and sending a sultry wink my way.

Fuck me. I'm not sure how long it will take for my possessiveness to wear off, but I love hearing her correct someone when they call her by her maiden name. It's not even the fact that she has my last name, hell I've considered taking hers a number of times, it's just the fact that the two of us sharing a last name tells the rest of the world that she's *mine*. Forever.

"My apologies and congratulations," Morgan says. "I'm joined by Mr. and Mrs. Wilson this morning to play the newlywed game. I'll be asking them a series of questions in which they'll each write the answer on their mini white boards before revealing their answers at the same time. Are you two ready?"

"Yep!" Scarlett exclaims, rubbing her hands together in anticipation before grabbing the white board from her lap. She's got a competitive glint in her eyes that's sexy as hell.

I'm obsessed with every little thing my wife does.

"Okay, question number one: Who is the better cook?"

I write out Scarlett's name on my white board and am shocked to see she's written my name on hers. "Come on, Red, that's not true. You're a helluva cook."

"Thank you, but I can't work a grill to save my life and you can do it all, so I think that makes you the better all around cook in our household," she admits.

"Aw, that's sweet. Ready for question number two?" We both nod in response. "Alright. Who is the better driver?"

I'm not surprised when she and I both agree that I am the better driver. Because I am. Without question. Like, it's not even close.

"Who is more romantic?"

We both turn our boards to reveal my name, and Scarlett's cheeks heat a bit. "He's got the whole random acts of kindness and thoughtful gestures thing down pat."

"Nah, you just like when I serenade you before bed," I tease, causing her cheeks to heat further.

"Who is Scarlett's celebrity crush?"

It better be me. Though I'm not really a celebrity. She turns her board and has my name written on it but I've just written me with a question mark beside it. "Nice!" I say before giving her a high five.

"Who said 'I love you' first?" Easy enough since it was me.

The questions continue to rattle off until they get more specific.

"What is Bennett's pet name for you?"

"Oh, that's kind of a hard one since you've got a few you use," Scar mumbles.

"Not a nickname, but a pet name. You know like sugar or sweetheart," Morgan clarifies.

Oh, this is going to make Scar's cheeks heat like never before.

We turn our boards and her pet name I use for her is revealed. Baby girl.

"What is Bennett's favorite activity that the two of you do together?"

Scarlett's eyes widen in panic as she clears her throat and looks over at me. "I-I um . . . next question?"

Oh, fuck. This is too good.

My brow quirks at her in surprise. "What's the matter, baby girl? You don't want them to know that my favorite thing the two of us do together is our pregame—" Scarlett cuts me off when she shoots out of her chair and holds her hand over my mouth. My chuckle is muffled by her hand and after giving me a stern look, she pulls her hand away but I snatch it to place a kiss on the delicate inside of her wrist.

At that, Morgan shows us mercy and says that's a wrap on our video for the day. I take Scarlett's hand in mine and lead her down the hallway to the elevator and press the up button.

"That was fun. What'd you think?" she asks me as we wait.

"I thought it was fun too. Though it made me eager for us to partake in my favorite activity. It is a game day afterall, Red." I pull her in close and place a quick peck on her forehead.

"Oh you think you're so slick, don't you? I'm not sure I should take you up to my office."

"That's fine, you don't have to. We could always take a detour to the locker room or the penalty box," I suggest, rubbing my hands up and down her back.

"You're dangerous," she tells me before stepping out of my hold and pulling me into the awaiting elevator. As the doors close, I press her against the wall and reach beside me to press the elevator stop button.

"Benny, what are you doing?" she asks, a bit breathless, perhaps a bit scared as well.

"Getting creative," I tell her as I lower myself to kneel before her. "I've got a pregame ritual to perform and a new wife to worship. Are you up for a little reminiscing of our first night together, baby girl?"

She's panting as she gazes down at me. "I don't recall you getting on your knees for me in the elevator that night."

"No, I suppose I didn't. But I've fantasized about doing this countless times," I admit shamelessly.

"Who am I to stand in the way of your fantasies?" Scarlett helps guide her pencil skirt up her hips to reveal a lacy pair of panties.

"Such a good fucking wife, making all of my devious dreams come true." I run my nose over her soaked panties before placing whisper-light kisses over her slit. Moving her panties to the side with one hand, I drag my middle finger through her drenched core before plunging it deep inside her tight pussy. Licking my lips, I inhale deeply before flattening my tongue and marveling at my first taste of her. "Fuuuck, baby girl. You still taste like me from this morning. Was your pretty pussy leaking my cum during our interview?"

A moan escapes her lips before she bites down on her bottom one and whimpers softly.

"Mmm," I hum in approval before making another pass up to her clit and lightly biting it. Placing her knees over my shoulders, I glance up at her with her back against the wall, her fingers curled in my hair, and demand, "Now be a good wife and come for me, Mrs. Wilson."

28

Scarlett

Five Months Later…

There is a slight breeze blowing into the suite where we're getting ready through the balcony doors, causing the sheer curtains to flutter in a way that relaxes me. I tighten my silk robe and take a sip of my coffee before running my fingers over the envelope Gemma just handed me.

The dusty blue envelope matches our custom stationary and color palette for our wedding today, and I get caught admiring the way my name looks in Bennett's chicken scratch handwriting.

Butterflies erupt in my belly as I open it to find a letter he wrote to me. We agreed to write each other letters to open on the morning of our wedding, and it's something I've been looking forward to most.

To my blushing bride (because I know you're blushing right now),

I know we're going all-out traditional with everything today, but I just had to let you know that last night was the worst night of sleep I've had in months because you weren't by my side.

Even though we're already technically married, I'm happy that we're doing the big, traditional celebration today with our friends and families present. I can't wait to have the entire world know that you are mine and I am yours.

Your grandfather gave me another sage piece of advice a few months back for our wedding day, and I thought I'd share it with you now since he unfortunately couldn't be here with us today. I can't tell you how sorry I am that things took a turn with his health so quickly; I just hope that when we get back, he'll enjoy the videos and photographs we share with him.

Joseph's advice to me was something I hadn't heard before. He suggested we take a moment to ourselves during the reception, just the two of us, to soak in the moments and gravity of this day. I think a part of him knew his health was declining, so he took me aside and told me this after our elopement. He said that his favorite moment from his wedding day with your grandmother was when they took a walk outside their reception hall together after their first dances were done, and they talked about their favorite moments from the day thus far.

So what do you say, Scar; will you take a walk with me as the sun begins to set behind the Eiffel Tower and tell me all of your favorite details from our wedding day?

I'll be seeing you soon, baby girl.

All my love,

Benny Boy

I set the letter on the table, and choke back a sob threatening to escape. My emotions have been all over the place since we had to make the tough decision to have my grandfather receive round the clock care as his dementia rapidly progressed.

Gemma is beside me in a flash with a tissue, rubbing my shoulders in a soothing way.

"I love you, Scar. I'm so happy that you found Bennett. And I know that Pop Pop is so proud of you and happy for you too."

"Thank you, Gems. I'm thankful I found him too. And I love you more."

"I'm serious, Scarlett. Ever since he came into our lives, you've been lighter. It's like he took one look at the weight of the world you carried on your shoulders and decided right then and there to help take on the load. Look, I know the two of you started out as some agreement—I overheard the two of you talking about it a month or so after he proposed. But I can tell the love the two of you share now is more real than any love story I've ever seen." Gemma's pale green eyes shine with sincerity.

I take a deep, stuttered breath, still consumed by the emotions brought on from his letter, but I'm also shocked to find out she knew about our agreement for months now and hadn't said anything.

"There isn't a more perfect man to have brought into mine and Gunner's lives. You did an amazing job raising us on your own for so long, and I'm just so incredibly grateful that you now have a partner to stand by your side, to lean on when you need to, and to love you unconditionally through the good times and bad." Gemma wraps me in a tight hug I hadn't realized I needed so badly.

Squeezing her tight, I rub my hands up and down her back. "When did you get so wise beyond your years, Gemmy?"

With the loss of our parents and her diagnosis, she had to grow up a lot quicker than most kids, and my heart aches at the realization.

"Not sure, but someone must be doing one heck of a job raising me," she says, winking as she pulls out of my embrace. "Here," she says, handing me another tissue, "you'll ruin your makeup."

"I think it's a little late for that. But I'm sure Walker can touch it up for me. She's a magician when it comes to hair and makeup."

We walk into the other room to find McKenna, Dakota, and Alexa have joined us and are taking their turns having Walker help them get ready.

"Alright ladies, do we understand our assignments for today?" I turn and ask them once Gemma has left the suite to give Bennett his letter from me.

"Are you sure you want to do this? Poor fella isn't going to know what hit him," Dakota drawls in her southern accent.

"Positive. And make sure you get video evidence of his reaction since I won't be there to see it," I tell them.

McKenna chuckles at his expense. "Poor fella is right. I can't wait to watch him drown in his misery. Happy wedding day, Benny Boy!"

My hands aren't shaking like I thought they would as I hold my beautiful bouquet with both hands. Even though I wish my grandfather was here at this moment to walk me down this aisle, I'll be forever grateful that we were able to share that moment together when he walked me down the aisle in Vegas.

As I wait for my queue, I can faintly hear Gemma's voice and the strum of her guitar through the wooden doors. I'm not sure I've ever been more surprised than I was when Gemma asked if she could sing a song while I walked down the aisle. And for her to be playing the guitar that Bennett has taught her how to play on makes me all the more emotional even thinking about it.

Gemma chose to sing "Crazier" by Taylor Swift and as the chorus hits, the doors open to the rooftop terrace where we're getting married.

All the air escapes my lungs as I take in Bennett standing at the end of the aisle in a black tux. He looks so devastatingly handsome waiting for me beneath an acrylic arbor with white flowers climbing up the sides and the Eiffel Tower behind him in the background.

Not even a moment later I hear a matching gasp as Bennett sucks in a shaky breath. He brings his fist up to his mouth, and the sight of him bending at the waist because he's so overcome with emotions is enough to bring me to my knees.

When his head lifts and his gaze connects with mine once again, I'm left breathless. The way he's looking at me now—with such reverence and devotion—makes me wish I could run down this aisle to him. But I don't because I'd likely trip over myself in my haste to get to him. Besides, my knees are now shaky and knocking together as I place one unsteady foot in front of the other to get to him.

I'm not sure how many guests are in attendance, or what the floral arrangements along the aisle look like because I'm too enraptured—too overcome with emotions—at the sight of my husband standing at the end of the aisle, wiping stray tears from his cheeks as he waits for me.

Who would've thought that my big, burly husband would've become such a sap in only a few months time? I tease him about it quite often. He says it's just "dusty" and therefore his eyes water, but it's been happening more and more since we got married in February.

I've just made it to the end of the aisle, the beaming smile on my face matching his own, when Bennett extends his arm out to help me up the two steps of the stone altar.

Handing my bouquet off to Gemma once she takes her place beside me, I turn to face Bennett, holding both of my hands out for him to take in his. Instead, he surprises me by pulling me into his chest and catching my lips in a slow, fiery kiss that leaves me even more breathless.

There's a loud "whoop!" from I'm pretty sure Jackson and laughter follows from the guests.

Griffin, who is officiating our wedding, gasps beside us. "*You're supposed to wait until I tell you to kiss the bride,*" Griffin mocks in a voice that sounds eerily similar to Bennett's. "See, now he gets it. It's hard to wait, isn't it?"

A giggle slips past my lips when he breaks our kiss to subtly flip off Griff.

Griff lets out a huff before welcoming our guests. "Dearly beloved, we are gathered here today for the *second* ceremony of matrimony to join together Bennett and Scarlett. The couple wants to thank you for making the trip to be a part of their big day."

Griffin continues his opening remarks, but the words sound like background noise to me as I hone in all of my focus on Bennett's features. We didn't have a first look, so this is the first time I'm able to take him in since the groom's dinner last night. He looks so strikingly handsome in his black tux with his black bowtie. His facial hair is neatly trimmed and his hair is perfectly styled with the relaxed texture that has me itching to run my hands through it.

He's taking me in just as intently, his eyes rove over me like a caress, causing goosebumps to pepper my skin.

I'm pulled from our mutual perusal when my grandmother joins us on the altar to do a reading my grandfather helped us pick out for the ceremony before his health declined, when he had more lucid days.

Bennett patiently wipes my tears as they fall down my cheeks, only letting go of my hand so we can each pull my grandmother in for a hug once she's finished the reading.

We each take our turns repeating the declaration of intent that we wrote together with the help of Dakota so it sounded more polished. Now comes the part I've been most nervous for. The exchange of our vows.

Griffin has Bennett go first, so when he unclasps one of my hands to reach into his jacket pocket for his vows, I hold onto his other hand with both of mine, loving the way his big hand eclipses mine.

Benny clears his throat. "Scarlett, we may already be husband and wife, but that doesn't mean I'm not nervous as hell standing before you and our closest friends and family to declare and vow my undying love to you. But that's exactly what I'm going to do. Because I love you, and I want the rest of the world to know that too. I love you more than I ever thought it was possible to love another. And I promise to continue loving you every day for the rest of our lives. I'll cherish you, and us, and this family we're building until my last breath, and in every life hereafter.

"You are the very best part of me. Calling you my better half doesn't even scratch the surface of the role you play in my life. You knocked me on my ass seven years ago, and when you came back into my life a year ago, I decided right then and there, I was never letting you go again." He shifts on his feet and takes a deep breath. "And now here we are. Don't ever say I'm not determined."

I cut in. "And stubborn. Don't forget that."

Unable to help himself, Bennett pulls me in again for a quick kiss. "And stubborn. But not too stubborn to know that a happy wife leads to a happy life." He takes my hands in his again and smiles down at me.

"But declaring my love to you isn't enough right now. So before our friends and family, I want to secure my hopes and dreams for our future in these vows. Scar, I vow to not only love, honor, respect, and cherish you, but also to serenade you every night before falling asleep with you in my arms. I vow to always take care of you, Gemma, Gunner, and any additions we make to our little unit. I vow to always carry the weight with you when life's challenges come our way. You will never need to stand alone. I vow to fill up your water cup when you forget before bed." That earns him some chuckles from the guests. "I vow to also fill up your gas tank when it's running on empty and your tires when they're running low on air." He looks away from the vow booklet he's holding and winks at me. "Matter of fact, I vow to fill up whatever needs filling."

Bennett squeezes my hand in his and continues, "From this day forward, your happiness is my happiness, your sorrows are my sorrows, and your aspirations are my aspirations. My heart beats for yours until the end of time. I love you, Little Red."

At this point, as tears steadily stream down my cheeks, I'm cursing myself for not having gone first because I'm not sure how the heck to follow that.

Bennett

July

My gaze hasn't strayed from my beautiful bride since she walked down the aisle to me in her stunning dress several minutes ago.

Scarlett's dress falls off her shoulders and clings to her chest and torso before falling into a long satin train at her waist. My favorite detail is the thigh-high slit that allowed her leg to peek out as she walked, showcasing the light blue heels with a satin bow she's wearing.

And now, as I've just recited my vows to her and reach in my pocket for the tissues I've stored there, I can't help but feel like the luckiest man in the world to call this enigmatic woman mine for the rest of our lives.

Scarlett blushes before saying, "I'm not sure why I decided to go second."

That earns her a chuckle from me and the guests. Taking a deep breath, she begins, "Bennett James, my god you look dashing." I squeeze her hands in mine and resist pulling her in for another kiss as she continues. "I can't begin to put into words what you mean to me. Before you came into my life, I was struggling to find purpose outside of being a young, single guardian to my two younger siblings. Never did I think I'd find someone as amazing as you. Thank you for showing me what unyielding love and devotion look like. There are too many times to count when you've simply shown up for me, Gunner, and Gemma without anyone asking you to. You've gone above and beyond what I had hoped for in a life partner."

She pauses as her chin begins to wobble and her eyes glass over with unshed tears. "I love you so much, baby girl," I whisper to her.

"I love you too," she mouths and takes a deep, settling breath. "My vows to you may seem ordinary, but I'd argue that nothing between us has been ordinary from the day we met. So as simple as they may be, I vow to love, honor, cherish, and respect you. Vowing my undying love to you for the rest of our lives is as simple as breathing air. Vowing to honor our marriage above anything else is as easy as putting one foot in front of the other. Vowing to cherish you is a privilege I don't feel worthy of. Vowing to respect you until my last breath gives me the same amount of joy as picking out my new favorite pair of shoes."

She bites down on her quivering lip. "I'll never be able to thank you enough for stepping into our lives and filling pieces of our puzzle I didn't even realize were missing. I love your patience, your kindness, your thoughtfulness, and even the way you're grumpy around anyone else but me, Gunner, and Gemma. I love the way you manage to bring me back down to earth and calm the storms you may not even realize are brewing beneath the surface. You are my stabilizing force that keeps me pointed in the right direction. Your arms are my safe place and your heart is my home. Today we celebrate with our friends and family the start to our eternity. I will love you until the end of time, Benny Boy."

I blow out a deep breath to try to fight back the sob that wants to escape before Griffin says it's time to exchange rings. I turn toward where Jax is standing with his hands on Gunner's shoulders as my two best men.

"Alright, it's your time to shine," Jax says to Gunner.

"Here you go, Benny. Love you so big!" Gunner exclaims as he places the rings in my palm.

"You did perfect, Champ. Love you even bigger," I tell him as I kneel down and wrap him in a hug.

After we exchange rings, Griffin grabs the mic and stands off to the side. "I now pronounce you husband and wife . . . once again. You may now kiss the bride . . . again."

I don't hesitate a moment as I cup Scarlett's face with one hand and grasp her waist with the other. The moment our lips crash against each other, I silence her sweet moan as I bend her back into a dip. When we break the kiss, I take her hand in mine and bring it to my lips.

"Bennett and Scarlett want to thank you all for joining them to celebrate this most joyous day. It is my absolute pleasure to present to you, for the first time, Mr. and Mrs. Carlisle," Griffin announces, taking the guests by surprise. There are looks of confusion and shock, but all I can do is smile down at my wife's blissed-out expression. Damn right I decided to change my last name so my wife and I could have the same last name as Gemma and Gunner.

We just told them last month that we've been approved to adopt them and we're planning on making things official when we get back home after our honeymoon. But first thing's first, we wanted to all share the same last name, and I would never ask them to make that change for me. I was more than happy to do that and can't wait to wear CARLISLE on my back next season.

Holding up our joined hands, we start to make our way back between the rows of family and friends here to celebrate us, but I'm unable to resist the urge to kiss her again. So midway back up the aisle, I pull her in and dip her across my body for a kiss that feels like it displays every emotion I'm feeling right now.

Euphoric happiness swells my chest and clogs my throat as I walk hand in hand with my bride.

Our first dance is announced as we make our way onto the dance floor. With Scarlett's hand in mine, the opening chords of our first dance song "Feels Like Home" play. But instead of Chantal Kreviazuk's voice playing over the speakers, there is an all too familiar voice singing the opening lines as she sits at the piano on stage.

"Bennett, what did you do?" Scarlett asks incredulously, eyes wide as she takes in the singer.

Smiling to myself, I rasp, "I had a surprise up my sleeve. It turns out you and Gemma made quite the impression with Taevin Gray at her concert, and her cousin just so happens to be a buddy of mine."

"What? Since when?" she squeaks, and I don't think I'm imagining Gemma's gasp and excited squeal over the sound of the music.

"Since he and I were neighbors in our condo building for a few years. Anyways, I called him and cashed in on a favor he owed me," I explain as if it's no big deal, when I know the possible repercussions my scheming may cause a major fallout for my little brother.

"Does Taevin know you? She looks like she's seen a ghost," she says, nodding over my shoulder as I spin us around to get a glimpse of Taevin's face that has gone a ghastly shade of white as realization and recognition sinks in.

"She may or may not have dated Jackson in high school. They were each other's first loves." I shrug, feigning indifference, but Scarlett stares back at me, jaw open as if what I just admitted was a total bombshell, which I guess to her it kind of is.

"You've been keeping secrets?" she asks, sounding bewildered by this new development.

I'm so entranced in this moment with my wife, that I hardly register Jackson making his way across the room toward the side of the stage. "I'll explain later, Red. For now, let me put those dance lessons my sister gave us to good use." I put some space between Scarlett and I before spinning her back into my arms.

As Taevin sings the last lines of the song, I dip my bride and watch as her copper curls nearly touch the floor before slowly lifting her head to brush her lips against mine. The kiss is short and sweet, yet it evokes every feeling inside my chest.

"Are you ready to take that walk together, Scar?" I whisper the question against her lips as she crashes her lips back against mine.

Moments later, Scarlett playfully drags me out of the venue and across the street, my hand in hers, as she smiles back at me with nothing but sheer bliss. Her smile hits me straight in the chest, and I've never seen a more beautiful sight than the look of the setting sun illuminating her silhouette. The golden glow of the fading sun causes her hair to look like a fiery blaze.

"So, what was your favorite part?" Scarlett asks me as we settle onto a bench beneath the Eiffel Tower.

"Well, a few of my favorite parts were what led to this pocketful of polaroid pictures of my bride dressed in very sexy lingerie posed in positions I'd love to have her in later this evening," I admit with nonchalance, though I nearly keeled over from lust and need for my wife each time one of the bridesmaids brought me another polaroid.

"Is that so? Who gave those to you?" she questions in a sugary sweet voice.

"McKenna, Alexa, and Dakota came around almost every hour, on the hour to hand them to me. You wouldn't know who put them up to that, would you?"

She mock-gasps and feigns innocence. My Little Red is such a little liar.

"Well, whoever it was that put them up to it, I should thank them. And I'd also like to thank you for the gift you gave me with your letter earlier. I especially liked the engraving on the whiskey glass. What was it again? I believe you promised to always be by my side. Or on top of me. Or under me. Or on your knees in front of me. Apparently, wherever I need you to be," I tease her as I pull her against my chest and cradle her head in my hands.

"All teasing aside, can you believe today? It was perfect," I tell her as I stare down into her whiskey-flecked eyes that never fail to captivate me.

"It's been everything and more than I could've ever dreamed growing up. And you're the main reason why. Thank you for giving this to me. I'm not referring to the wedding in Paris, I mean this life we've started together. You've shown me that while it may be a risk to open my heart and love someone, it is more lonely and heartbreaking to close myself off and never have loved at all. You are my best friend, Bennett, and I can't wait to live out our dreams together for the rest of our lives." Scarlett's words sink in and sear my soul like a hot brand I'll proudly wear forever.

"What was your favorite part of the day today, my beautiful bride?" I ask her as I pull her closer to me.

A wide smile eclipses her face. "Besides seeing you at the end of the aisle, probably that as I walked down I saw Gunner standing beside you and heard Gemma's voice guiding me to you."

At the mention of that, a wide smile of my own mirrors hers. "She did so amazing and her rendition was so beautiful. Did you know she came up with that all on her own?"

Scar shakes her head. "I didn't. She's amazing. They both are. I can't believe we get to officially adopt them when we get back."

My chest expands just thinking about it. "I know. The only thing that would've made today better would've been to be able to celebrate them officially being ours. But that momentous occasion deserves a celebration all on its own."

Nodding her head in agreement, Scar nudges her shoulder against my chest. "That, and perhaps if we would've had the Stanley Cup table instead of the cake table like you originally wanted."

Throwing my head back, I let out an exaggerated sigh. "Ah, yes. But you know what, we made it to the third round which is the farthest our team has ever made it in franchise history. Next year we've got a few more pieces to move around and then the cup is ours. I can feel it."

Scarlett hums in agreement and turns to look at me. "Well study up this season, Cap. Your apprenticeship starts next summer."

"I can't wait. That just means I'm one step closer to watching you live out your dreams, Red."

"I've told you this before, but in case you forgot I'll tell you again. This life we're building together is my dream. I love you," she tells me.

"I love you too. We went from temporary to eternal in less than a year's time. Where do we go from here, my love?" I ask her as I tuck a stray strand of hair behind her ear, rubbing the freckles on the lobe of her ear as I do.

Scarlett hums in contentment, her gaze locked with mine. "I don't know, but I've got a sneaking suspicion that we've yet to even scratch the surface."

I know she's right. Each day feels exciting and new with Scarlett. I'm hopeful for our future and for the life we'll continue to build beside each other.

"I love you forever and always, Little Red." My voice is thick with emotion as I think of what our future has in store for us.

"Watch yourself, Benny Boy, I just might hold you to that." Scarlett winks at me and a dazzling smile lights up her face.

I thank my lucky stars that I met this woman seven years ago. Call it fate, call it divine intervention, I'm just glad to call her mine for the rest of my life.

Epilogue

JACKSON - JULY

The opening chords of "Feels Like Home" by Chantal Kreviazuk play, which is the first dance song Bennett told me he and Scarlett had picked out, but what I wasn't anticipating was the voice that begins singing the lyrics.

I'm standing at the bar with my back to the stage, but I don't need to look to know who is singing right now.

No, not as her melodic tone floods my system and wraps around me like a warm embrace—a voice I'd know anywhere, anytime, because it's the voice that haunts me in my dreams.

Chills unwillingly work their way down my spine as the beautiful tone sinks into my very being.

But this can't be right. I must be imagining things as I've often done over the past decade. *She* can't be here. Not in Paris. Not at my big brother's wedding. She'd never do that.

She wouldn't, would she?

Turning around as if in slow motion, I'm shocked to find her on stage beneath one of the spotlights playing the piano and singing with her eyes closed, lost in the lyrics that are currently cutting me with each line she sings.

I black out everything happening around me, my sole focus tunneled in on the woman with raven hair that spirals down her back, nearly touching the piano bench she's sitting on.

This isn't right. This can't be happening. Not after all this time. Not here like this.

And then reality smacks me in the face like an uppercut to the jaw, causing my world to come to a standstill. She opens her eyes and turns her head to the side to smile at the happy couple dancing on the dance floor only for her face to go ghostly white as she takes in the groom, or rather, as she realizes *who* the groom is.

Without missing a beat, she turns her focus on the ivory keys beneath her fingers as she sings the last lines of the song.

Rushing past everyone, shoving a wide-eyed Griffin and Carson out of my way, I cross the dance floor, hardly comprehending the fact that my brother is dipping his bride as the song comes to a close.

The singer stands abruptly and tries to rush off stage but I'm there before either of us can realize what's happening.

My chest is heaving as I try to grapple the waves of emotions crashing into me.

What the actual fuck is *she* doing *here?* This has to be some sick joke, or maybe a revenge plot by Bennett for all of the crazy shit I've put him through over the years. But if it is, my brother's gone too far this time.

I look into her deep brown eyes that once looked at me with reverence as if I was her sole salvation. Those same mahogany eyes that stared back at me full of tears as the only girl I've ever loved broke me—broke *us*—without a moment's pause so she could pursue her dreams. Without me.

Taevin Gray left me and became a household name—a country star so bright that she now sells out stadiums in order to fit the large crowds of her adoring fans.

And even standing here before her a decade later, I can't help but fight the feelings resurfacing. My pathetic heart is at war with my head, screaming for me to walk away just like she did.

Like she tried to do once more just now.

Run. I should run. I need to run.

But I don't have more than a moment to attempt an escape because not even seconds after our gazes lock, Taevin pales further and her eyes roll to the back of her head.

"Tae!" I shout as I move to catch her before her head hits the ground. Her limp weight feels like nothing in my arms, causing a sharp chill of fear to run down my spine.

I search the faces surrounding us, begging for someone to help. One of the wedding guests calls out that she is a doctor and comes rushing up to us, ordering me to set her down and move back so she can examine her.

Shoving people aside, a man who claims he came with her as her date kneels down beside her. I make my way over to the guy who looks oddly familiar, though I can't place him.

"What's the matter with her? What'd she take?" I ask, pulling him up by the lapels of his suit jacket.

He looks taken aback by my accusing tone. "Take? What are you talking about? She doesn't use." He pauses to scoff, somehow looking down his nose at me though he's several inches shorter than me. "She's not an addict. You of all people should know how the media can twist a story to fit their narrative. And you've played right into their hands." He shakes his head at me. "Such a disappointment, Jackson."

My eyes narrow at him in confusion and anger. "Who the hell are you and how do you know who I am?"

"I'm Kyle Blackwood, Tae's manager and one of her closest *friends.*" I don't miss the emphasis he puts on their label as friends, but it doesn't mean I have to like the guy.

There is commotion behind us as the Paris paramedics arrive and begin transferring Taevin onto a stretcher.

Pushing my way past those surrounding her, I shout, "Step aside so I can get in the ambulance with her."

"No, I'll go," Kyle has the nerve to tell me.

"Over my dead fucking body," I growl out in a lethal tone that says I'm not fucking around.

He lets out a deep sigh. "Just stop making a scene, Jackson. I can't let you go, she'd never forgive me."

I get in his face to show him how serious I am. "I said step aside."

He crosses his arms, looking as if he'll refuse to let me by him. "I can't. And *you* can't."

"The fuck if I can't. Step aside and let me be with my wife!"

"Your what?" Kyle's eyes nearly bulge out of his head, and it'd be funny if I wasn't ready to kill the fucker standing in my way. Guess he isn't as close with Taevin as he thought.

Murmurs echo behind me at my declaration, and I hear my younger sister, Walker's voice ring out above the rest.

"Jax, did you just refer to Tae as your wife?" she asks incredulously.

Fuck. This is not how I wanted this to go.

But I don't have time to waste worrying about anything other than getting to Taevin right now.

"Move or I swear to god I'll hurt everyone standing in my way," I bite out in a chilling tone.

Bodies move out of my way, and I make it out of the back of the reception venue to where the paramedics are loading Taevin into the back of the ambulance. Taking my phone out of my pocket, I use a translating app to inform them I'm her husband.

Next thing I know, I'm sitting in the back of an ambulance, holding on to her limp hand, and praying, for the first time in over a decade, that she is okay as we race through the streets in a foreign country.

"Please be okay, Thorn," I beg aloud while silently pleading.

Come back to me, baby. Stay so you can cut me all over again.

Extended Epilogue

Scarlett – Two Years Later

"Are you sure she should even be here?" Gemma asks Bennett as they set down bins on the kitchenette counter.

I huff out a breath, annoyed that they're talking about me as if I'm not in the same room as them. "*She* is right here, thank you very much. And *she* feels just fine and wouldn't miss her baby sister moving into college for anything in the world."

Gemma and Bennett share a frightened look before glancing back at me. "Good! I didn't mean to upset you, Scar. I'm so glad you're here to share this moment with me, I just wasn't sure if you should be walking up all these flights of stairs while you're twenty-eight weeks pregnant in the middle of an August heat wave."

"Now that I'm up here in your room, we'll let the guys do the heavy lifting and I'll help you unpack and set up your room." I fan my face which is drenched in sweat while taking in her two-bedroom suite with a living room and kitchenette. "You're so lucky. I didn't get a suite my freshman year, I had to share a shoe box sized room with my roommate who was a complete stranger. We got along just fine, but I'm so happy you're rooming with Eva."

Gemma gives me a genuine smile. "Yeah, me too. And Eva said Colt will be here in a few minutes so he can help Bennett unload the rest of the bins."

"Oh, I didn't realize Colton went to Abbott U," Bennett cuts in.

"That's because he hasn't for the last two years. He just transferred this year after playing the last two seasons in Boston at Emery."

I bite my lip, but the timing seems uncanny considering Colton was one of Emery's leading scorers for their hockey team last season.

"What made him transfer?" Bennett asks before I can.

"The coach for Abbott recruited him heavily, and with his sister committing here and Nathan playing for Minnesota, it was kind of a no-brainer for him," Gemma explains.

I shoot a look at Bennett that I hope says *oh, how lovely*.

"That's great," I tell her.

"Is it?" Bennett asks, which has me shooting him another look that says *poker face, dammit!*

I've told him countless times that the more we show our distaste for Colton, the more she'll naturally run right into his arms.

Bennett clears his throat. "Right. That's quite the coincidence, Gems. But I'm sure you'll be so busy with your studies and meeting other freshmen, that you'll hardly have time for Colton. Besides, AU has a huge campus."

"It's actually the craziest of coincidences. Because he's a transfer, Colt is living in our same dorm since they're co-ed. And he and I are both even in the same philosophy course together."

"You're shitting me," Bennett mutters.

"Afraid not, big guy!" Colt says as he comes up behind Bennett and pats him on the shoulder. I fight back a fit of laughter when Bennett gruffly shrugs him off.

Completely undeterred, Colt moves toward me and rubs my belly like he has a death wish as my husband moves to swat his hand away.

"Don't touch my wife," Bennett growls and Colt shoots his hands up in surrender.

"I was just checking in. How's the baby watch going?" Colt asks me.

"Checking in on what?" Gemma asks him, humor lacing her tone.

"On my fave little mama and our new babe. When do you guys find out what you're having?"

"We already know. Everyone else will find out when *our* baby decides to make an appearance. Now, please don't ever reference my wife as your favorite little mama again. And it's *my* baby. Well, ours. Scarlett and I are the ones who made the baby."

"Thanks for the health lesson, Cap. Not sure we've gone over baby making much in anatomy and physiology yet."

Bennett shoots me a pleading look. "For fuck's sake, Red, I think I'm gonna kill him."

"Murder trials are long and if you miss the birth of our first born I'll wind up in prison for killing you. Now, play nice." I turn to face Colt. "Don't touch an overheated pregnant woman without her consent or you might lose a hand you're fond of. Colt, be a dear and help Bennett grab the rest of Gemma's things from the car."

Bennett pulls me in and places a chaste kiss on my forehead. "God, I love you, baby girl," he whispers for only me to hear.

"Love you too, Daddy," I whisper back and a low grunt rumbles through his chest. I shoo them out of the suite so I can have a quick chat with my sister.

"Gemma, can you shoot me straight?"

"Always." She hesitates, "Well, I lied. That color of sundress does make you look a bit washed out, but I figured that's because you've been so careful with your sun exposure during your pregnancy. And there probably isn't too much that fits you right now. So I lied. I'm sorry."

I bring my hand to my forehead, feigning annoyance. "Not what I was referring to, but good to know. I meant about Colton. Are you two . . ."

When she continues to stare back at me blankly, I decide to just come out with it.

"Are you two sexually active?"

A loud thud followed by the sound of a box dropping on the plank floors is all I hear before an "Oh fuck!"

Slowly turning around, I find a wide-eyed Nathan Connelly staring back at me. He shifts his weight side to side sheepishly, likely from secondhand embarrassment.

"Sorry, ma'am," Connelly says.

"Ma'am?" I question. "Nathan, you ma'am your elders, not someone who is only old enough to be your big sister."

"Sorry, Scar. And sorry, Gems. I'll just put this in Eva's room," he says and scurries into the room on the left.

"So?"

"Scar! You can't just ask me that. And like I've told you a million times now, Colton and I are *just friends*. He's like an older brother to me," Gemma whisper-hisses.

"Okay. And if that were to change—if feelings were to develop—you'd tell me right? I just want you to be safe after everything that's happened. Just because you're at college now doesn't mean I'll worry any less."

"You've got my Dexcom notifications, along with about a half dozen other people. Eva gets them too, so I'm good."

"I get them too, Scar. And I'm actually taking a few hybrid classes this fall part-time, so if Gemma ever needs anything or a ride back home to visit, I can help," Nathan cuts in when he comes back out from Eva's room.

"That's so kind of you, Nathan," I say just as Gemma says, "That's completely unnecessary. And since when do you get my Dexcom notifications?"

"I've gotten them for the last two years. Bennett gave them to me the night of your hospitalization when I found you at the rink." Nathan shrugs as if it's no big deal, but looking over at Gemma and the figurative steam blowing from her ears, I'm going to guess that's anything but the case.

"You what?!" She's seething mad, and Nathan is clearly wiser than his brother because he has the wherewithal to step back. "Are you trying to tell me that for the past two years you've been, what—*monitoring* me? I'm not your problem, Nathaniel Connelly."

"It's just Nathan, and you know that. And I wasn't monitoring you, I was keeping an eye out for my little sister's best friend. Who just so happens to be the sister of my team's owner. Who also happens to be one of the most stubborn people alive."

"Can you just cut the shit, Nathan? Why didn't you tell me? Oh my god—" she cuts off and gasps. "No. It wasn't why you . . . Tell me you didn't . . ." Gemma stutters to a stop.

Nathan puts his hands out in front of him and steps toward Gemma as if he's approaching a wild animal. "Don't go there right now. Just forget we ever had this conversation, Ruby. I'll see myself out, and I'll keep my distance. Promise me that whatever story you're spinning in that pretty head of yours stops right now."

Okay, my level of confusion is off the charts right now, and I know it's not solely due to pregnancy brain. Did he just call her Ruby?

"How can I not? Did you seriously—" before she can finish her sentence Nathan spins on his heels and marches out of the dorm suite.

"What the hell just happened? What am I missing here, Gems?"

She shakes her head to herself and clears her throat. "Just forget about it, Scar. I know I'm going to." On that note, she storms into her new bedroom and slams the door shut behind her.

Seriously, teenagers!

Looking down at my growing bump, I mindlessly rub my belly and say, "Promise to go easy on your mama, okay? As you can see, I've already been through the thick of it with these teenage years."

Strong arms wrap around my waist and long fingers intertwine with mine. "You should put your feet up, Mama. I've got a few more loads to bring up and then I'll grab us some lunch. What are you craving?"

I bask in Bennett's strong embrace and breathe a contented sigh of relief. "Our little one is craving Chinese again."

"Oh I could fuck with some chicken fried rice right now," Colton declares from the doorway.

Bennett's answering growl of annoyance vibrates against my back. "Fuck. Off. Colton," he tells him and I can't help the giggles that slip free.

After Benny convinces me we should let Gemma have some time to herself to get settled, we say our goodbyes and I'm not surprised when I cry the entire way home. My hormones have made me highly emotional, which doesn't bode well for moving my little sister into college.

"Let's get you upstairs, Red," Bennett suggests after he cleans up our Chinese food littering the kitchen island. "I'll rub your feet and you can take a nap while I bring Gunner with me to the store. Do you have anything you want me to grab while we're there?"

"Could you add more kiwi to the shopping list?" I ask, practically drooling just thinking about how good a kiwi parfait sounds right about now.

"Anything for my girls," he says as he wraps his arms around me and rubs my belly.

A few minutes later when I'm set up in bed, Bennett begins to rub my feet and calves, fretting over me because he thinks I overworked myself this morning. "Can you believe we're going to have a baby girl in only a few months?" I marvel, mindlessly rubbing my belly.

"I always had a feeling we'd have a girl first," he surprises me by admitting.

"You're already so great with Gemma, I know our little one hit the jackpot with the best girl dad in the world."

"Thanks, Red. I hope she looks just like her mama and acts like her too. Speaking of her impending arrival, we should probably settle on a name. Or at least narrow down the list."

"What do you think of Everett? I kind of like the idea of our kids' names ending in 'ett' like ours," I suggest, holding my breath to see what he'll say.

"I love it, and it goes perfectly with the middle name we decided on after your grandfather," he points out.

"Everett Josephine," I hum, completely content at this moment.

"Our little Ever girl is going to turn my world upside down just like her mama," he sighs and I can't help but fall a little more in love with him right here and now.

The way he's looking at me has warmth spreading over my body like a warm embrace. Bennett's love and devotion to not only me, but this family we've built together is something that still leaves me speechless. My love for him grows with each day, and I'm eagerly awaiting for the day when he'll hold our baby girl in his arms for the first time. He said he hopes she looks like me, but I've been envisioning a baby girl with a head of chestnut hair and hazel eyes and a grin just like her daddy's. Either way, she'll be the most loved little girl in all of existence.

Also by Grayce Rian

Also by Grayce Rian
The Off Ice Series
What It Was
(Griffin & McKenna's story)
What It Should Be
(Carson & Dakota's story)
What It Must Be
(Bennett & Scarlett's story)
What It Could Be
(Jackson & Taevin's story)

Acknowledgements

First and foremost—thank you, my dear readers. As an indie author, my dreams wouldn't be a reality without your support!

To my forever best friend: thank you for loving me each and every day. Your unyielding support means the world to me.

To our three children: you have changed me in inexplicable ways, all for the better. I will never be able to express how much and how fiercely I love the three of you.

To my parents and two big sisters: I love you all immensely. Thank you for allowing me space to grow, for your unwavering support, and fostering my creativity growing up!

I have to thank my amazing in-laws. One of the biggest bonuses to marrying my husband was gaining the large, loud, and loving family I married into. Thank you so much for your support and love!

I want to give the biggest thanks to my incredible editor Ciara, aka my most compatible musical bestie. I can't wait to work together on so many projects to come!

To my book designer, Kateryna: wow, your creativity amazes me! You were such a joy to work with and your enthusiasm for this project had me so much more excited. I cannot wait to work on the rest of the covers in this series together!

Samantha: Becoming friends with you has been one of the best surprises on this indie journey. Thank you for being a critique partner and for all of our plot brainstorming sessions!

Hannah: You're the best friend I never saw coming! Thank you for being an alpha reader, for sharing your creativity, for your spreadsheet skills, and all your words of wisdom. I cannot wait to hug you again hopefully so soon!

Ginsa: Stop it right now! I cannot wait for what we have in store together. I want to shout it from the rooftops! ILY so big!

Brit: Holy moly! I am so glad to have met you through Hannah. Thank you not only for the amazing content you've created for my socials, but also for the friendship and late night chats! I feel like we could talk for hours on end without running out of things to say!

To my betas: I couldn't have shaped this book into what it was without your input and feedback! Brittany, Chelsea, Morgan, Rose, Sariah, and Sam.

To Sam, Ginsa and Jess: Thank you for being my safe place and the best author support system. You're each so talented and I love that I get to cheer you on as we share in this journey!

About the Author

Grayce Rian is a contemporary romance author living in Wisconsin. *What It Must Be* is the third standalone novel in the Off Ice series.

Grayce's stories perfectly combine spice, angst, and sweetness to make readers swoon. When she's not writing about your new, favorite book boyfriend, you can find her with her high school sweetheart, chauffeuring their three kids to every activity imaginable, or with her nose buried in a book.

Grayce fell in love with reading and writing at a young age and pursued the creative outlet as a minor in college. She contributes a lot of her creativity and passion for reading to her mother, and Grayce now shares the same love for fictional escapes with her three children.